NOT HIS
WIFE

BOOKS BY L.G. DAVIS

Liar Liar

Perfect Parents

My Husband's Secret

The Missing Widow

Stolen Baby

The New Marriage

The Stolen Breath

Don't Blink

The Midnight Wife

The Janitor's Wife

THE LIES WE TELL SERIES

The New Nanny

The Nanny's Child

BROKEN VOWS SERIES

The Woman at My Wedding

The Missing Bridesmaid

NOT HIS WIFE

L.G. DAVIS

Bookouture

Published by Bookouture in 2025

An imprint of Storyfire Ltd.
Carmelite House
50 Victoria Embankment
London EC4Y 0DZ

www.bookouture.com

The authorised representative in the EEA is Hachette Ireland
8 Castlecourt Centre
Dublin 15 D15 XTP3
Ireland
(email: info@hbgi.ie)

ISBN: 978-1-80550-131-2
eBook ISBN: 978-1-80550-130-5

PROLOGUE

Red and blue lights flash against the old farmhouse and the nearby barn. The sirens stopped a while ago, but not the flashing.

Police are everywhere. Crime scene tape flutters between trees like Halloween decorations.

It looks like something from one of those true crime documentaries.

I lean against my car, parked at a safe distance, my trench coat pulled tight around me as I watch the chaos unfold. I shouldn't be here. But something pulled me back, some sick need to see it for myself.

Reporters hover near the edge of the property—some speaking into microphones, and others just watching, eyes wide with the thrill of it all.

Not long ago, this place smelled like cinnamon, chocolate, and fresh bread. Laughter spilled from the kitchen, and the sound of someone humming carried down the hall. That old rocking chair on the porch didn't watch the sunsets alone.

Now there's only silence, broken by static-filled radios and barked orders. The officers move in tight groups across the grass.

A detective emerges from the shadows, his face pale and grim, one hand clutching his radio.

Then I finally see it—a stretcher with a black body bag on top.

My hands are slick with sweat, and I shove them into my pockets, pressing my nails into my palms. But my heart won't stop pounding, and the tension inside me coils tighter, making my stomach twist.

I don't take my eyes off the covered shape as two paramedics roll it slowly across the dry, uneven grass, toward a white van parked near the fence. Its rear doors are wide open.

Then the hairs at the back of my neck rise.

Someone's watching me. A woman, standing off to the side. She's staring at me like she's trying to place my face.

Like she knows the truth: that everything unfolding here tonight is because of me.

ONE

CORA HARRISON

Tuesday, July 9, 2019

I open my eyes to find a strange man smiling down at me and stroking my cheek. "You're awake. Welcome home, darling. How are you feeling?"

The room is dimly lit and he quickly opens the blinds and comes back to place a hand on my forehead. His touch is warm and gentle. But I flinch away.

The space is large but modest, with simple furniture and muted colors. Pale-blue wallpaper decorates the walls, a little worn in places. The air is filled with his cologne, pine and cinnamon. There are also traces of lavender, from somewhere in the room.

When I turn my head, I notice a framed wedding photo on the bedside table. The man in the photo is the one sitting on the bed next to me, and the bride has dark, oval eyes and a curly updo with whisps of ringlets framing her heart-shaped face.

There's a desk leaning against one wall and a small mahogany dresser on one side of the window with another framed photo resting on it. I try to squint for a better look, but my headache slams against my temples.

I close my eyes again and the sheets rustle as he stands up. "It's okay, my love. I'll get you some water."

"Where am I?" I ask when he's back. My mind is spinning as the stranger helps me sit up in bed to take a drink of water, cool against my parched lips. I reach up and gulp like I haven't had a drink in months.

"Easy now." He gently pulls the glass away, setting it down on the bedside table. "Oh love, I'm so glad you're awake. I've been so scared." He leans his head down as if to kiss me, but I tense up and turn away.

Who is this man?

I press my head deeper into the pillow, my heart pounding.

He straightens, running a hand through his hair, and the locks fall right back into place. I watch as the sunlight reveals shades of dark brown and a hint of natural bronze highlights. Some strands fall forward, emphasizing the sharp angles of his jawline. His eyes, the color of rich, turned earth, mirror my own confusion and he opens his mouth and then closes it again.

"Cora, I... I know you're scared," he says finally. "But don't worry. Everything is going to be fine. I'm here."

He places his hand on mine, but I pull away. "Who are you?"

There's a deep furrow between his eyes. "It's me, baby." He moves closer again, running a hand down my cheek. "I'm your husband, Evan."

He picks up the framed photo on the bedside table and shows it to me. "This is us."

I blink, hoping that once my eyes adjust, I'll recognize the two faces looking back at me and it will all come flooding back. But right now, there's a void where my memories should be, my identity.

I don't even remember our names. *Evan. Cora.*

Nothing.

"I'm sorry. I don't know who you are."

A vein pulsates in the middle of his forehead, but he clears his throat, and forces a smile.

"You were in a coma for two weeks, and when you woke up, you spent four more days drifting in and out of consciousness. The doctor said you might experience temporary amnesia, so I was expecting... but I never imagined... I never thought you'd forget who I am."

Evan is attractive, with well-defined features, and dressed in blue and silver satin pajamas. Still confused, I take in his perfectly shaped nose, which turns up slightly at the tip, and the neatly trimmed beard outlining his mouth.

I don't remember him. Not at all.

"What happened to me?"

"There was an accident. You were trying to hang a large and pretty heavy photo frame on the wall at the top of the stairs, and you fell. I don't know what you were thinking, not asking me for help. But, Cora, I'm happy you're here, it could have been so much worse. You'll be okay now."

The name he keeps calling me repeats in my head, but it still doesn't feel right. I feel a sudden, extreme urge to get up.

I gather up all my energy and try to push myself out of bed, but Evan puts a hand on my chest.

"Where are you going? You just returned from the hospital yesterday. Doctor Rowe said you need complete rest."

"I just need to move," I say, and he lets me pull myself to my feet.

Honestly, I have no idea where I want to go. I only want to figure out what's happening to me.

Step by step, I move toward the dresser with Evan beside me. On my way, I catch a glimpse of the adjoining bathroom and, like the bedroom, everything inside appears old and in disrepair. The sink's edges are a little chipped, the bathtub has turned a dingy cream, and the wallpaper is faded and peeling.

There's not much on the smooth surface of the bedroom dresser—just a wooden boar bristle brush, a small bottle with an amber liquid inside, a single hairpin, and the photo I noticed from the bed: a portrait of Evan.

Sitting down, I stare at my reflection in the round, gold vintage mirror.

Looking back at me is a woman with long, curly hair in a messy bun above her head, deep, dark eyes, thick eyebrows, and full lips. I can't remember myself, but I can see I'm the same woman as the one in the photo next to the bed. The bride. I know it has to be me, but she's a stranger too, and she looks lost, like me.

I push myself to my feet again and move to the window. Gazing outside, I'm taken aback by the emptiness. It's farmland, but there are no animals or even houses in sight, just vast fields that stretch far into the horizon. In the distance, a shimmering lake.

There is a quiet beauty, and the leaves of the few trees shivering in the wind make it look like the land itself is breathing. The way the sunshine bounces off the surface of the lake is breathtaking. Everything looks peaceful, untouched. Almost like it isn't real.

A barn stands tall in the distance, its blue paint faded by the sun and rain.

"Where..." My voice drifts off.

"We're in Cedar Hollow, baby, North Carolina?" He says it like a question, then he cocks his head to one side, expecting me to say something. When I don't, he continues. "We moved here seven months ago from Charlotte. You always dreamt of living on a farm. You said your grandparents owned one and you loved visiting them as a child. On our wedding day, five years ago, I vowed to make that dream a reality—and I did. I finally fulfilled that promise when I bought Thistle Creek Ranch."

I take in his words, but the person I am at this moment doesn't seem suited for farming. It doesn't feel right.

Evan continues, his arm keeping me balanced. "You could have stayed in hospital for longer but I think this will be the best place for you to recover, surrounded by nature. Do you remember what month it was before you were unconscious?"

"June?" I say without even having to think about it.

"That's right. Now it's the ninth of July. Thank God you remember something."

"Except my name," I whisper.

"It will all come back, I promise," he assures me.

I scan the room, hoping to find something that will help me remember, but my eyes land only on mismatched furniture. In one corner, there's a large armchair made of brown and cream suede, its seat area worn and creased.

"I know there's not much to see right now, but when you get back on your feet, we'll turn this place into a home. We'll get some animals and maybe plant a garden. You love cherries, and you've always dreamed of having cherry trees. We'll make that dream come true. I promise."

If this is my home, why do I feel so out of place? This land, while beautiful, doesn't feel like it has ever been my home, or my dream.

I've heard of people having accidents that cause them to forget parts of their lives, but this much? I can't remember my home, my own husband, or even my name.

Evan appears to be a good man, a loving husband, and I feel awful that I can't remember him. If I were in his position, I'd be devastated.

"Evan, how old am I?"

"Thirty-six," he replies. "Three years younger than me."

That sounds about right, and as he says it, I remember that I was born on December seventh.

As Evan stands there looking helpless, tears well up in the eyes of the woman in the mirror.

All I want to do is run away from her. From me. But there's nowhere to go—because according to this man and the photo on the bedside table, this is my life.

And this stranger is my husband.

TWO

The kitchen cabinets are faded mahogany, and the countertops are speckled granite, chipped in places but still sturdy. There's even an old cast-iron stove, and next to it hanging from the wall are well-used copper pots and pans.

Evan told me as we came downstairs that this farm last belonged to an older couple. After the husband died, the woman sold it to us with most of the furniture, and we haven't had the chance to repair or renovate it yet, especially the dining room, which we have barely used at all.

There are details around us that do feel familiar to me as we walk through—the slight creak of the floorboards underneath my feet and the dish towels hanging by the sink, their edges decorated with a strip of lace and patterned with tiny blue flowers that have faded with time. But even as recognition tugs at me, I still don't feel at home, or like this is a place where I could ever belong. It kind of feels like I'm trespassing.

Evan did not want me to come downstairs, insisting that I should stay in bed and he would bring me breakfast, but I need to have a look at my surroundings. I'm desperate for a clue that would lead me to my memories.

When we go to sit down, I'm surprised to find an elderly woman—probably in her seventies—seated at the round kitchen table, sipping from a fine china teacup. Her hair is in two long braids, and her weathered face is lined with age, but looks so soft. A cane rests beside her, propped gently against the edge of the table.

"This is my beautiful aunt, Mary." Evan pulls out a chair for me. "She's been living with us for about two months now."

Another member of my family who is a blank in my mind.

"Hello... Good morning," I say to her, my throat a little scratchy as I inhale her strong floral and musk perfume.

Evan moves to the stove, and I sit down, smiling tentatively at Mary. She stares back at me and says something so quietly I can't hear her. There's something unsettling about the way she acts. She isn't fully present. Like me.

Evan sets a plate in front of me—scrambled eggs, bacon, sausages, and toast.

As we eat, the silence is punctuated by the clatter of cutlery and the occasional slurp of tea from Aunt Mary, who is still staring at me, making me even more uncomfortable, and I'm mindful of Evan too as he watches me from across the table.

Finally, the atmosphere shifts when someone else walks in, a woman who looks to be in her early thirties. She has straight, jet-black hair that brushes her shoulders, with black eyes to match. Even before she says a word, her personality fills the room. There's a radiance about her, a vibrancy that was lacking in the room until now. She's like a breath of fresh air.

"Oh, Lina, I was wondering where you were." Evan looks relieved as he smiles at her.

"I was straightening out Mary's room." She glances at me with a beaming smile that lights up her entire face. "Good morning."

"Lina, this is my wife." Evan gets up and comes to stand

behind me, placing his warm hands on my shoulders. "She came home from the hospital last night. I'm so glad she's back."

"Hi." I manage to smile, shaking her hand. Lina's grip is firm. "I'm... I'm Cora." The name still sounds foreign on my tongue and to my ears.

"Nice to finally meet you, Cora." Her voice is soothing.

"Lina started with us two weeks ago," Evan continues as he sits back down. "I brought her in soon after your accident to help with Mary."

"That's right," she confirms. "Mr. Harrison said you used to take care of Mary yourself, but I can assure you she's in good hands. I'm here if you need anything at all, I'll be visiting Mary a few times a week."

"Thank you."

Lina gives me another warm smile before turning her attention to the older woman. "You've barely touched your food, Mary. You need to eat to keep your strength up."

Mary looks up at her. "I'm not hungry." She folds her arms across her chest.

"You don't have to eat everything, but at least try a little." She pierces a piece of bacon and holds it up for Mary to take a bite.

Mary mumbles something incoherent again, but manages to eat a little more.

Evan smiles at his aunt, then looks over at me. "Are you okay?" He reaches out to take my hand but then seems to change his mind. "I know everything must feel confusing right now, but we'll figure it out together. You're not alone in this. I will take on fewer clients while you're recovering."

"Thanks. What do you do for work?"

"I'm a psychologist and author." His eyes flick at Lina then back at me. "My focus is on behavioral psychology, and I'm writing a new book that explores how people can reshape their sense of self. But I'll be working from home for a while. Before your accident, I worked too much and didn't give you enough..." His voice trails off as he glances at Lina. "My wife has temporary amnesia. But I'm sure she will make a full recovery."

Lina smiles at me with genuine warmth. For the first time since I woke up, I feel almost okay, surrounded by people who care for me, even if I don't remember them.

Soon after, Evan goes to write a few chapters of his book. While Lina gives Mary her medication and gets her comfortable on the porch, I clear the table.

"You really don't have to do that," Lina says when she returns and joins me at the sink.

"It's all right, I'm more than capable of doing some household tasks. I don't want to be treated like an invalid." I wring out the dishcloth. "This is making me feel a little more normal. I just wish I could remember anything about who I am, my past, my life."

Lina is silent for a beat, then she puts a hand on my arm. "Why don't you try to enjoy the present? Your memories will come back when the time is right. Forcing yourself to remember will only make you more stressed."

"You're right. I'll do my best." I glance behind me at the door. "What's wrong with Mary? She doesn't seem... okay. Is it just her age?"

"She has dementia. She used to live in a care home in town, but you and your husband decided to bring her here to live with you." She runs a hand through her hair and it swings back into place, a silky, black curtain. "Evan said it was your idea. You wanted her to be surrounded by family, by love."

She makes me sound like a good person, and I like it.

Lina leaves soon after lunch, and I sit with Mary in the living room as she watches a TV show, a documentary about birds.

Every now and then she points at the screen and murmurs something. I try to engage her in conversation, but I don't really get anywhere.

Finally, Evan comes to take her to have her daily nap, but I offer to do it instead, assuring him that I'm fine. At first, he's hesitant, then he lets me. But as I take Mary's arm, he follows us to her room, which is downstairs.

The room is sparsely furnished, with a double bed accompanied by a nearby chair, and a white leather Bible sits on the bedside table. A dresser leaning against one wall shows off a collection of perfume bottles and a framed photo of a younger Mary in business clothes. By the window—that overlooks the sprawling fields, the barn, and the lake—is an old armchair.

I carefully tuck Mary into bed, but she barely acknowledges me. When I'm done, Evan comes to kiss her forehead, just as his phone rings. He takes it from his pocket and looks up at me. "This might take a while. Make sure you get some rest, my love." He exits the room with the phone to his ear.

"I will. You go ahead."

When his footsteps have faded away, I move closer to the bed and peer down at his aunt. "Mary, do you remember me?"

She stares at me for a while, then, without warning, she throws back the covers and struggles to her feet. My breath catches as she moves to the window, her back rigid, her bony shoulders rising and falling with each breath.

"This isn't your home," she says without turning around. "You don't belong here. Get out now."

A cold ripple spreads through me, but I keep my composure. I'm careful not to do anything that might upset her. I know how disorientating it is when you can't remember anything. "What do you mean, Mary?" I step toward her. "I'm Cora, Evan's wife. This is our home. It's all okay."

"You're not his wife," she counters and keeps staring out the window. Then, as suddenly as she left it, she goes to climb back into the bed, pulling the blanket all the way up to her neck. "Margaret?" Her confused eyes lock onto mine, squinting as though she can't see me well. "Don't let them take you to the barn. Get far away from here."

THREE

I pull Mary's door shut, then stand there, gripping the doorknob as her words repeat inside my head and a cold weight settles in my stomach.

Who is Margaret? And what was that about the barn?

I head to the living room and walk to the window, staring at the barn, a simple structure bathed in sunlight. I draw in a breath and try to shake off the unease.

Mary is confused, that's all. Dementia does strange things to a person's mind. And yet... something about the way she said it, the urgency in her voice rattles me more than I want to admit. It's also sad that she can't remember who I am, her nephew's wife.

I rub my arms and step out of the living room.

Needing a distraction, I follow the sound of Evan's voice to where he is, in a room at the far end of the hallway. His office door is slightly open and he's sitting at his desk. The moment I enter, he ends the call.

"Sorry if I'm disturbing. I was just—"

He closes the laptop in front of him and stands. "You can

never disturb me. I was just about to start another chapter of my book. That was my editor on the phone, and we went through some notes on the manuscript. I was hoping you took a cue from Mary and also went up for a nap."

"I don't need a nap. I feel fine."

"Well, why don't you keep me a little company here for a bit then?" He strides to a long leather couch and pats the space next to him. I take a seat and study the room, which doesn't match the rest of the house at all. Evan's office is elegant, filled with beautiful furniture that looks and smells brand new.

The walls are lined with bookshelves filled to the brim with hardcover books of various colors and sizes. There's a glass desk in the middle of the room, with stacks of neatly organized papers and a sleek black laptop sitting on top of it. There's also a billiard table on one side of the big room, made of polished oak with a deep-green felt top.

A small silver safe is tucked away in a corner next to the desk. This room is definitely more modern. It even smells new, of fresh leather, wood polish, and a hint of coffee. His large, cushioned swivel chair seems particularly inviting, and it's upholstered in the same rich leather as the couch.

"I like your office." I run a hand over the seat of the couch, feeling the smooth, cool texture. "It's so different from the rest of the house." Instead of the lake, this room overlooks the front of the farmhouse, where a midnight-blue Volvo XC90 and a rust-colored Chevy pickup sit parked beneath a large, leafy tree.

In the distance I spot rolling hills, but these windows don't overlook the barn like mine and Mary's do.

"Since this is where I spend a lot of time writing and working, I took the liberty of designing it myself, but you wanted to be responsible for the rest of the house. Do you remember, Cora, that you are an interior designer? And you're so talented. I'm sure that once you recover, this place will be brimming with your own personal touches." He chuckles as he seems to remember something. "You could never even watch a movie without analyzing the set design, the colors, the layout. You noticed the smallest details, the way everything was arranged. It was... one of the things I loved most about you."

"An interior designer?" I repeat. Yes, that feels like something I would love to be. No wonder I was so focused on the aesthetic of the rooms. "Was I employed at a company?"

"You used to be in Charlotte, but when we moved to Cedar Hollow you quit. You planned to start your own company. You were talking about building a website and an online presence, but then you got hurt. But you *will* get better, my love, and you'll make all your dreams come true. Right now, I don't want you worrying about work, just focus on healing. It's important that you remember who you are and the beautiful life we built together, the things you love, the things that make you *you*. Like how you always insisted on doing a full stretch as soon as you got out of bed every morning, or how, no matter how tired you were, you always read at least one chapter of a book before turning in for the night."

A part of me is desperate to hold on to the version of me he's describing, but it still feels distant and fuzzy. I focus on something concrete instead.

I glance out the window, in search of something familiar, and then back to Evan. "Is this farm far from downtown?"

"Not really, it's only a fifteen-minute drive. Cedar Hollow is a small town, but it has everything we need, and the people are friendly enough."

Although I can't recall much about myself or my past, the name of this town, Cedar Hollow, when he first said it to me, *did* ring a bell. I choose not to tell Evan, as I don't want to upset him by admitting I remember the town but not him. "Are your clients willing to drive up here?"

"No, I will be holding online sessions until you're better. I want you to have all the peace and quiet you need. The only client allowed in this room for now is you."

"Thank you. You're so thoughtful."

"You don't have to thank me. I'm your husband." He pats my hand.

"Okay." My eyes drift to his bookshelves, then to his desk, where a book is displayed, on a little stand. The author name on the cover catches my eye.

Evan Harrison.

"You wrote that?" I point at the book before standing up to get it. I pick it up, and as Evan watches, I read the title: *The Dynamics of the Mind*.

"That's impressive."

"Thank you," he says, joining me and gently taking the book from me, returning it to its rightful place. "The one I'm working on now is a follow-up and it's a bit ambitious. It requires much more research than my last."

"Really? Tell me more about it."

He clasps his hands together and a smile plays at the corners of his mouth. "It's a study about how people respond to shifts in their environment. It's all about the subtle ways the mind adapts, even when we don't realize it. The mind is so much more flexible than most people realize. You'll see. Once you're feeling better, you'll be amazed at how adaptable you can be."

"Sounds like a big topic to tackle." I glance again at his book and wonder how long it took him to write. Writing a book must take so much willpower and patience.

"It *is* a huge topic, and my publisher thinks it'll be ground-breaking." He sits back down. "But don't bother yourself with the complexities of my boring work. Let's focus on getting your health and memories back."

"Yes, please." Back on the couch, an idea comes to me and I

perk up. "Was I on social media? If I was, maybe it could help me remember things."

His expression lights up. "That's a fantastic idea. You weren't very active on there, but maybe you'll find something useful."

He crosses the room and fetches a gray laptop from his desk. "This was yours." He sits down with it on his lap and a wave of excitement washes over me. I'm so anxious to find out more about my life.

Luckily, there's no password to get into the laptop. Evan opens Facebook and pulls up my profile: *Cora Harrison*.

The profile picture is a silhouette of me standing alone in a field at sunset. It's beautiful, almost like a painting.

The account is set to private except for my friends list, but I don't recognize any of the profile names.

Evan opens the login screen, types in the username, and hands the laptop to me, waiting for me to enter the password. I stare blankly at the screen.

"You can't remember it," he says flatly.

I shake my head. "Do you know it... maybe?"

"No." He sighs.

I close the laptop, place it on the couch next to me, and press my palms against my temples as tears spring to my eyes. This is the first time I have cried since waking up to this strange new life.

With the back of my hand, I swipe the tears away, hoping Evan didn't see because even if he's supposed to be my husband, I feel uncomfortable crying in front of him. But he did see, and now he's wrapping an arm around me.

"Sweetheart, you're going through a lot. It's okay to let it out." He pulls me close and as I cry into his shoulder, I notice that his scent is starting to feel more familiar and comforting.

"I have an idea," he says when we finally break apart. He reaches for the laptop again and flips it open. "Let's log into my account instead and look at your page from there." He goes ahead and does just that, then pulls up my profile again. "There we go."

Holding my breath, I scan the photos, dozens of them, most of them with Evan and some of us and Mary, and other people I don't recognize, but a lot of them are nature shots. A beach with jagged cliffs in the background, a snowy mountain scene, a cityscape lit up at night. In some of them, Evan and I are standing hand in hand, wrapped in the beauty of these breath-taking places.

I focus on one of us taken at the edge of a cliff, the ocean stretching out below us and the sun shining bright behind us. My head is resting on Evan's shoulder as both of us look out over the water. I can almost feel the wind on my face as I stare at it, like I'm still there, standing beside him, looking happy and content. I wish I could rewind back to that day, that moment.

"That was taken at the cliffs near Mendocino. You said you'd always wanted to see that part of the coast. We went there to celebrate our second wedding anniversary and rented a little cabin for the weekend. It was perfect." Evan leans closer, his voice softer. "Do you remember that weekend trip, Cora? The way the light reflected off the ocean at sunset. You loved it so much, and the fresh seafood we ate on the first day... You said it was the best meal you'd ever had."

I stare at the photo, trying to pull something more from it, and although I do feel a connection, the memories are like distant dreams, too hazy to grasp.

I scroll through a few more photos and stop to stare at one where we are on the beach at sunset. Close by is a man in his late thirties, a woman in her forties, an older couple leaning into each other, a group of people laughing together. They all look like they're on the same trip with us.

"Who are these people?" The tip of my finger lands on the

older couple. "Are any of them... are they family? My parents? Where are they?"

"Those are people we met on the trip." Evan's expression darkens for a moment, enough for me to notice before he turns to look away. "Cora, your parents—" He looks down at his hands before meeting my eyes again. "You fell out with your parents when you graduated from high school, before we met, and you haven't been in touch for years. I don't know all the details; you didn't want to talk about them or your childhood."

"I don't understand." I close the laptop and turn to my husband. "How? What happened? Did you reach out to them after my accident? Did they come to see me at the hospital? Will they visit here?"

"They've been out of your life for years, my love. A year after we got married, I asked if you wanted to reach out. You said no, that you didn't need them. So, I tried calling them myself. Since my parents are not alive, it would have been nice to have family in our lives. But the numbers didn't work." He pauses to reach for my hand. "You were upset with me when you found out what I tried to do. You said they didn't deserve to be in your life, Cora. And over time, I learned to respect that."

It's like a punch in the stomach. This is the time anyone would need their family most, and I am estranged from mine? What happened that was so terrible we decided not to speak again?

I swallow the hot lump in my throat. "What about siblings? Do I have any?"

He shakes his head. "Like me, you were an only child. It's just... been you and me."

Suddenly tears spring to my eyes, blurring everything. I feel a sudden surge of affection for this man who stood by me, even when my parents turned their backs. "Were we happy?" I whisper.

"Yes, Cora. We were very happy. I know it's difficult for both of us right now. But we'll get through this."

After leaving Evan's office, I return to Mary's room, still thinking about what she said to me earlier.

To my surprise, she's out of her bed again and is sitting in the armchair by the window with a book in her lap. She barely acknowledges me as I enter and pull up a chair to sit next to her.

"Hi, Mary, what are you reading?"

She looks up then and for a moment just stares at my face before turning the book over to reveal the cover.

"*Echoes of Silence*," I read.

"It's poetry," she says. "It's soothing for the soul."

Hearing her say more than a word or two to me surprises me, and I take the opportunity to get the conversation going. "How about I read a few of them to you?"

This time she says nothing, but she hands me the book, and that's a good start.

The first thing I notice when I flip it open is the name written inside. Margaret.

"Mary, who is Margaret? Is she a friend of yours? Was this book hers?" For Mary to remember this woman and keep her things close must mean something.

"Who's Margaret?" Mary repeats the question back to me and points to the book. "Please, can you read something?"

She's definitely confused and there's no point in bothering her with questions. I make a mental note to ask Evan instead.

For the next few minutes, I read several poems, but my favorite is one about a quiet lake at dawn, where the mist hangs low over the water like a whisper, and the poet speaks of the world slowing down and the beauty of silence. As I read it, I watch Mary's face relax and her lips part as she stares out the window.

I finish the poem and wait, unsure if I should read another.

Finally, she speaks. "I love them all, but that one reminds me of when I was a little girl. The evenings were so quiet and still, peaceful. I loved to sit by the lake with my grandfather. He was a good man, my pawpaw."

Her words hang in the air, and I place the book on the table. "I'd love to hear more about him."

For a brief moment, Mary's eyes seem to clear, and I catch a glimpse of the woman she must have been; strong, vibrant, full of life. "It's not important anymore. What's gone is gone."

"Mary, what did you mean when you said this isn't my home, and I should get out?"

"I meant nothing by it," she says after a brief hesitation, still looking out the window. "Don't mind me, dear. My mind doesn't work as well as it used to. I used to be as sharp as anything. Oh yes, I was a very successful businesswoman once. I saw the world, but I never thought of living anywhere else. Cedar Hollow—my hometown—always had my heart."

Before she can go on, there's a creak behind us. I turn to see Evan in the doorway.

"I'm afraid she tends to jump from one topic to the next without warning," he says. "It's the dementia; some days she's more present than others."

I look at Mary, who's in her own little world again. "She said something weird about me not belonging here, and I was asking what she meant."

"I'm so sorry she said that to you." He takes a deep breath and gestures for me to leave the room with him.

"The first time you met my aunt, she didn't warm to you." He closes Mary's door and we walk side by side to the stairs, but we stop before we climb them. "She was always protective of me. You have to understand... she practically raised me after my parents died. You were the first woman I ever introduced to her, but she didn't think you were good enough for me." He sighs. "I remember she said something similar to you that day, that you don't belong in my life. I'm so sorry she's regressed back to that. But don't let that bother you. I'm sure there will be days when she remembers who you are, how much you loved her, and also how much she loved you. She really warmed up to you since we got married."

"Thanks for explaining. But she also keeps mentioning someone named Margaret. She was reading her book of poetry when I came into the room. That name is written inside."

Evan pinches the bridge of his nose. "Margaret is the woman who lived here before us. We bought the farm from her."

"And Mary knew her?"

"I don't think so. It's likely she heard the name mentioned by someone from a neighboring farm, someone who knew her. Also, Mary has always loved poetry. She must have found the book of poetry lying around somewhere and took it." He rubs the back of his neck. "The other day, she forgot who I was. I know she can't help it, but I wish she could focus more on her real memories. I hate seeing her mind fool her into thinking people she didn't even know are friends. Watching her losing touch with what really matters hurts."

I put a hand on his arm. "I'm sorry, Evan. Is there anything I can do? How about I make you a cup of tea?"

"Definitely not. I want you to rest."

"I've been resting all that time I was in the hospital. You really don't have to worry about me. Aside from a few aches here and there, and a broken mind, I'm really okay."

"That's good to hear. But don't worry about making tea for me. I think I should get back to work. If you need anything at all, or some company, you know where to find me."

. . .

When Evan is back in his office, I head to the kitchen, and ten minutes later, I'm standing next to the stove, holding a cup of green tea in my hands. The steam curls upward, filling the air with the refreshing scent. As I lift the cup to my lips and take a sip, it occurs to me what just happened.

I made this cup of tea and didn't even stop to think where everything was—the tea, the sugar, the cups. I did it all on autopilot. My body moved as though it had made tea inside this kitchen a hundred times before. A feeling of déjà vu washes over me and adrenaline pumps inside my veins, making me breathless with excitement. I'm remembering.

I glance down at the cup in my hands, a brown ceramic with a faint crack running along its rim. The way it nestles in my palm also feels familiar, like I've held it before.

With hands wrapped around my cup of tea, I walk to the dining room, where the heavy curtains are drawn, blocking out the sunlight, so I pull them open.

The air inside feels stale as though the room hasn't been used in months. A large, rectangular dining table is in the center, surrounded by mismatched wooden chairs, some of them with delicate flower or vine carvings along their backs. They look like they're waiting for someone, and they've been waiting for a long time.

In the air, I sniff the faint hint of wood polish and something floral. Is it Margaret's perfume, maybe?

I take a sip of my tea and, walking past a glass china cabinet, I approach a side table near the window, where a small brass plaque is sitting. It's engraved with the letters M & R, and beneath the initials are a delicate pair of doves in flight. Margaret must be the M and her deceased husband the R.

Next to the plaque, I spot a pair of reading glasses with a silver chain attached to them. That's weird. They look like someone had set them down a few minutes ago and never came back for them. If they were Margaret's, why would she leave such precious things behind, like that book of poetry that Mary found?

I circle the room slowly, my attention drawn to the walls, where faded landscape paintings hang, but I feel like I'm invading someone's privacy, so I step out for now. I keep walking through the house until I find myself standing in front of a door that won't open.

I reach out, testing the handle, but it's locked. As I'm about to walk away, I hear something, a faint, muffled chirping. It sounds like birds.

It's so distant that at first, I'm not sure I've heard it at all. But as I press my ear closer to the door, it comes again, faint but distinct.

Definitely birdsong.

There's no way I'm imagining this. Why would there be birds in the house, and why is the door locked?

I step back as questions swirl around inside my head, the mystery gnawing at me.

I can almost see the birds in my mind's eye, small, frantic creatures, fluttering wildly around, their tiny claws scraping against wood as they fight for a way out, beaks tapping against the walls in desperate confusion. They're a dozen, or maybe more.

Trapped.

I blink, shaking the vision from my head. I'm being ridiculous. There aren't birds locked behind this door. I'm not in a movie.

Even so. I heard something, and this door is locked for a reason. An involuntary shiver trickles down my spine as I try the handle again.

"Cora, what are you doing?" Evan's voice makes me jump.

"I was looking around, trying to see if anything feels familiar."

"I understand. But you have to remember that this will still feel like a stranger's home since we haven't really made it our own yet." He glances at the door. "That's the basement. It's under renovation and unsafe. I keep it locked to keep Mary from going down there. Everything there is too dilapidated and the steps are dangerous. I'm taking a coffee break, do you want to join me?"

Reluctantly I walk after him, but first I pause and listen again at the door, my stomach churning.

I can't hear the birds anymore.

FOUR

Wednesday, July 10, 2019

Standing in front of the bathroom mirror, I touch the right side of my head, my fingers brushing over a tender spot. I try to recall the fall because maybe that memory is the bridge that connects the two halves of my life, the one I can remember only vaguely, like a dream, and this one, with its blank canvas, waiting to be filled.

My instincts tell me I was a fighter, a person with a determined spirit, and right now I'm determined to overcome this challenge. Depending on Evan for everything bothers me.

Yesterday was especially difficult as I had to ask him so many questions and it pained me to see his disappointment when I couldn't recall yet another detail about our past.

Sure that today I will remember something important about me and my life, I splash my face with cold water, then jump into the shower.

There's a knock on the door just as I step out of the bathroom. I'm really grateful that Evan sleeps in the guest room so I can have my personal space. I'm not comfortable sleeping in the same room, not yet.

Putting on a dressing gown and wrapping it tightly around myself, I go to the door instead of asking him to enter.

"Morning, sweetheart. Doctor Rowe is here to see you." Doctor Rowe is our family doctor and Evan said he would be coming today to see how I'm doing.

"Thanks. I'll be down in a bit."

Evan places a hand on my cheek and peers into my face. "Are you feeling okay?"

What he really wants to know is, do I remember anything? Do I remember him?

"Better than yesterday."

"That's good. I'll go and get a bit of writing done and will check on you in a bit." He gives me a kiss on the cheek and then walks away.

Ten minutes later, I'm sitting in the living room opposite the doctor, an older man with a bushy beard, little hair on his head, round glasses, and a friendly face.

He asks me a few questions about how I'm feeling, and I tell him everything, down to the little details. He listens quietly, jotting down notes.

"When will I get my memories back?" It's best to address the elephant in the room.

"It's different from person to person." He runs a hand up and down his beard. "Sometimes they come back in a rush, sometimes piece by piece, and sometimes they never do, I'm afraid."

My heart sinks, and the headache I thought was giving me a break this morning returns with a vengeance. I rise to my feet, my head spinning.

"Are you all right, Cora?" Doctor Rowe places a hand on my arm. "Does your head hurt?"

"A little. I'll be right back." I stumble out of the room and manage to hold it together until I reach the kitchen, where Mary is sitting, eating a bowl of cereal while scribbling in her journal. Evan thinks it's a way for her to jot down memories of her life as they come to her, trying to hold on to whatever she can before it slips away.

Yesterday morning she forgot her journal outside on the porch and I snuck a look inside.

I didn't like the idea of reading her personal thoughts, her memories, but I couldn't stop my hand as it reached for the book, opening where her blue ballpoint pen served as a bookmark. For a woman whose hands tend to shake a lot of the time, her cursive handwriting was remarkably steady and neat.

When I was about six or seven, Mama made me a dress for my birthday. I can still remember choosing the fabric with her in town. I wanted to touch every fabric roll in the store, but Mama guided me to the ones within our budget. In the evenings, we worked on the dress together. When it was finished, it was the most beautiful thing I'd ever seen, yellow with bright-green clovers on the hem.

Margaret mentioned that dress the other day. Said we could recreate it on her sewing machine. Her mother was a tailor, you know. She learned everything from her. But we never got the chance. They took her away before we could even start.

I thought about that entry all day yesterday, wondering which parts of Mary's memories were real and which were distorted by the dementia. And who were they, the ones who took Margaret away?

Evan said Mary couldn't have known Margaret, but the way she wrote about her in that journal, it feels like she not only knew her but had known her since childhood.

I almost asked her more about it, but then she would know

that I read her journal. So, I said nothing. But I do plan on keeping my eyes open for any signs of a sewing machine.

"Morning, Mary," I say now, pouring myself a glass of water. Either she doesn't answer or she speaks too low because I do not hear her.

I swallow down a painkiller and leave her alone to return to Doctor Rowe, who I find talking in hushed voices to Evan. They both stop immediately as soon as I enter.

As I get back to the couch, Mary comes in and trains her gaze on the TV. She probably wants to watch one of her game shows, she loves *Who Wants to Be a Millionaire?*

Evan rises to his feet and takes his aunt's arm. "Aunt Mary, how about we go for a walk and give the doctor and Cora a moment?"

Mary glances at the TV again and looks about to protest before changing her mind and nodding.

"We don't mind having her here," I say. "We could go and sit somewhere else."

"No, it's fine." Evan puts an arm around his aunt's shoulders. "Fresh air would do her a world of good."

As I watch them leave, my heart softens toward this man who is taking care of his aunt with so much love. Taking on a dementia patient—whether you're related to them or not—cannot be easy. Now he has my memory loss to deal with as well.

Once they leave, I bring my attention back to Doctor Rowe.

After drumming his fingers against his thighs for a while, he pulls a handkerchief from his pocket, dabbing at the sheen of sweat gathering on his forehead. His gaze drifts toward the door, his jaw tightening.

I tilt my head. "Everything all right?"

"Sure, yes. Of course." He shoves the handkerchief back into his pocket, then straightens. "Let's continue, shall we?"

He prescribes me sleeping pills, then he gets to his feet. I offer to walk him to the door, but he declines.

I remain on the sofa, where Evan finds me later.

"Everything is going to be okay," he says as he comes to sit down next to me. "You and I, we will get through this together."

I shift, creating distance between us. "I'm not upset, Evan, just frustrated." I wish I could speed this whole thing up. I'm feeling betrayed by my body. "I'm so sorry it's taking so long. I know how hard this is on you, and I really do appreciate you giving me the space I need to remember and recover."

"Hey, you don't need to thank me for anything. You're my wife, I love you. I'm not going anywhere." He gives me a kiss on the forehead, and it feels almost natural.

In that moment, we hear a vehicle approaching. The deep rumble of an engine, the crunch of tires against gravel.

When we step onto the porch, a dusty blue Ford pickup truck rolls to a stop in front of the house. The woman who steps out is dressed in faded denim overalls over a plain T-shirt, her dark hair twisted into a messy bun. She looks to be in her late thirties.

A boy, about five years old, sits in the truck's passenger seat, watching us through the windshield.

"Who is that?"

Evan folds his arms across his chest. "That's Sabrina. She owns a small farm not far from here. She used to deliver fresh eggs and milk. I'm not sure why she's here. I don't order from her anymore."

Sabrina doesn't have a basket of produce with her. She doesn't look like she's here to sell anything.

I watch as she steps onto the porch, wiping her hands on her overalls. Her face is tanned, her hands rough, like someone who spends most of her time working outdoors.

"I'm not here for business," she says to Evan. "I only wanted to ask about Cora." She hesitates as she glances at me. "I didn't expect to see you. Your husband didn't mention you were home from the hospital."

Something about the way she's looking at me makes me feel a twinge of familiarity.

I don't remember my own husband.

But I swear I know this woman.

FIVE

"Sabrina," Evan says, "I'm sorry I didn't reach out to tell you that Cora's back home. The last few days have been, well... challenging."

Sabrina's brow wrinkles as she looks at me. "I can imagine. How are you doing, Cora?"

"She's lost her memory completely," Evan answers for me and Sabrina's eyes widen.

"What?" She searches my face for some sign of recognition. "Cora, do you remember me?"

I swallow hard. There's something about her—her voice, her presence—that tugs at something deep inside me, but I can't quite grasp it. "I'm sorry, not yet."

For a moment, she studies me, then offers a tentative smile. "Maybe if we sit and chat, I'll say something that jogs your memory?"

Evan sighs. "The doctor just left," he explains. "He said Cora needs as much rest as possible. Maybe you could come by another time?"

Sabrina crosses her arms. "I hear you, Evan, but if I were in

Cora's shoes, I'd want to talk to someone who could remind me of who I was." She looks at me again. "Unless you want me to leave?"

"No, you're right," I say. "I'd actually like to sit and talk."

"All right." Evan squeezes my shoulder before heading back inside.

Sabrina gestures to the steps of the porch. "Come on, let's sit."

We settle onto the wooden steps, and in front of us, the boy kicks a soccer ball across the patchy grass.

"In case you don't remember him either, that's Owen," Sabrina says, "my little tornado."

I watch the boy chase after the ball, the warm breeze stirring his tousled hair.

"I really don't remember you," I admit. "But there's something about you that feels... familiar."

"Well, that's a start." She rests her forearms on her knees and exhales. "All right, let's start from the beginning. I'm Sabrina McCleary. We haven't known each other that long, but before your accident, you used to buy our milk and eggs and sometimes you stopped by our farm for a chat."

She lifts a hand and points toward the horizon. "It's not too far. You can't really see much from here, but it's a short walk. The house is yellow with a large metal peacock on the roof."

I squint in the direction she's pointing, but all I see is a blur of trees and open land.

Sabrina continues, "You used to drop by for one of my mother's delicious sweet iced teas. Jill—that's my mom—she makes the best sweet tea you'll ever have." A smile tugs at her lips. "And you were always so kind. You'd bring over a little something, cookies, chocolate, or something else my son might enjoy."

Sabrina suddenly pushes herself up. "Hang on a sec." She

walks over to her truck, and rummages inside. When she returns, she's holding a bar of chocolate and a novel with a creased spine.

She offers me the chocolate first. "I was going to give this to your husband so he could give it to you when you woke up from the coma, but since you're awake now... here."

"Thank you." I take it and run my fingers over the wrapper. There's something oddly comforting about it.

"And this," she says, holding up the book, "actually belongs to you."

I stare at the worn paperback. *The Rainmaker* by John Grisham. I don't recognize it, but the thought of it being mine stirs something inside me.

"You lent it to me," Sabrina explains. "The first time you stopped by our farm, I was reading a John Grisham book on the porch. You saw it and said you loved his books. That's how we got talking."

I run my fingers along the edges of the pages. "Did I read a lot?"

"Seemed like it." She smiles. "You were always curious about people too. Asked a million questions about the people of this town. Feel free to ask me anything at all."

I glance at her. "What else did I tell you about myself?"

"Well..." She tilts her head. "You liked the band Michael Learns to Rock. Said their music helped you unwind."

I don't recognize the name, but I say nothing.

"And you loved to travel. After university, you said you did a solo trip to Greece. Said it was the best experience of your life."

Something inside me stirs. Greece. Sun-soaked buildings, the scent of the sea... It doesn't bring up a full memory, but the thought of it makes my heart ache.

"You really don't remember your life?" Sabrina asks gently.

"No, but it's strange. Some of what you're saying—it doesn't feel completely foreign. It's like hearing about someone else's life, but, I don't know, a part of me wants to believe it's mine."

"I see what you mean. Maybe it'll come back in pieces."

Before I can say more, the front door creaks open, and Evan steps onto the porch, his eyes settling on me. "You okay?"

"Sure." I grip the book in my lap.

Sabrina takes that as her cue to leave. She stands, dusting herself off. "I should get going. I need to pick up some supplies in town."

Owen jogs over, tugging at her arm. "Can we go to the feed store now?"

"That's where we're headed, bud." She ruffles his hair and smiles at me. "Cora, when you feel up to it, you should drop by. My mom would love to see you. As much as she can anyway—her eyesight isn't what it used to be, but we're saving up for surgery."

"Sure, I'd like to come by."

"Wonderful." She gives my arm a gentle pat before heading toward the truck with Owen.

I thank her for dropping by and watch as she climbs into the truck, starts the engine, and waves before pulling away, kicking up dust as she disappears down the road.

After Sabrina leaves, I go into the living room to sit with Mary while she watches *Columbo*, and Evan disappears to his office.

When I spot Mary's journal next to her, my mind circles back to what she wrote about Margaret and the sewing machine. It doesn't make sense. Like Evan said, it has to be the dementia, mixing up names and memories.

After a few minutes of watching TV, I'm too restless to stay in one place, so I get up to do something, and the only thing on my mind as I walk out of the living room is finding the sewing machine.

I have no idea where to look, but I start with Mary's room,

one of the few places in the house I haven't really explored. The air smells of the Chanel no. 5 that Mary chose to wear today. Unlike some people who have a signature perfume, she seems to prefer a variety, judging from the many bottles on the dresser.

The wardrobe is the first place I check. All I find are a few of Mary's clothes—neatly hung blouses in faded pastels, three black skirts with pleats, a few knitted cardigans with pearl buttons, and a pair of floral slippers on the floor. Next, I open a padded storage bench by the window, containing only neatly folded bedsheets and towels.

On the verge of giving up, I sink onto Mary's bed.

Then, something catches my eye.

Near the doorframe, on the right side and at waist level, I notice some lines. I stand to get a closer look. Definitely faint lines, scratches maybe?

My fingers skim the bruised wallpaper. Something about the marks makes me pause. I take a step back, telling myself it's nothing.

This is an old house, and it will have its scars. So, pushing the scratches to the back of my mind, I leave the room and head back to the living room before Mary wonders where I've disappeared off to.

Columbo is still playing, but there's no one on the couch, or in the room for that matter. Mary is gone, her journal left behind.

Panic hits me instantly as I whip around, scanning the room. "Mary?" My groggy voice barely cuts through the low hum of the TV. No answer.

I promised Evan that I'd watch her while he worked. What if she went outside alone and got lost?

My mind racing with worst-case scenarios, I run to the kitchen, but she's not there, or in the dining room.

Before I run out the front door to check in the field, I look in the hallway leading to Evan's office and the basement.

My shoulders sag with relief when I spot her standing completely still in front of the basement door, her back to me, shoulders rigid.

"Mary, are you okay?" I go and put an arm around her.

"I was looking for the toilet," she says. "I guess I lost my way. And then, I thought... I thought I heard the birds singing."

SIX

Lina has just taken Mary for her afternoon nap and Evan is out playing golf. It's his way of unwinding, like his early morning billiards games.

When Lina returns to the kitchen I'm finishing up the last of my lunch—a broccoli and salmon casserole from the freezer.

"Cora, I was thinking, I could tidy up the house while Mary sleeps."

"You don't have to do that, Lina. I'm here. You're just here to care for Mary."

"I know, but I find cleaning quite relaxing actually, and I really don't mind." She tucks her straight hair behind her ear. "You don't have the energy to be cleaning right now, and your husband is so busy with work."

"You're so very kind. But that would really make me feel terrible."

"No need for that. We all go through tough times and we have to learn to accept help. That's one thing my mom told me when I was growing up, to never reject help, and right now, Cora, you need it."

"I've been cleaning up here and there and I'm still standing."

"Accepting help doesn't mean you're weak. Let me do this."

"All right then, but please only do a little tidying up, no major cleaning." I soften my tone. "I guess what I'm trying to say is, thank you." I smile at her. "I was thinking that I might go out for a little walk." Since I woke up after the accident, I haven't gone beyond the porch.

"I think that's a wonderful idea." Lina is already filling a bucket with soapy water. "You do just that."

I fetch my John Grisham novel and take it with me outside.

The fields stretch out to the horizon, a vast expanse of green and gold, and the air is crisp and clean, carrying the faint scent of hay. I breathe in deeply, relishing the sensation of the warm wind and the soothing touch of the sun on my skin.

But the sound of birds reminds me of the basement. I mentioned it to Evan, and he said the birdsong must have been coming through an open window somewhere. I know he must be right, but it really sounded like it was coming through that door.

I don't want my mind to run wild again, but I can't shake this feeling that there are things he's not telling me. Things he doesn't want me to know about that house.

Last night, I brought up the scratches I found on the door-frame in Mary's room, hoping for a simple explanation, and he didn't seem surprised at all. He simply confirmed that the house is old and wear and tear like that is normal.

"Probably came from moving furniture around over the years," he mused.

I set my eyes on the distant sparkling lake. The grass brushes against my legs as I tread through the fields, and the world feels expansive and free. Despite my mind still holding my memories hostage, I definitely feel a lot physically stronger today.

With a smile, I take in the beauty around me. When Evan told me that it had been my dream to live on a farm, I could not imagine it, but now, as I drink in the vast openness, I'm starting to see why someone would crave this kind of life, so far from the chaos of city life.

With my book tucked under my elbow, I reach the edge of the lake, where there's a lone wooden bench. The water glimmers like a sheet of glass under the bright sun and there is a family of ducks, paddling toward the reeds at the lake's edge, leaving a trail of ripples.

I open my book and start to read, but I'm finding it hard to lose myself in the words. Looking up, I watch a single leaf drift from a nearby tree, twirling and floating in the breeze before landing on the water.

After watching it float for a while, I pull out my phone—a new iPhone Evan gave me, since I couldn't remember the password to my old one either—and go online.

I type Evan Harrison into Google.

There are articles praising his work, interviews where he talks about the science of human behavior. Even a feature in a business magazine with the bold headline: *The man who knows you better than you know yourself.*

His name is everywhere, and he clearly has a glowing reputation.

Scrolling through the articles, I see something about his latest book, *The Dynamics of the Mind*, which was published two years ago. The launch got a lot of attention, but the reviews are all over the place. Some call it brilliant, that it's a game-changer in psychology. Others seem more critical. One article in particular stands out for me:

Is Doctor Evan Harrison's research pushing ethical boundaries?

I click on it.

Doctor Harrison's new book explores how people's thoughts and behaviors can be shaped in ways they don't even realize.

The piece then gets too technical for me, so I gloss over the middle part until I reach the last paragraph.

Supporters praise his work as innovative and thought-provoking, applauding his willingness to explore the mind in unconventional ways. But critics argue that his methods border on manipulation, with some questioning the ethical implications of how far he's willing to go in the name of research.

Rereading that last sentence, I think of the way Evan speaks to me, the way he knows me. The way he always seems to anticipate my thoughts before I can even voice them.

I exit the article, but there's a knot in my stomach.

He's a psychologist and it's in his nature to read people, to grasp what they are going through so he can better help them. That's his job, isn't it? So why do the critics have a problem with that?

I don't want what I read about Evan to influence me while I'm getting to know him. His professional life has nothing to do with his personal life. All this means is that he's damn good at his job, and I should be proud of him. The fact that he is a good husband is the only thing that should matter to me right now.

Pushing the phone back in my pocket, I try to read my novel again, but don't even make it past the first page before getting to my feet.

I cannot allow myself to relax when there's so much going

on inside my head. It's not just questions about Evan, and my past. It's this *house*, that's supposed to be my home.

There's something going on inside it and I won't be able to rest until I figure out what it is.

The birds. The basement. The scratches. Margaret.

Setting off walking again, I soon find myself at the old barn.

As I open the large, squeaking door, I wonder how it must have looked filled with livestock. I also wonder about Margaret and her husband, picturing them tending to the fields and breathing life into this place year after year. Was it difficult for her to let it go?

It's a little dim inside, the only light filtering in through the cracks between the wooden planks. It smells of old wood and damp straw. There are cobwebs clinging to the rafters, the feed troughs, and stretching in thick strands between the wooden beams.

A few tools are scattered around—a rusted rake leaning against the wall, a spade coated in dried dirt propped beside it. In the corner, an empty wooden crate sits half-open next to an old white bike with a woven basket.

The floorboards are cracked and slightly raised in places, making each step feel unsteady.

I pause inside, wrap my arms around my body—feeling a chill—and look around. A faint glimmer catches my eye near a pile of old hay.

Something small, half-buried in the dirt.

I crouch down and brush away the debris, revealing a broken necklace chain. The metal is sturdy, thicker than most chains you'd wear, and it looks a little rusty in places. I hold it up, studying it, wondering what kind of force it took to break it, what stories it has to tell.

Unsure what to do with the broken chain and not wanting to drop it back onto the ground, I slip it into my pocket to decide what to do with it later.

Then I wipe my hands on my jeans and hurry toward the door. As soon as I'm out in the open, I allow the fresh air to rush into my lungs.

Inside the house, I'm surprised to find Lina in my room, and as soon as I enter, she quickly closes a drawer of one of the bedside tables.

"Ah, you're back," she says, her eyes shifting away from mine.

"Yes. Are you looking for something?" I know I gave her permission to clean, but rummaging through drawers is a different matter. I can't help but feel a little violated.

"No, just... tidying up in there." Her eyes still avoid mine.

"Right," I reply, even though I'm well aware that the drawers she closed only contain a notebook and a pen I keep by my bedside for jotting down important thoughts before they slip away. That's a habit I picked up from Mary's fixation on recording her fleeting memories. "Thanks, but don't bother with this room. I can take care of it," I assure her. "Actually, I can handle cleaning the entire upstairs. You don't need to bother with it. You have enough on your plate."

"True." Lina leaves with a stiff posture, and I get to work.

Since my memory is not the most reliable right now, I grab the notebook and sit at the desk, jotting down everything I found out about this house, including those scratches I saw in Mary's room. I also write down one question:

Did Margaret have a sewing machine?

As soon as I finish and my head feels emptied, I remember the broken chain still in my pocket. I don't want to lose it, so I put it in one of the bathroom drawers.

I can't bring myself to throw it away. It might have belonged to Margaret, and if she ever comes back for the things she left behind, she might want it.

I go downstairs just as Evan's car pulls up outside. Lina rushes out of the house, says goodbye to him and drives off.

Going to greet him, I tell Evan about Lina cleaning the house, and his face darkens. "That's not her job. I'm paying her to take care of my aunt and nothing else."

When he sees that his outburst has shaken me a bit, he quickly pulls himself together and comes to take my hand. "I'm sorry. It's just that we had a cleaning lady before and she stole a few things, and it's left me wary of anyone touching our stuff."

I accept his explanation, but he's been so kind and gentle that seeing this angry side of him throws me.

Later, hoping to reconnect, I head to his office to sit on the couch while he works on his new book.

But as I turn the corner in the hallway, a movement catches my eye, and I stop.

Evan is walking fast toward the basement door at the far end, with a large duffel bag that hangs over one shoulder.

It must be heavy; he looks like he's leaning to the side.

He unlocks the door and slips through it, shutting it behind him without once looking back. Then I hear the metallic click of the lock sliding into place, and I realize I've been holding my breath.

Moving as silently as I can, I creep toward the basement door and press my ear against it.

For a moment, all I hear is my own breathing. Then a faint creak, followed by the soft thud of Evan's footsteps descending the stairs.

And then I hear nothing else.

I remain there, listening and waiting, but there are no other sounds. Just silence.

What's he doing down there?

The way he shut the door so quickly and locked it behind him looked like he didn't want anyone to see him.

Minutes tick by as I wait for him to come back up. Five. Fifteen. Twenty.

Still no sign of him.

I need to do something—anything. With one last glance at the locked basement door, I go to the dining room.

Pulling open the drawers, I rummage through them to distract myself, hoping for some clue about Margaret, the woman who lived here before us.

Most of what I find in the drawers is junk, like old grocery store receipts, loose paperclips, and several pens. But then I spot something.

A slim planner from a year ago, wedged at the back of a drawer. It must have fallen and gotten stuck there.

It has a pink flamingo on the cover, but it looks old, its edges curling slightly. I pull it out and flip through the pages.

Most of the notes scrawled inside are ordinary—reminders to pick up prescriptions, doctors' appointments, little things that seem trivial.

But then I notice something odd.

Between January and August, every single Wednesday has the same note written in small, neat letters:

Visit Meadowbrook.

Meadowbrook? The name rings no bells, but something about it makes my pulse quicken.

Is this a place? A surname?

Acting on instinct, I grab a pen from the drawer, but there's no paper nearby. Instead, I press the tip to my palm and scribble down the name before I can forget it.

As I cap the pen, a sound makes me freeze.

Evan.

I shove the planner back where I found it and straighten up, smoothing my hands down my sides. Then I head out of the dining room and almost bump into him walking down the hall, pushing what I think is the basement key into his pocket.

"Sweetheart, are you okay? Were you looking for me?"

"No." I keep my voice casual and my posture relaxed. "Were you doing some work in the basement?"

"Yeah. I went to fix something. It's a crazy mess down there... all dirt and dust. I should get cleaned up."

But I'm sure there isn't a single speck of dust on his clothes. No smudges of dirt, no grease stains. Nothing to suggest he'd been tinkering with anything down there. And he didn't bring that heavy bag back up with him.

"I should really go and have that shower. I'm all sweaty," he says.

No, you're not.

He's lying. What is he not telling me?

I need to find a way to get my hands on that key.

SEVEN

I'm sitting on the bedroom floor, rummaging through all my handbags in search of my old phone's password so I can get access to my contacts, my friends and former colleagues. Yesterday, Evan gave me the phone numbers of three of our mutual friends in Charlotte so I could reach out to them, but only two picked up. Melinda and Julian. Both were friendly enough, but understandably they did not know how to communicate with me. There was an awkwardness in their voices, a hesitation, as if they weren't sure what to say or how to act. Neither of them kindled a spark in my memories.

I pull out old receipts, scraps of paper, and other useless things. Unsurprisingly, there's no notebook or a piece of paper with any passwords written on it. My frustration mounts as I go over to the desk and open my laptop. I attempt again to log back into my Facebook account, trying numerous combinations, including suggestions from Evan—our wedding date (August 5, 2014), my birthday (December 7), his birthday, and various other ideas. No luck.

A twinge of disappointment tightens my chest. Then an idea forms.

I decide to create a new account. I type my full name—Cora Harrison—into the registration fields, and choose an avatar for my profile picture for now.

Once the account is set up, I scan through the list of almost one hundred people who had been following my original account. I pick a few names and start typing out a message to them.

> *Hi, I wanted to let you know I'm having trouble getting into my old account, so I've set up this new one. Hope you're doing well. Cora*

I hit send and pause for a moment, staring at the screen. Then, deciding to send more friend requests later, I start clearing up the mess I created. As I gather up the scattered contents of the bags, I remember what I wrote on my palm the other day. What with me spending the last two days watching to see if Evan will return to the basement and searching endlessly for the key to open that door, I completely forgot about it and it's long washed off. But now I remember it.

Meadowbrook.

Whispering it under my breath, I go back to my laptop and type it into Google. But all I get are random results, so I narrow my search to Meadowbrook, Cedar Hollow, North Carolina. This time, I get a hit.

Meadowbrook Assisted Living Facility. A care home for the elderly.

I stare at the screen. Whoever wrote those notes in that planner visited an elderly care home every Wednesday in 2018. Why does this feel important?

I grab a pen and jot down the phone number, and the second I finish, I hear the doorbell ring. It'll be Lina and I'm a bit nervous to see her after catching her going through the drawer last Friday.

As I descend the stairs, I hear raised voices in the kitchen.

My heart lodged in my throat, I move slowly. Walking past the living room door, I catch sight of Mary on the couch, a game of chess on the coffee table in front of her. Evan had been playing a round with her earlier. Next to Mary is her journal as always. She's holding a pen in her hand, but instead of writing, she's staring at the door, her head cocked to the side.

Earlier, I read another one of her entries, this time about fireflies—little specks of light that she and her grandfather, Pawpaw, used to love catching. I find the memories of her childhood soothing, and every chance I get, I can't help reading. Her stories draw me in, tugging at something deep inside me. Maybe it's because, on some level, they remind me of my own childhood—one that might have been similar to hers.

When I flipped the page, I found something unsettling, though—an entry about an old rocking chair that's missing the person who used to sit in it.

That old rocking chair on the porch creaks every time the wind moves it, like it remembers her sitting there, watching the sun slip behind the trees, her hands resting easy on the worn wooden arms.

I wonder what she thought about during those quiet moments in that chair. Did she count the days behind her or the ones ahead? Was she waiting for something?

Sometimes I forget what it was like. She sat there every evening, didn't she? That's what she told me. Maybe she still does. But I haven't seen her lately. I'll check tomorrow. Maybe she's resting.

Don't you miss your old chair, dear? Won't you come and sit in it again? It's waiting.

I'm not sure if the person she referred to was Margaret or someone else, and as usual, her thoughts are confused and tangled together. I do know there's an old wooden rocking chair on this house's porch, and after reading I went to sit in it, staring out at the fields, wondering if that's where Margaret used to sit. With that thought, I felt goose pimples push through my skin.

"Like I said, Lina, you're only here to tend to Mary," Evan shouts at Lina, causing me to snap back to the present.

His tone is harsh, and as I move closer to the door, I catch sight of Lina through the crack, and she looks upset.

"I was just trying to do something nice for you and—"

"I get that, and I appreciate your gesture," Evan interrupts in a softer tone. "But this is our home, and you need to respect that. And my aunt needs you more than the house does."

I hate that Evan is making such a big deal of this. It seems a little controlling and out of character. But then, I only know what I've seen of him in the few days since I woke up.

"All right. I understand," Lina responds quietly and Evan sighs, his hand rubbing at the back of his neck. There's a silence, and I wonder if I should make my presence known. But before I can muster the courage to step inside, Evan speaks again.

"I'm sorry, Lina. I shouldn't have snapped at you like that. It's been a stressful time lately, that's all."

"Thank you. I really just wanted to help. I didn't mean to overstep any boundaries."

"I know. I appreciate it, truly. And you're great with Mary. For now, if you do feel the need to clean, you can help out with Mary's room."

"Okay. I apologize again if I crossed any lines."

"It's fine. Let's forget about it." With that, Evan turns and heads to the door, and it's too late for me to slip away unnoticed. As he opens the door wider, he smiles. "Hey, sweetheart." He reaches out to touch my arm. "I'm heading out to do some grocery shopping."

"Great. How about I come with you?"

"I don't think that's a good idea. You're starting to recover your memories and going out there might overwhelm you. Give it a few more days and we'll see how you feel then."

My cheeks fill with the heat of frustration, but I nod. "Right. Can you pick up some of that fresh orange juice you bought last time?"

He kisses my forehead. "Of course. I'll see you soon."

Soon after, I'm standing in the doorway, watching him drive off.

"You don't have to worry about it," Lina says as she hands me a cup of green tea in the kitchen, after I apologize for getting her into trouble with Evan. "Why don't we sit down for a bit and have a chat?"

"I'd like that." I sip my tea. "Do you like what you do, Lina?"

"More than anything. I love helping people. And Mary—she's a sweetheart."

"I can't even imagine how hard it must be for her. I mean, I've lost my memory too, but at least there's still some hope. To think that Mary doesn't have that hope, it's devastating."

"What you're going through is tough too. Going through that trauma and losing your memory like that..." Lina shakes her head. "You're strong though, I can see that in you. Don't forget to give yourself credit for the progress you're making. Also, you're so lucky to have someone who loves you so much, taking care of you the way Evan does. Some of us are still searching for that special someone to love and trust."

Trust. I run that word over in my mind and I think back to seeing Evan going into the basement on Friday and lying to me about it.

· · ·

After I spend some time in my room, checking on my new Facebook account and writing down my thoughts, I go to Mary's room. She's sitting on the bed scribbling in her book. I begin helping Lina fold her clothes and put them away in the closet.

Lina tells me a little about herself, that she likes to paint, sketch, and to practice martial arts in her free time. She also enjoys exploring new cafés and restaurants, especially when she visits different towns and cities.

As much as I'm interested in getting to know her better, I eventually steer the conversation toward something that's been on my mind.

"Lina, have you heard of a care home here in town called Meadowbrook?"

Lina lowers her voice. "It's where Mary was before you brought her here."

So then, if the planner I found belonged to Margaret, perhaps Mary really did know her. But if Margaret's visits to Meadowbrook were to see Mary every week, they must have been old friends.

Why didn't Evan know? Or if he did, why did he lie?

EIGHT

Tuesday, July 16, 2019

The next afternoon, while Mary is in the living room journaling and half-watching one of her shows, I tell Evan I need to have a word with him, and we sit on the couch in his office.

He reaches for my hand, but I pull it away.

"Cora, is something wrong? You look upset."

"Not upset. Just confused."

"Right." He leans back and crosses his arms. "What's on your mind?"

"I know Mary used to stay at Meadowbrook before we brought her here, and I found out Margaret—the woman who used to live here—visited that place every week early last year. I'm wondering if maybe she was visiting Mary."

He presses a fist to his forehead. "How... where did you...?"

I cut in, keeping my voice steady. "That doesn't matter. What I'm trying to say is—"

He stands abruptly and shoves his hands into his pockets. "Cora, I don't know why you think this is important, but Aunt

Mary gets confused a lot. Like I said before, she didn't know Margaret. Just let it go. Don't get caught up in something that's only going to upset you—or my aunt. Now, I'll go play a round of chess with her before her nap."

I paste a smile onto my face. "Fine. I've got a few things to do anyway. I might go out to the lake later. Get some air."

"Sounds good, but how about waiting until after Mary wakes up? We could all go for a walk together as a family."

"No, I think I'll go alone, if you don't mind. I need some time on my own."

I walk out onto the porch and ease myself into the old rocking chair. It creaks beneath me, the same low groan I've heard before.

More than ever, I'm convinced Evan is lying about Mary and Margaret not knowing each other. What I can't figure out is why.

I glance toward the edge of the property, peering into the distance, trying to make out other farmhouses, our neighbors.

I know what I have to do next.

When Mary is asleep and Evan is inside his office, I walk out into the sunshine, but instead of heading to the lake, I hurry to the barn, where there's that bike with the woven basket. I push it out of the barn and climb onto the cracked seat. It feels awkward at first, but then I start pedaling and it's easy. And just like that, the wind catches in my hair and a rush of freedom surges through me.

I don't care if Evan sees me cycling off. I'm a free woman, after all, and I can go where I want, when I want. I ride for what feels like hours, the countryside stretching before me in search of the yellow house with a peacock on the roof.

It won't be hard to find it since it seems there's only one main road that leads from our farm to the town and I'm heading in the direction Sabrina had pointed when she came over. The sun warms my skin as I pass fields of wildflowers, their bright colors cheering me up. The scent of sweet honeysuckle wafts in the air, mixing with the earthy smell of fresh grass.

As I round a bend, I pass only one farm before spotting a small stand by a wooden gate, fresh produce and jars of preserves laid out under a colorful canopy. There's a familiar figure standing there, chatting with an older woman, whose hands are busy with a crocheting project. Sabrina.

My heart skips. I've found it without even really looking. Sabrina looks up as I approach and hop off the bike.

"Cora!" Her face lights up. "What a surprise." She's wearing denim overalls again but underneath is a vibrant floral blouse. Her hair is in a French braid that snakes its way over her shoulder.

"Hi Sabrina, how are you? I was hoping we could have a chat," I say, my voice lighter than I feel.

"Lovely." She steps forward, motioning to the wooden bench beside the stand. "Come sit down. We've got fresh sweet tea."

As I sit, she introduces me to her mother, who I must have known before the accident.

"That's my mom, Jill. I told you about her."

"Hi, Jill," I say and the woman looks up at me briefly, but her eyes are clouded and a little unfocused behind the round glasses. I wonder if she recognizes me since Sabrina mentioned last time that her eyesight is not that good.

Sabrina pours me a cool glass of sweet tea and hands it to me. It's a pale-yellow color, with a sprig of mint bobbing at the surface. I take a sip, grateful for the tangy sweet taste that lingers on my tongue.

"Where's Owen?" I glance around for the little boy and his ball.

Sabrina smiles. "He's at preschool in town. He was sick the other day, but it turned out to be nothing, a little cold is all."

"I'm happy he's fine again." I take another sip. "You have a lovely farm." I scan the fields around us with chickens here and there, and a couple of goats munching on the grass. "It's more alive than ours." There are even fruit trees dotting the landscape, heavy with nectarines, peaches, and plums. A distant barn stands tall and proud, and it looks freshly painted with a coat of bright red and white paint.

"Thank you." Sabrina's gray eyes brighten as she smiles. "It's a lot of work, but it's worth it. I work as a waitress at the Bluebird Diner in town two or three times a week, and the rest of my time is spent here. Not much free time, I'm afraid. But I like to keep busy."

"And it's only you and your mom doing all the farm work?" Jill must be in her late seventies or early eighties and I can't imagine her contributing much.

"No. My brother Raymond was in the army, but he moved back home almost two weeks ago to help out. Ray is out in the field now, tending to some new seedlings we've recently planted."

I lean back slightly, soaking it all in. "Y'all did an amazing job. It really is beautiful here."

"That farm of yours was once a beauty as well until—"

"Richard died," Jill suddenly speaks up, her voice unexpectedly sharp. "Has Margaret come back home yet?"

A rush of adrenaline hits me so hard that I snatch a breath. "Margaret?"

Sabrina looks uncomfortable as she busies herself with arranging the trays of fruits for selling. "Margaret Tookes. She and her husband, Richard, used to own the farm before you."

Jill's hands stop moving. "Margaret loved that old farm," she says under her breath. "She would never have sold it."

I'm thrilled to be getting all this information without even asking many questions. Margaret is finally a real person and not just a name in Mary's journals or on her lips.

"When Richard died," Sabrina adds, "Margaret was devastated. She grieved him deeply. My mom and Margaret were very close. They had this routine, having tea and cakes together every week. But one day, Mom came over for their regular tea, and Margaret was gone. Your husband Evan opened the door and said that Margaret had sold the farm."

I feel a knot tighten in my stomach when Jill suddenly jumps to her feet, her face flushed with emotion. "Margaret wouldn't have left without saying goodbye!" she insists, her hands trembling as she rubs a silver locket that hangs around her neck. "She used to sing in the big city, you know. She was a star, Margaret Lewis was her name then. But she gave it all up when she met Richard. She always said the farm was a piece of her heart, where she could be with him. When he passed, the farm was all she had left. She wanted to live there with his memories until she went to join him."

"Could it be she couldn't handle the farm on her own?" I suggest. "Or the memories became too painful after her husband died?"

Jill shakes her head vehemently. "No! She would never have left without telling me. I know it. We've been friends for over forty years."

She walks back toward the house, mumbling something under her breath. Sabrina watches her go, her expression sad, then turns back to me.

"I'm sorry. Mom... she's still upset about Margaret. It's been hard for her."

"I... I feel guilty," I admit after a pause. "The farm was a gift from Evan, to me. Do you think he pressured Margaret into selling it?"

"I don't think so, Cora. I really don't. Margaret was getting older, and she wasn't well. I actually worried about her being alone on that big farm. Maybe, like you said, she couldn't handle it anymore. Maybe she went somewhere to be taken care of."

I try to swallow the tightness in my chest. Sabrina's words help, but they don't erase the discomfort gnawing at me. Something's wrong, I know it is.

Before I leave, I ask her one last question. "Do you know if Margaret was friends with my husband's Aunt Mary?"

Sabrina offers a half-smile. "This is a small town. Most people tend to know each other, whether they want to or not."

When I arrive home, the house is quiet except for the distant sound of Evan's voice behind the closed door of his office.

I slip inside and then upstairs into my bedroom where I grab the laptop and sink onto the edge of the bed. My hands feel clammy as I type the name into the search bar: Margaret Lewis.

Jill was right.

Margaret was an up-and-coming country singer in her day. Fairly popular. Her name appears in a handful of old articles, mostly from entertainment archives. In her twenties, she had a promising career, a few charting songs, a steady rise to stardom —until her thirties, when everything stopped.

The reason? Love.

She fell for a fan—his name isn't mentioned—and seemingly vanished from the limelight as she was taking off. Some say she *did* give it all up for love, while others speculate that she just slipped into a quiet life, alone and far from the flashing lights.

The last real mention of her is decades old.

And then, I stumble across a grainy photo in an old online forum post from more than ten years back.

She was beautiful. Soft, blonde curls framing her delicate heart-shaped face, full lips.

Her bright eyes tell me she's the kind of person who would give up everything for someone she loved. Richard Tookes?

I remember the brass plaque in the dining room—engraved with her and her husband's initials. Like Jill, I'm finding it hard to believe that she so easily gave up this home, which held so many memories of her beloved husband.

NINE

After Mary is in bed and I've searched the house again for any sign of a sewing machine, which keeps niggling at my mind, I settle in the living room to watch some TV.

A few minutes later, Evan walks in and tells me he has a surprise. He reaches out a hand, takes mine, and escorts me to his office, which is lit up by candles and a green picnic blanket is on the floor. A bottle of sparkling cider sits in an ice bucket, its label reflecting the flickering candlelight. There are fluffy cupcakes, strawberries dipped in chocolate, a plate of cheese and crackers, a large pizza box, and a bowl of popcorn.

"I know you've been feeling crappy all day, so I wanted to do something special to cheer you up." He motions for me to sit on the blanket.

"Oh Evan, this is so sweet. I love it." He's trying so hard to make me happy, to feel like myself again. His effort is touching, and it warms my heart. Even though I still have a lot of questions and still wonder why he doesn't want me to know about Mary and Margaret, I put that aside for now and reach for his hand, squeezing it lightly. Maybe there is an innocent explanation for everything.

When he lifts the cover of the pizza box and I see the pepperoni pizza with extra cheese, my stomach does a happy flip. He picks up a slice and hands it to me. It smells heavenly, of melting cheese and spicy pepperoni. I take a bite and savor the flavor.

We eat in comfortable silence, and he pulls out a stack of photographs and hands them to me. More wedding photos. I look beautiful, in an ivory gown with a trail of lace following behind. Evan is dashing in his black tuxedo, a look of pure bliss etched on his face as I walk down the aisle toward him.

"I wish I could remember," I whisper, my fingers tracing over the glossy surface of the photos. "I'm so sorry." I look down at my wedding band, so desperate to reclaim the past. The ring is elegant, a delicate gold band with a single dazzling diamond. But it feels slightly loose on my finger.

Evan smooths a hand over mine, his touch as comforting as ever. "Don't be sorry," he whispers. "Just because you can't remember doesn't mean it didn't happen or that it didn't matter. Our love is here, right now."

Smiling, I stare at his face, taking in his features, and for a fleeting moment, something flickers in my mind. I almost, almost recognize him. But then it's gone. My memories are like fireflies, like glimpses of light that are impossible to catch.

Evan is a very handsome man, and I can imagine having fallen for him. Tonight, he's neatly put together as usual, wearing a crisp white T-shirt and dark-blue jeans. In spite of myself, I reach out and hug him.

"Thank you for doing this."

He hugs me back tightly, holding on until I pull away.

"You're very welcome." He bites into his slice of pizza. "I know you had a rotten day, and I know it's devastating not being able to remember. I wish I could fix all of this for you, for us."

"You're doing a very good job." I take a bite of my own pizza.

As we continue eating, I sip my cider and observe him over the rim of my glass. "Was it easy for you to buy this place?" I ask, keeping my tone light, as if I'm making casual conversation. "From Margaret?"

He shrugs. "I bought it through a real estate agent, so it was pretty straightforward." He reaches for a napkin and wipes his mouth. "Didn't really know much about her."

For a second, I consider telling him about my conversation with Jill and Sabrina, but something stops me. He doesn't even know I went over there, and I want to keep it that way. As much as I feel close to him tonight, I also feel independent, more in control somehow. There's something freeing about having my own thoughts, my own little discoveries.

"It's kind of strange," I say, swirling my drink. "That she left behind so many memories—the furniture, the belongings... everything except for photos, of course. I haven't seen a single one around yet."

"This is our home now," he says lightly. "You should focus on us, on your healing. Not on things that don't matter."

His words are gentle. But I sense a tension, hidden well beneath them, and I notice his eyes have gone cold.

After dinner, Evan insists on cleaning up and I head to bed, thinking about Margaret and the husband she loved, here in this home.

Later that night, well past midnight, I wake with a start. My eyes open and my breath catches in my throat.

Mary is standing in my room, holding her journal. Moonlight from the window outlines her fragile figure; I must have forgotten to close the curtains.

"Mary?" I whisper. "What are you doing here?"

She hugs her journal to herself with one arm while gripping her cane with the other, then slowly walks toward the door.

Evan said that Mary had a serious fall at the care home, which is why she now relies on a cane to move around.

"Mary, it's all right. Talk to me." I rise and go to her, then help her back to sit on the bed.

"I heard something. Someone crying. Is it her?"

"Who, Mary? What do you mean?" Goose bumps rise on my arms, and a cold, tingling sensation travels down my back.

"I don't know." She shrugs and steadies herself, pushing up to her feet. "Good night."

She makes her way to the door, and I follow to ensure she reaches her room safely.

Then in the hallway, I pause and listen. I think I hear it too —a faint, distant sob. I strain my ears, but the sound fades away, or perhaps it was never there at all.

TEN

Two days later, I hear it again: a woman crying in the dead of night.

I open my eyes and my heart leaps into my throat.

There's no sound; it must have been another bad dream. My mind is on overdrive since I spent the last two days thinking about the people who lived in this house before us.

I had been dreaming about Margaret Tookes. In one of my dreams, I was at the lake, and she approached me wearing a blue dress. Her lips moved, and she spoke to me, but no matter how hard I tried to listen, I couldn't catch a single word. It was as if she were whispering, her voice swept away by the breeze from the lake.

I close my eyes again, but then I hear footsteps outside my door.

Thud. Thud. Thud.

Now that was definitely not in my mind.

As I grip the sheets, the sound grows louder, inches from the door now. My heart pounds in my chest like a drum. When the sound stops and nothing more happens, I take a deep breath and slide out of bed.

Carefully, I tiptoe toward the door, every creak from the old wooden floor echoing in my ears. I pause, hand hovering over the doorknob, and listen.

It's not as if I'm living in this house alone. It could have been Evan walking past my door.

There's nothing for me to be afraid of, I tell myself. But the fear clings to me like a second skin. Still, I force myself to turn the knob slowly until the door swings open to reveal someone standing there.

"Goodness, Mary. You scared me." I clutch my chest and try to catch my breath. "What are you doing up here?"

Mary is standing there, leaning on her cane. She looks disoriented, as if she was also ripped out of a deep sleep. Evan will not be happy to know that she's been climbing the stairs in the dark.

"I heard you crying," she says.

Could it really have been me crying in my sleep?

"I'm okay, Mary, it was just a bad dream" I say, trying to reassure her.

After a pause, she nods. "My nephew is taking me to the country club tomorrow for lunch." She pushes her shoulders back, standing taller. "I used to be a member there for many years, you know. In fact, I was one of their best and most respected members." She beams at me. "Did I tell you that I was a very successful businesswoman back then? I was someone they would call a hotshot these days."

"Yes, you did. But wow, Mary. That must have been exciting."

"I sure had a good time." Her smile fades again. "But despite having all the money in the world, I never had kids of my own or a husband."

She speaks without looking at me, her eyes distant.

"At least you have your nephew."

Evan told me that his mother died while giving birth to him, and his father—who never remarried—passed away from a stroke when Evan was just fifteen. With no siblings or other relatives remaining, Mary, his mother's sister, is the only family he has.

As I study Mary's face, I wonder if Evan and I want kids. We have been married for five years, so there must have been talk of it. Or perhaps we were one of those couples who chose not to have children.

"Yes," Mary sighs, bringing me back from my thoughts. "My nephew is a good boy, always looks out for me. I don't know what I would do without him."

"You would have been just fine. Now, let's get you back to bed."

She does not resist as I guide her to the stairs. When I tuck her in and read her a verse from her Bible, she reaches under her pillow and hands me a folded piece of paper.

"What is this?" I ask, unfolding it.

The grainy black-and-white photo featured in the article shows Mary, who was probably in her early fifties, receiving an award for top businesswoman of the year. Her hair is styled in a neat updo, and she's wearing pearls and a perfectly tailored pant suit.

The headline of the article reads: *Providence and Guardian Insurance CEO Honored for Excellence in Business.*

"That's wonderful, Mary," I say, and she reaches to take it back from me.

"I was quite something, wasn't I?" She stares at it, her hand shaking a little. "I had power, respect, and influence. But not any longer." Her voice drifts off and her eyes cloud over.

"You still are quite something, Mary. Now get some rest."

On my way to the door, my eyes linger on the scratches by the doorframe again.

. . .

Instead of heading straight to bed, I wander into the kitchen to grab a drink.

I open the fridge and I'm about to reach for the large carton of fresh orange juice that Evan put in there yesterday evening, but it's not there so I pour a cup of milk, warm it slightly in the microwave, and drizzle in a bit of honey.

It's comforting somehow, that I know exactly where everything in the kitchen is located. The cups hang above the sink, the plates sit underneath near the stove on the left side, and the silverware is arranged neatly in the drawer next to the fridge. I'm even aware of the honey's exact spot in the cupboard above the coffee maker.

It's all muscle memory. Even though my mind can't recall the past, my body seems to, which is encouraging. It's only a matter of time before everything else falls into place.

Focusing on the present moment, I take a sip of the milk, savoring its warmth and sweetness on my tongue. It's a reminder of a childhood I can't quite remember but instinctively know existed.

Cradling my cup of milk, I make my way upstairs. I wonder why Evan didn't wake up when he heard me crying. If my crying were loud enough to disturb Mary, surely he would have checked on me? He would also have heard me and Mary talking in the hallway.

I reach my door but change my mind and head in the direction of Evan's instead. To my surprise, I find it open a crack, but the light is not on inside. Without thinking, I push the door open a bit further and when I see no movement on the bed, I switch on the light only to stare at an empty room.

Evan is not on the bed, or in the bathroom.

I go to the window in his room that overlooks the front of the house and peer out. His Volvo is still parked outside.

Unable to stop myself, I head back downstairs, and after knocking on his office door, which is locked, I go to the base-ment door.

I press my ear against it, straining to hear any sound from the other side, but there's nothing, and no light coming from under the door either.

Where is my husband?

ELEVEN

Friday, July 19, 2019

I wake up shortly after Evan and knock on his office door. Instead of inviting me in, he comes to the door. Normally, he appears polished and distinguished, his hair perfectly in place and often dressed sharply. But today, he looks like he hasn't slept at all, with dull eyes, faint dark circles, and still wearing his satin pajamas. I guess he doesn't have any meetings this morning.

"Morning, sweetheart," he greets me, surprised to see me. "You're up early today."

"Yes, I didn't sleep well last night. I had an awful dream and ended up waking Mary."

"What did you dream about? Are you okay?"

"I can't remember the details, but I cried in my sleep." I step into the office and Evan closes the door. "Mary heard me and came to my room."

"She climbed the stairs? She knows she shouldn't do that on her own. She could fall, like she did at that home." His eyebrows furrow together to form a deep grove. "I worry about her safety. That's why I moved her into a room downstairs."

"Don't be upset with her. She wanted to check on me; she was worried. I'm sure she was careful, and she's okay."

Evan crosses his arms with his hands tucked into his armpits. "I'll talk to her later about going upstairs. But for now, let's focus on you. I'm sorry I didn't hear you last night. I was fast asleep, or I would have come to see you."

"Don't worry about it. It was only a bad dream. Nothing serious."

A part of me wants to say I know he's lying, that he wasn't in his room late last night, but I hold back. Instead, I smile and add, "At least I didn't wake up the entire house."

"No, you didn't." He chuckles, then shifts gears. "Are you hungry? Lina is already here, and she made more breakfast than Mary can eat." He pauses, studying my face. "I'm taking Mary to a doctor's appointment later, and then to lunch at the country club. Would you like to join us? We could spend some time together as a family. What do you say?"

"No, you two go and have a nice time together. I'm sure she'd love to have you all to herself." I want to leave this house, but there are things here I need to explore when no one is here.

"I really don't like the idea of leaving you alone," Evan remarks. "I'll ask Lina to stay until Mary and I get back."

Knowing I'm not going to be able to convince him otherwise, I sigh. "All right, Evan. If that will make you feel better."

At eleven, before Mary and Evan are set to leave for the doctor's appointment, a grimy white truck parks outside the house. A man in blue overalls and a black cap enters, carrying a toolbox. Evan greets him, and they both head down to the basement. Soon I hear banging and drilling and after some time, they return upstairs.

Observing them, unnoticed, from the kitchen doorway, I watch Evan hand the man some money. "Thanks, Pete, for fixing some of the mess down there. I'll likely need to call you back soon. That basement might require a complete renovation. I plan to convert it into a gym for me and my wife once she recovers."

The knot in my stomach begins to loosen as relief fills me. I understand now.

The reason he doesn't want me to see the basement is because he's planning a surprise reveal of the gym.

So, the basement, at least, has an innocent explanation.

But what about the rest? Evan lying about where he was at night? This strange business about Margaret, and her friendship with Mary?

After Evan and Mary leave, I check my new Facebook account and I'm disappointed to see the friend requests I sent out still haven't been accepted. I go downstairs to find Lina, my hand gliding along the handrail, worn smooth from years of use. Somewhere in my buried memories, I remember that the third step from the bottom creaks.

Lina isn't in the living room or the kitchen. As I'm about to call for her, I hear the sound of cupboards being opened and closed. I follow the noise to Evan's office. The door is open, and Lina is behind his desk, staring at the screen of his laptop before rummaging through one of the drawers. Then as if sensing my presence, she slowly raises her head.

A blush spreads across her cheeks as she shuts the laptop. "Hi, Cora, I didn't realize you were awake."

Of course you didn't.

"What are you doing?" I'm still standing in the doorway, watching her.

She steps away from the desk and approaches me with a

bright smile. "The last time I was here, I misplaced one of my bracelets, and this morning Mary mentioned she thought she saw it in this room."

I don't buy it. How could she possibly find a bracelet inside my husband's laptop?

But as she walks out of the office and wraps an arm around me, suggesting we have a drink and enjoy a friendly chat, I accept.

I know she was looking for something, but then again, so am I.

I really feel like there's a secret in this house, and maybe Lina senses it too. I wonder if I should use her to help me find out what it is. Either way, I won't be telling Evan about what I saw.

TWELVE

Monday, July 22, 2019

On Monday morning, Doctor Rowe comes over to the house to check on me, and I take the opportunity to ask him if there's any way to expedite my memory recovery.

He rubs his chin, then clears his throat. "I suggest patience and rest. Everything you lost, or at least most of it, might come back."

Might. What would I do if I never got all my memory back? How can I live the rest of my life having lost most of it?

He goes on about how important rest is for my brain. But how can I relax in a house I know is hiding secrets?

Suddenly, without thinking, I blurt out, "I've been hearing strange noises at night, and seeing things. And I'm not sure whether they're real or whether I've made them up."

Evan is sitting on the couch on the other side of the room, watching us. I see him lean forward, listening intently.

Doctor Rowe looks over at Evan, then turns back to me. "It's normal for the mind to play tricks on people recovering from trauma, particularly head injuries."

After Doctor Rowe has gone and Evan has closed the door, I clear my throat. "Evan, what are you and Doctor Rowe not telling me? I saw you looking at each other and I feel like there's something important you're keeping from me."

Evan buries both hands into his hair and sighs. Then he wraps an arm around my shoulders and ushers me in the direction of his office. He sits me down on the couch and sits next to me.

"Sweetheart, you're still recovering. That's why I didn't want to overwhelm you with the truth right away. I really wanted you to have a fresh start."

"What are you talking about?"

He rakes a hand through his hair and clears his throat, debating what to tell me or how much of it to share. Then he looks me straight in the eyes. "Before the accident and your memory loss, you suffered from bipolar disorder. It's something you've had since you were a child. Sometimes you saw things that didn't exist."

I didn't imagine it then, the look the doctor gave him.

I sit there, frozen. Devastated.

I almost wish I hadn't brought it up, hadn't demanded to know. Sometimes ignorance truly *is* bliss.

"Come here." He pulls me into a hug. After a long moment, I'm the first to pull away. I look him in the eyes. "Was I in any kind of treatment?"

Evan stands up, goes to one of the drawers at his desk, and pulls out two pill bottles. "This is lithium, a mood stabilizer," he says, sitting back down and placing one bottle in my hand. Then he hands me the other one. "And this is olanzapine, an antipsychotic." He sighs and leans back. "I think you should also get on something for anxiety. I'm pretty sure you still have a bottle of Xanax somewhere in the house. Maybe in the bathroom cabinet? I'll have a look later."

My stomach churns as my fingers tighten around the

bottles. The labels are crisp with my name printed on them. "Why did I stop taking them?"

"Since the accident, I didn't want you to take that medication. You said you didn't feel like yourself when you took them and I wanted you to feel normal, even for a little while. I thought that might help you recover your memories more quickly."

I stare down at the medication in my hands. "And Doctor Rowe? Was he okay with me stopping?"

"It was your psychiatrist back in Charlotte who prescribed your medication, but Doctor Rowe knew about your condition as well, and he was against you taking a break. But I resisted because I wanted you to get your memories back as soon as possible. And you were doing quite well, actually. But now... I don't know. Maybe we don't have a choice. If you're starting to see things that aren't there, maybe we should handle this before it spirals out of control."

With tears in his eyes, he takes my hand and kisses it. "I'm sorry, baby, that you have to go through all of this. But we'll get through it together. We did before."

"Okay," I whisper. "Thank you for being here for me."

"Always." He shifts in his seat and swallows loud enough for me to hear. "Now that you know, there's something else I haven't told you."

"What is it?" My eyebrows shoot up. What worse thing could he possibly have to tell me?

"You didn't fall while hanging up a photo frame." His voice is hesitant. "I lied to you. You had an episode, you were manic. It had been building for days. You were convinced that someone was watching us, that the house wasn't safe. You weren't sleeping much, and you barely ate." He hesitates. "That night, you said you saw something at the top of the stairs. I was trying to calm you down, but you screamed and backed away too fast. You lost your balance and you fell down the stairs."

"Oh my God." I try to picture it, seeing myself pacing around, confused and frantic, seeing and hearing things that weren't there. Is that what's happening to me now?

"I didn't want you to know," he continues. "I didn't want to remind you of your... the illness. But you need to know the truth; then you can decide how we handle this. It's your life, it's your health, and it was not okay for me to withhold that information."

"You're right," I say through gritted teeth, almost angry at him, but not really.

In truth, I'm angry at the situation. Furious that I have to deal with more than memory loss, that I have to come to terms with this as well.

The loss of control is what unsettles me the most.

THIRTEEN

Friday, July 26, 2019

In the last few days, I've kept myself busy around the house and trying to solve the mystery about Margaret. I haven't allowed myself to stay still long enough to think about my mental health.

Today after dinner, I tell Evan that I want to tackle the dining room. "I want to pack up the previous owners' stuff and make it feel a little more like ours."

Evan pauses, his hands dripping over the kitchen sink as he washes the plates. "Is that a good idea?" He accepts a dirty plate from me. "Are you sure you're not taking on too much?"

Something inside me ignites. "Yes, it's a good idea, Evan." My tone is sharper than I intend. "You said I planned on renovating the house anyway. I might as well start now."

He reaches for a dish towel and dries his hands, taking a few steps toward me. "It's just... it's getting late, darling. Start fresh in the morning. Why don't you go and watch a movie with Mary? I'm sure she hasn't settled on one yet."

"No, I have enough energy to start. I want this place to feel like home." I peer through the doorway leading into the dark dining room. "Doesn't it feel weird being surrounded by strangers' things?"

Evan sighs. "But there's a lot to do in there. I'll help you."

"No, you go and work on your book." I walk in the direction of the dining room and stop, turning again to face him. "You could get me some boxes and bubble wrap."

"Your wish is my command." He bows and walks out.

Evan is right. Taking on this project might be a lot of work, but for some reason, I feel like being alone with Margaret's things. I want to get to know her better, to figure out why she left them all behind. To feed my increasing curiosity.

By the time Evan comes back with the boxes, I've already cleared one shelf of crystal glasses and figurines.

"Thanks." I barely look up as I stare at a beautiful crystal horse figurine, its surface catching the light and sparkling like a diamond.

I sense instead of see him hesitate for a moment in the doorway, then he's gone and I'm left alone with Margaret's memories.

I work for over two hours straight, opening drawers, pulling down the heavy curtains, discovering what little I can about Margaret and her husband.

In a cabinet in the corner, I find a stack of old recipe books with yellowed pages and handwritten notes in the margins. Tucked in the back is a square metal tin filled with faded nature postcards from Nantucket, Maine, and Seaside. There's a whole bunch of them, none addressed to anyone. I'm guessing these were their favorite holiday spots.

There are also several lavender sachets and a stack of linen napkins. I bring my attention to the engraved brass plaque I saw last time, my fingers tracing the letters as my chest tightens. Poor Margaret. She must have been devastated when Richard died.

I carefully wrap up the plaque and keep going. Even with

an ache blooming in my back and my arms feeling leaden, I push through it, unable to pause, not wanting to think.

It's close to eleven when Evan walks back in and insists I stop for the day.

"Sweetheart, you've done enough." He points to the boxes. "Let me carry those to the basement for you."

"No worries, I can do it myself. Please go and unlock the door for me." I reach for a box, but as I lift it, he steps forward.

"Cora, you know it's not safe down there. And you look exhausted. I don't want you falling again."

I feel suddenly frustrated. "Sometimes you forget we're not children, me and Mary."

Evan stares at me, his lips parted as though he's about to say something. But he doesn't. Inhaling sharply, he takes the box from my arms and leaves.

And that's when Mary wanders in, barefoot, in her pale-blue nightgown. She was supposed to already be in bed, but she must have heard us talking.

She stops in the middle of the room, eyes sweeping the mess around me, before they land on something near the fireplace.

She picks up a sterling silver vintage candle stick. "I gave this to Margaret one Christmas."

"You did?" I cross the room to stand in front of her.

"Yes, she was very pleased." Mary squints at the candle holder like it might unlock a forgotten memory.

I clear my throat, trying to sound casual. "Mary, why don't you tell me more about your friend Margaret? What did she look like?" I hope she can answer me quickly before Evan comes back and takes her back to bed.

Mary's face brightens and her eyes immediately look clearer. "She had the most beautiful black hair. It was long, like a raven's wings."

"Is that so?" Disappointment burns through my chest. From the photo online and the descriptions of her in the few articles I found, Margaret was a blonde, unless she colored her hair, of course.

"Oh, yes. She always wore it up in one of those fancy clips. And her eyes..." Her smile falters. "They were green. No—hazel. No, wait... blue, I think."

"She sounds like a beautiful woman," I say in a flat voice.

Maybe Evan was right. Maybe I *am* chasing after something that's not real. "Mary, I heard Margaret was a singer once. Did she have a beautiful voice?"

Mary snorts out a laugh. "Lord, no! That woman couldn't hold a tune to save her life."

I laugh too, but it catches in my throat.

FOURTEEN

Monday, July 29, 2019

It's been a week since Evan told me about my illness and I've continued taking the bipolar medication. Given the circumstances I've been mostly fine, keeping busy with the house.

After clearing out the dining room, on Friday night and Saturday morning, I decided to deep clean the rest of the house. While cleaning the living room yesterday, I came across a small photo album tucked behind some old books.

Inside were pictures of Margaret with a man I assume was Richard. He was tall, with dark hair, hazel eyes, and a neatly trimmed beard. They looked so happy and in love. In most of them, Margaret leaned into her husband, obviously feeling safe and protected in his presence.

It was a welcome glimpse into a life that felt honest and full of love, and I felt sad for Margaret, that she lost the man she loved, the man she felt safe with.

I also came across a business plan for the interior design company Evan said I planned on starting. I pored over it in bed last night, trying to get into my own head, to connect with the version of me who wrote it. The name I chose for my company —Fieldhouse Interiors—felt fitting. Seeing the color palettes, sketches, and pictures of logos, I could see how passionate I must have been about starting my business.

I wanted to continue my cleaning mission again today, but the exhaustion has finally caught up with me, and I feel sluggish. But mostly, I feel so sad, like there's a heavy blanket weighing me down. I felt like this yesterday too, but not enough to put the brakes on.

Right now, even if I wish I could be up and about, doing things around the house and searching for pieces of Margaret, I'm lying on my bed, staring at the white ceiling with Evan sitting next to me on the bed, holding my hand. He doesn't say anything, just sits there, stroking my fingers absentmindedly. The frown on his face makes the lines between his eyebrows deepen, and I know he is struggling as much as I am.

I wish I could grab a remote control and fast-forward to a time where I remember everything about him and our lives. I've been home three weeks now, and still nothing. My bipolar label now defines me more than my own past.

Shouldn't the medicine I took earlier be working by now? My exhaustion feels so deep, and the sadness weighs heavier than yesterday. I'm desperate to find a way out.

"I'm here, sweetheart," Evan says eventually, tightening his fingers around mine. "I know you want this to be over, but you really need to be patient with yourself."

He is patient with me every single day. Why can't I give myself the same kindness? I want to pull my brain from my head and piece it back together.

"I don't know what to do," I whisper. "I feel like I'm broken."

"You're not." He puts a gentle finger on my cheek and brushes it softly. "You're perfect to me. I love you, Cora."

I wish I could tell him I love him back, but I'm still not there yet.

"You don't have to say anything." He attempts a smile, but in his eyes, I can see the shards of his broken heart.

So, we continue in silence. He watches me, and I wish he would stand up and leave because there's nothing I want more right now than to be alone. The longer he stays, the worse I feel, because I can't give him what he so desperately needs—his wife back.

Finally, he leaves my room, and I stay in bed for another hour. The only time he returns is to bring me food, but the tray lies untouched on my bedside table.

Finally, I pull myself out of bed and walk the short distance to the bathroom. But my head feels so light, like it's floating on my body, and the room tilts. By the time I reach the bathroom, my vision starts to blur at the edges.

When Doctor Rowe came over again last Friday, he said I was progressing quite well. But I feel as though I'm losing myself.

Returning to the bedroom, my eyes fall on the pills on the nightstand.

Before I can stop myself, I reach for a bottle of antidepressants. Even though I already took a pill this morning, I pop open the lid, pour out another, and swallow it down.

Inhaling deeply, I finish getting dressed in a gray sweatshirt. My fingers feel numb as I push my feet into the fuzzy slippers that have been discarded at the side of my bed.

I find Evan in the hallway, having just come upstairs. "I was about to check on you." He comes to press a kiss to my cheek, leaving a tingle there. "Is there anything you want? Anything at all that I can do for you?"

"No, thank you. What I need is to get out for some air." I make my way toward the stairs.

"That's a great idea. Let me get changed out of this suit, and I'll join you."

"No. If you don't mind, I'd like to be alone. I'm sorry."

"Right, okay." He pushes his hands into his pockets. "I understand."

As I head downstairs, my thoughts drift to Margaret and how she must have walked up and down these stairs. Did she move slowly and with grace, pausing slightly on each step? Or did she hurry, taking two at a time, eager to get to where she was going?

I'm becoming a little obsessed with the woman, and I think about her a lot of the time. When in the living room, for example, I sometimes wonder which of the spots on the couch was her favorite, or when in the kitchen I often find myself studying the worn-down patches of linoleum by the stove, imagining her cooking. What was her signature dish? Did she hum while she cooked, or was she the quiet type?

"Are you sure you're okay on your own?" Evan asks from the top of the stairs when I reach the bottom.

"Of course. You have to stop worrying so much."

If I were in his shoes, I would probably do the same. But he shouldn't get used to me feeling low; today is an exception and I'm determined to get back on my feet soon.

Once I step outside, I inhale and the scent of damp earth and grass fills my lungs.

I walk toward the lake, the rippling water soothing as it sparkles in the sunshine.

Sitting on the bench with my legs pulled up to my chest, I stare out in the distance, seeing nothing, and trying not to think of anything, to stay calm and present. And for a moment, I feel almost normal, like I belong in this life, in this moment.

Then, out of nowhere and without warning, the same dark

thoughts creep back in, teasing me. What if I never get my full memory back? Or what if remembering is worse? What if my life was so terrible because of my illness that my memories are better left in the past?

Unable to handle my racing thoughts any longer, I get up and make my way back to the house. But I find myself taking the long way, wandering around the farmhouse, letting my feet take me wherever they want. I'm not ready to go inside yet.

That's when I see the trash cans in an isolated part of the property, covered by a tin roof. The two large containers are old and weathered, their colors faded to a dull gray. They're also stuffed to the brim, which makes it hard for their lids to close completely. A green trash bag is leaning against the side of one container, unable to fit inside.

A memory flickers. Earlier in the morning, Evan had carried the same kind of bag from the basement. Could that be it? Is it filled with some of Richard and Margaret's belongings?

My stomach knots as I step closer. Am I really about to go searching through garbage? My rational mind warns me against it, but my curiosity is stronger. I can't help but think about what I might find, a piece of Margaret's life, discarded like trash. Even though I never knew her, after hearing her story I find myself feeling a little protective of the things that belong to her.

With a deep breath, I step forward, reach for the green bag, and tug it open. The scent of old paper and dust rises, making me wrinkle my nose.

Inside, I find scraps of torn and shredded papers, fragments of someone's life.

Most are unrecognizable. Then, I find a black-and-white photo that's not completely destroyed, a beautiful woman with hair in an intricate updo, wearing a wedding dress. She's radiant, frozen in time, her face filled with joy as she looks to the side at her groom. But the groom is gone, torn away.

Who is this woman, and why destroy this photo? I want to

think it's Margaret, but this woman looks different from that photo I saw online or the one in the album I found in the living room. Even in black and white, this picture is clearly more recent.

Before I can dwell on it any longer, I look down and notice something that has fallen from the bag—a silver heart-shaped locket with another tiny heart engraved on its surface. It's slightly tarnished and its chain is missing.

I remember the heart locket Jill wears around her neck and has a habit of rubbing when she's talking. If I'm not mistaken, it matches this one.

As I pick it up, the rusty chain I found in the barn comes to mind. Could it have once belonged to this locket? If so, why are they separated?

I am about to open it to look inside when a sound startles me: footsteps.

I quickly shove the locket and the half-torn photo into my pocket, then hurriedly stuff the garbage back into the bag, but before I can close it, Evan appears. His eyes flick to the trash bag, then to me, both eyebrows raised in confusion.

"What are you doing out here?"

"The bag had fallen over," I say quickly and straighten up. "I was fixing it."

I force myself to hold his eyes, praying he doesn't notice that my hands are shaking. God knows why I'm so scared in this moment, but I am.

"I was about to make coffee," he says after a long moment. "Do you want some?"

"No, thanks. I think I need a shower."

I step past him, forcing myself to walk casually, even though my pulse is thudding in my ears. My instincts are screaming at me not to tell him about my growing obsession with Margaret. I don't have my memories, but I do have my intuition, and I am going to have to trust it.

Inside, I go straight to my bedroom and lock the door, then sinking down onto the bed, I pull the locket from my pocket and pry it open.

I stiffen when I see the photos inside.

Three women. Two on the left and one on the right side.

On the left is a photo of Margaret and Jill, probably in their forties or fifties. I recognize them instantly. Their arms are around each other, faces lit with laughter. I already knew they were friends—Jill's grief made that very clear.

It's the photo on the right that steals the air from my lungs.

Mary.

She's smiling faintly in the photo, her eyes softer than I've ever seen them. In this photo, she's older than the two women in the other picture—mid-sixties maybe—and her hair is loose around her face. I press the locket shut, but the images are burned into my mind.

FIFTEEN

Tuesday, July 30, 2019

It's late afternoon and Evan isn't home; he's out doing some errands in town, and honestly, I'm relieved.

Not only because of his constant hovering, though that's part of it. But mostly because I've been finding it hard to even look at him since I found that locket yesterday. Since I knew without a shadow of a doubt that he lied to me about Mary and Margaret. He's close to his aunt and always has been. There's no way he wouldn't have known about a friendship that close.

I was so tempted to confront him yesterday, and I almost did. But the thought of hearing another lie spill from his lips made me change my mind.

My gut tells me that what I found out is only the beginning, a thread I've only just started pulling on, that I've barely scratched the surface of something much bigger.

So I'll wait and act like I know nothing, like I believe him. When the time comes for me to confront him, I want to have the full story, to know why he lied. All of it.

For now, I'll keep my silence.

Lina is here, and I find her in the kitchen, moving with quiet efficiency between the cabinets and stove. She has made lasagna for lunch and it's on the kitchen table.

Evan has loosened up and now pays her extra to clean and tidy whenever she can, probably thinking it would keep me from going on a cleaning spree again. The only places she doesn't go are his office and the basement.

"Cora, you came in time." She beams. "Why don't you sit down? Let's eat."

Mary is already sitting at the table, her open journal next to her.

We share a quiet lunch, none of us saying much, and when we're done, Lina takes Mary for a short walk before her nap, leaving me sitting at the table.

Mary forgot her journal again, open at her most recent entry, and I pick it up.

There's something wrong with this house. Too many shadows in the corners. And I think the walls listen. I listen too. I hear things sometimes, even when I try not to.

Mama said once that every house has a memory, but I think this one has secrets too, the kind that don't want to stay buried.

Some mornings I wake up and feel like I've forgotten something important, like I left the oven on, or the door unlocked. But it's not that. It's something else...

After that last sentence, Mary must have lost the memory thread, because it ended so suddenly. Frustrated, I close the journal and start clearing the table.

When Lina and Mary return from their walk, I offer to take Mary to her room, where I help her out of her cardigan and pull the blanket over her legs.

Then I sit on the edge of the bed. "Mary, do you like staying here?" Her eyes narrow in confusion, and I gently touch her hand. "It's just that... sometimes I feel like something's off here. I'm wondering if it's just me."

For a second I think she might say something important. But she only gives me a weak smile and says something entirely different.

"Pawpaw used to teach me how to swim. I must have been eight or nine. Maybe younger. He held my hand so tight I thought it might snap right off." She gives a quiet chuckle. "We swam in the lake behind our old house, the one with the creaky porch and the apple tree in the yard."

And in that instant, she's somewhere else, in another house that probably feels more at home than here.

"I should get some rest, dear. That walk sure did me in. I don't have the strength I used to." She yawns and closes her eyes, her hand curled on the blanket.

I sit with her a moment longer, willing her to remember something else, to open her eyes and say more. But she doesn't.

Communicating with Mary is always hit or miss. Mostly miss.

Back in the kitchen, Lina is rinsing the last of the plates and I start wiping down the counter.

"You're really not great at taking it easy, are you?" There's a hint of humor in her voice.

"I rest enough, believe me. But if I rest as often as my husband tells me to, I'll forget how to function. That man treats me like I'll break."

"I totally understand what you mean. Maybe you need to get out of the house for a bit. Do things you love. Go into town."

"Evan thinks I'm safer here, safer from myself, I guess. Did he mention to you that I have bipolar?"

"Yes." Lina looks me in the eyes. "But you are your own person, Cora. Don't let anyone tell you otherwise. And something like that doesn't have to define you."

I turn her words over and over in my mind. She's right. To

prove that, I tell her I'm going out for a walk, and I cycle to Sabrina's farm, the locket and the torn photo inside my pocket.

Sabrina's brother, Raymond, is the one who opens the door, and I introduce myself.

He's a tall, broad-shouldered man with rugged looks. His tanned skin is lined at the corners of his eyes, evidence of countless days spent beneath the open sky. His beard is thick and black, matching the hair tucked under a dusty baseball cap. His clothes—faded jeans and a checkered flannel—are a little worn and his boots are caked with dry mud.

"Hi, Cora." His voice is deep and calm as he leans against the porch railing, arms crossed. "It's nice to meet you. Sabrina mentioned you recently got back home from the hospital."

"Yes. Nice to meet you too, Raymond. I... Is Sabrina in? I was hoping to—"

"Sorry you came all this way." He shifts his weight and wipes his hands on his jeans. "She's working in town today. Won't be back till later in the evening."

Disappointment tugs at me. "Oh, I see."

"She told me about your memory loss. I'm really sorry you're going through that. If you ever need anything, let us know. We're here."

His kindness feels genuine and so different from the suffocating concern I get from Evan.

"Thank you."

I'm about to turn and leave, thinking I should head back before Evan comes home, but then something catches my eye. Through the kitchen window, I see Jill sitting at the table, her hands folded in front of her. Her silver hair is pinned back, and her eyes are staring into the cup in front of her.

I glance back at Raymond. "Would it be okay if I said hi to Jill?"

"Of course. Come right on in."

He steps aside, allowing me into their home. The inside is warm, cozy, and lived-in, with floors that are scratched hardwood and covered by woven rugs that look like they are handmade.

The walls are a collage of memories, covered with dozens of family photos, some in mismatched frames. Pictures of Sabrina and her parents are scattered among them, but most of the space is dedicated to one person, Owen.

In almost every frame, Sabrina's son is grinning. A little boy with dark curls and wide, mischievous eyes. In one picture, he's perched on a red farm tractor, his small hands gripping the wheel, his face beaming with pride. Raymond stands beside him in that one, a protective hand on the boy's shoulder.

"You have a beautiful family," I say to him. "Owen is so adorable."

Raymond's expression softens. "Yeah. Unfortunately, that wasn't enough to keep his father from deciding to leave him and my sister when he was one." He lifts his cap and shoves a hand through his hair. "Sorry, I didn't mean to—come on, let's go to Mom."

As he leads me away from the photos, my heart goes out to Sabrina. It can't be easy being a single mother. But I'm glad her brother has stepped up to help her out.

The kitchen is small but welcoming. A round wooden table sits in the center, still holding signs of lunch—crumbs on plates, a half-empty glass of sweet tea, a bread basket lined with a blue-checkered cloth. The air smells of garlic, butter, and something faintly sweet, like cinnamon. A window above the sink lets in a warm glow of afternoon light, and through it I watch sheep graze peacefully in the field.

Jill is sitting at the table, her thin hands resting on her lap now, her hair pinned neatly back. When Raymond mentions that I'm here to see her, she turns and a bright smile spreads across her face.

"Cora, dear," she says warmly, motioning for me to sit.

"I'll get you some tea," Raymond offers.

Jill bobs her head approvingly. "Yes, Ray, bring her some of the chamomile. The one I like."

He chuckles. "Yes, ma'am."

After Raymond has brought the tea and left the kitchen, saying something about fixing the fence before sundown, I know this is my chance.

My hands tremble slightly as I pull the locket from my pocket. The moment I place it in Jill's palm, her frail fingers close around it instinctively. I watch her expression shift. Tears gather in her eyes as she strokes the metal, her fingertips searching and feeling.

"This... this was Margaret's," she whispers as her thumb traces the engraved small heart on its surface. "She would never leave this behind."

She turns it over, her fingers moving along the edges. Then she stops. "Where's the chain?"

"I don't know. It must have broken off." After finding the locket, I searched for it in the bathroom drawer where I'd left it, but it was gone.

My bedroom and the adjoining bathroom were the areas I'd cleaned and decluttered the most, so I probably moved it without realizing. I searched everywhere and didn't find it.

Jill's already dim eyes darken but she says nothing, pressing her thin lips together as she opens the locket and frowns. She squints at the photos.

"Who is this?" Her voice is uncertain as she tilts the locket toward me, clearly not able to make out the details.

"This?" I point to the photo on the left. "That's you and Margaret. And this one on the right"—I point to the other side —"is Mary."

Jill's fingers brush over the image of Mary. "Who is Mary?"

"You don't know Mary?" I ask, confused. "When I saw the photos, I thought the three of you must have been friends."

Jill shakes her head but keeps her gaze fixed on the locket, her lips pressed tight, as if trying to pull the memory from the fog. "Mary... Yes, I remember. I do know that name. Margaret mentioned her a few times—a school friend she reconnected with. Margaret wanted us to meet, but we never got the chance. She said her friend wasn't in good health. That she was—"

"In a care home?" I prompt.

"Something like that." Jill closes the locket but continues to hold on to it. "She seemed very fond of her."

That explains the planner. Margaret was definitely visiting Mary at Meadowbrook. Maybe they reconnected before Mary went to live there.

I shift my chair closer to the table, leaning in. "Jill, I know who Mary is. She's my husband's aunt. She lives with us on the farm."

Jill's head snaps back, and her entire body stiffens, as if the words physically shocked her. "I need to speak to her. She might know where Margaret is."

"I don't think she does, Jill. She has dementia. She doesn't remember much of anything anymore."

Jill opens the locket again, her fingers brushing lightly over the tiny images, her mind lost in thought.

I really hoped she might shed more light on their friendship —anything that might help me understand why Evan's been keeping it from me.

I pull out the bride photograph, sliding it across the table, hoping since it's a little larger, she might make something out. "Jill, do you know who this is?"

"A bride? I see the dress, the veil... but the face... it's a little blurry."

I hesitate. "Could it be Margaret?"

Jill shakes her head instantly. "No. Margaret never wore a wedding dress. She wore a white cocktail dress with sunflowers on it, the same one she wore on her first date with Richard. She wanted to be different, she said. She didn't believe in all the fuss."

A lump forms in my throat as I think of the woman she's talking about, someone brave enough to do things her way and not follow the status quo. "Could it be her daughter?"

"Margaret and Richard never had children. They longed for them more than anything, but it wasn't in the cards. They only had each other."

So, if the woman in the wedding dress isn't Margaret, then who is she?

"Something happened to her." I'm taken aback when Jill suddenly rises from the table and begins pacing, clutching the locket to her chest.

Then she stops and looks directly at me as though her full sight has suddenly been restored. Her eyes pierce through me. Her grip on the locket is tight, her knuckles bleaching white.

"Something awful happened to my dear Margaret. I'm sure of it."

SIXTEEN

Evan made spaghetti and meatballs for dinner, and the three of us eat the meal in silence because Evan and I are not really on talking terms.

Earlier, I wanted to be the one to make dinner and when he went on again about how I should take it easy, I snapped and told him that I'm fed up with being treated like a child and feel trapped in this house. He looked hurt, but I didn't take it back.

The silence suits me. I'm too distracted to make small talk anyway with my mind replaying what Jill said to me.

I use the silence to watch my husband, to really observe his mannerisms.

The way he cuts his food. The way he chews. The way his lips press together when he's lost in thought. The way he drinks his water, gently swirling it in his glass before taking a sip. The way he glances over at me every so often, as if checking I'm still here.

A flicker of recognition touches me, and my stomach flips.

I know him. I've seen him like this before. I remember... something.

But the memory is like a whisper. It's there, and then it's gone with my next breath.

After dinner, we all watch a movie together, an old black-and-white film that Mary insisted on seeing, about a woman who starts a cupcake business in her small town that becomes an unexpected success and transforms her life.

I guess the movie reminds Mary of when she was a businesswoman herself. She clutches her blanket to her chest, her eyes shimmering in the soft glow of the TV screen.

Evan is pretending to watch, but he has his laptop on his lap and keeps typing away.

When the movie ends and the credits roll, I turn to him. "Let me put Mary to bed tonight."

"Sure."

Mary allows me to escort her to her bedroom, and as I sit on her bed with her tucked in, she's suddenly especially chatty. Lost again in memories of her childhood, which must have just surfaced.

I'm about to read her a Bible verse that she likes every night, but she keeps talking about Christmas as a child.

"The house smelled delicious, like mint and cinnamon." Her eyes stare into space, seeing things I cannot see. "Mama and I used to bake cupcakes and share them with the neighbors. We did that every single year."

My breath catches as I picture her memories in front of me, but then I wonder if the movie was what brought on the memory, that the emotions she showed were not from craving her life as a business executive, but it was the cupcakes that tugged at her heartstrings.

I can see it. The warm kitchen. The laughter. The scent of peppermint and sugar in the air.

It all makes my mouth water. The picture she paints is so

vivid. And for the first time all day, I feel at peace, as though Mary's memories are a hug wrapping around me.

As I finally stand to leave, a slip of paper falls from my pocket onto the bed.

It's the torn bride photo. Before I can pick it up, Mary snatches it up and stares at it.

Then, without warning, she brings it to her chest and shreds it to pieces, ripping it apart with shaking hands.

I stare at her in horror as the remnants flutter down, landing on her quilt. "Mary, why did you do that?"

She doesn't say anything. Instead, she stares down at the shreds in her lap. Then, she brushes them from the bed, lies down and closes her eyes, her back turned.

I say nothing as I pick up the pieces and make my way out of the room.

SEVENTEEN

Mary's mood and reactions can be unpredictable sometimes. But why did she tear up that woman's photo?

After taking a moment to collect myself, I make my way back to the living room. The TV is off, and Evan is lost in thought. His laptop is next to him, and his phone is on his lap, lit up as if he just got off a call or was messaging someone.

When I enter, he looks up and beams, closing his computer, patting the space next to him.

"Evan, I'm really sorry about what I said earlier," I say, sitting beside him. "I know you're trying to help me, and you didn't deserve that."

"I'm sorry too." He takes my hand in his. "I don't want you to feel like I'm treating you like a child. I only want to protect you, not make you feel stifled."

"I know." In a moment of clarity, I realize how much he truly cares, and I feel like a horrible person. "I shouldn't have snapped at you like that. I know this is hard for you too."

"It's even harder for you." He gives my hand a squeeze. "I can't even start to imagine what you're going through. You're handling it better than most people would in your position."

"That's because of you. I couldn't do this alone. I guess what I'm trying to say is thank you."

"You're welcome," he says, and our eyes meet and hold. Am I imagining it or are our heads moving toward each other?

I'm not imagining it. Evan is only a breath away and any second now, our lips will meet.

Just in time, I pull away as the bride in the photograph climbs back into my thoughts. Reaching into my pocket, I pull out the shreds and put them on the coffee table, face up. Then, I carefully try to piece them back together.

"What's that?" Evan asks.

I look up. "Do you recognize this woman?"

He leans in, studying the broken image and even rearranging it a little to try and make sense of it. Then he shakes his head. "No, I can't say I do. Who is she?"

"I don't know either." The weight of disappointment settles in my chest. It's not Mary then. I thought she could be since some people looked very different when they were younger.

"Well, where did you find the photo, and why is it all torn up?"

"I was tidying up and came across it." I make sure to keep my voice neutral. I don't tell him exactly where I found it. If I did, he'd know I was going through the garbage the other day, that I had lied to him about it. "It was half-torn when I found it, but—well, do you recognize her?"

Evan's expression shifts slightly. It's barely noticeable, but I see it. A flicker of something, discomfort, maybe? But then he smooths his features, his voice even when he responds. "I don't know her."

Suddenly my whole body freezes. How could I have been so blind?

He was the one carrying that trash bag. Probably the one who filled it up.

He could have been the one who tore up that photo.

And if he was, then he already knows where I found it.

My heart pounds, but I force myself to stay calm. His reaction doesn't match up. If he had destroyed the photo himself, wouldn't he have been more guarded? More careful with his answer? Instead, he just looks at me, waiting, like he doesn't suspect a thing. Maybe the bag was already filled by someone else when he decided to throw it away.

He shrugs. "Maybe it belonged to the previous owners."

I want to tell him I know it's not Margaret in the photo, but I can't. He doesn't even know that I know what she looks like, that I googled her. If I say too much, I'll only make him suspicious.

"Maybe," I say, "though, I find it strange that she would leave behind any photo, and tear it up for that matter."

Evan's jaw tightens slightly, a hint of annoyance, but it's there. "Cora, I really think you should focus your energy on getting well. I need you to get better... for you, for us." He reaches for my hand again and we sit in silence, staring at the lifeless TV screen.

He doesn't try to kiss me again, and I feel a little guilty.

"Evan, I know it's hard for you, and I'm really sorry I can't fully connect with you yet. I need time."

"Honey, I understand." He clears his throat. "But it does hurt sometimes, you know. I can't help it." He kisses my hand before letting it go, then he stands and walks out of the room.

After a few minutes, I follow him to the kitchen, where he stands with his back turned, gripping the edge of the sink, his head bowed and his shoulders shaking.

Perhaps sensing my presence, he turns around slowly, smiling through his tears. Then he opens his arms to me, and I walk into them.

. . .

After saying good night to Evan, I head to my room, change into my pajamas, and climb into bed with my phone. I stare at it for a few seconds before switching it on and signing into my Facebook account, even though I planned not to for a while. I wish I hadn't. I'm still friendless. That's it. I won't bother anymore.

I roll onto my back, staring at the ceiling as I let the phone fall onto the bed beside me.

Is there a chance that before I lost myself I wasn't the nicest person, and my Facebook friends only stayed connected out of politeness or curiosity?

I could really use a friend right now, someone who is not Evan, to talk to about Margaret and everything else spinning around inside my head.

I suddenly grab the phone and, chewing on my bottom lip, I go to my pretty much non-existent contacts list and stare at Lina's number.

I could talk to her, right? When she gave me her number she said I could call her any time, that she was there for me.

She picks up immediately.

"Hey, Lina, it's me, Cora. I'm sorry for calling so late. I just... you said—"

"Oh, Cora, it's totally fine. It's nice to hear from you. Are you okay?"

"Yes, umm... You said I can call if—"

"Of course. What's on your mind?"

I grip the phone tighter. "I found a torn-up photo the other day. A wedding photo of a woman, and then, today, Mary tore it up even more when she saw it. Her reaction was so strong, like she hated her."

Lina hums thoughtfully. "Dementia patients react in unexpected ways. Sometimes they lash out at things that trigger memories. It's also possible that the woman in the photo meant nothing to her and she reacted out of frustration or confusion."

I let her words settle. "That makes sense."

There's a pause and I hear faint sirens on the other end. Lina must live in the center of town where the noise of the city never truly dies down. "Is there anything else you want to talk about that's troubling you?"

"Yeah, I met a woman named Jill who lives nearby. She claims to have been a really good friend of Margaret, the woman who used to own this place. She thinks something happened to Margaret, that she wouldn't have up and left the farm like she did, especially without saying goodbye to her. I keep thinking about it, about why she would abandon her life here so completely, memories of her and her husband. He died a few years before she sold, and Jill said Margaret was determined to stay here forever."

"Did you talk to Evan?"

"Kind of, but he keeps telling me to focus on my health."

"He loves you, Cora. That's why he doesn't want you to stress yourself out." Lina is silent for a beat, then says, "But if your gut is telling you something isn't right, you should trust it. And if you need someone to talk to about your discoveries, I'm all ears."

We talk a little more, Lina chiming in with her thoughts and encouraging me to keep digging if that's what my instincts are telling me.

"Thanks, Lina, for listening." I pause. "Can you not tell Evan about our talk?"

"Of course. I won't say a word."

After we say our goodbyes, I stare at the darkened screen of my phone. For a brief moment, I feel lighter.

I still won't tell Evan anything, for now at least. But I will definitely dig deeper into the mystery of Margaret Tookes and that bride in the photo.

Even if it's just because piecing together the secrets in other people's lives will distract me from the fact that I can't remember mine.

EIGHTEEN

Wednesday, July 31, 2019

I'm sitting out on the porch, my John Grisham book open on my lap, trying to read, but my thoughts are too scattered, and I'm too energetic, fidgety. I've only made it to chapter three, and I'm not really absorbing the plot.

I reach for my phone, scrolling through the texts Lina and I have been sending back and forth, discussing the mystery of Margaret Tookes.

I've just sent her a photo of the locket that I found when, suddenly, the door to the porch opens, and Evan bursts out. His face is pale, and his breathing is uneven, his chest rising and falling erratically.

He grips the doorframe as he meets my eyes.

"Is everything all right?" I ask, my heart starting to race.

"She's gone," he croaks, his voice tight, and panic oozing from his entire body. Even his hair is a mess, sticking out in all directions.

"What do you mean? Who's gone?" I shut the book on my lap, my pulse jumping. "Evan, who are you talking about?"

"Mary." He rushes back into the house, and I follow to find him pacing around in the hallway. "I went to check on her, and she's not in her room."

"But she was having a nap. How can it be that she's not there?" I sputter, trailing behind him as he storms into the room. He's right. It's empty, the bed neat and perfectly made.

"See? she's not here." He pushes his hands through his hair and continues to pace around, and then suddenly, he rushes out of the room again and bursts into the kitchen, with me right behind him. He looks almost crazy as he checks in the pantry, calling Mary's name.

"Mary is gone?"

"That's what I said," he snaps.

"Well, let me help you find her. She has to be in the house somewhere."

We search the house together again, room by room, but there's no sign of her.

"She's not here," I say, meeting Evan in the corridor again. "We should go look outside." Wasting no time, I hurry to the front door.

Evan stops me, grabbing my arm. "No. You stay inside. I don't want you over-exerting yourself."

"But I need to help you find her. Should we call the police?"

"No, not yet. I wouldn't want her to be frightened by them. It might be too much for her." He pauses to take a breath. "Fine, let's look together. But we need to split up. You look around the property and I'll drive around."

"Good idea."

Not long after, Evan jumps into the pickup truck and drives off with a screech of tires.

I draw in a deep breath as I scan the fields, which stretch wide under the sky. I narrow my eyes as I take in the distant lake shimmering in the weak sunlight. The only place I can think of to look is the barn.

My stomach tightens as I push the heavy wooden doors open. It's empty. She's not there.

I'm about to walk out, when a muffled sound catches my attention, a kind of shuffling. But I'm not really sure where it's coming from. I look inside the stalls, but they are all empty. Now I hear more than shuffling. It sounds like someone whimpering.

"Mary, is that you?" I call out, my heart pounding as I move deeper into the barn. The whimpering suddenly stops and I look around anxiously.

I glance at the closed windows and wonder if the sound may be coming from outside. I scan the shadowy barn once more, trying to make out any signs of movement. Nothing.

Outside again, I decide to check behind the barn, and as I turn the corner, I freeze. Mary is there, sitting on the ground with her knees drawn to her chest, her journal next to her.

"Mary," I call, relief pouring into every inch of my body. "There you are. We've been searching everywhere for you."

She doesn't seem to notice my presence, rocking back and forth. "Get her away from me. She wants to hurt me."

"No, Mary, I don't want to hurt you." I wrap my arms around the older woman's tense body. "We were so worried about you."

"She wants to hurt me," she repeats, and I pull back to see that her eyes are filled with real terror.

I attempt to help her stand, but she refuses, so I sit beside her to give her time to gather herself. She continues to murmur incoherently for a while longer, then she places her journal on her lap, sliding out the pen that sits in a little pocket on the side, and begins to write, finding comfort in her notes. As her hand moves across the page, I notice it leaving faint green paint. That's when I see that the tips of one or two of her fingers are covered in it.

"Mary, why are your fingers covered in paint?" I ask, but

she ignores me and continues writing in her journal. I give up and let her continue as I read over her shoulder.

I've never been a fan of thunderstorms. They're too noisy and chaotic, and like the sky is trying to warn us of something terrible that's about to happen. When I was ten, a bad one struck, shaking the entire house. The power went out, and suddenly everything seemed too big and too dark. Mama lit a lamp, and we huddled together. To soothe me, she told me a story I can't remember, but I do remember her voice. It was gentle and calm. By the time the storm had blown over, my fear had vanished. But sometimes, I wonder if that storm wasn't just the weather acting up. Sometimes, I think it was the beginning of everything that went wrong.

I never get to find out what went wrong, because Mary stops writing and seems to have forgotten her surroundings. Closing the book, she begins recounting again how her grandfather taught her to swim.

"That's wonderful," I say, relieved that she's communicating normally. "Were you a good swimmer?" I ask, but she does not respond, and I pull out my phone and call Evan to let him know I found her and she's safe.

"We need to get back in the house, Mary. Let me help you up."

She still refuses and harshly pulls her arm away from me. Fortunately, after about ten minutes of sitting there, the distant roar of a car engine makes its way to us. I glance over my shoulder and spot Evan's pickup navigating the dirt road.

Getting to my feet, I wave my hand wildly, catching his attention. The pickup skids to a halt in a cloud of dust, and he jumps out.

"Is she okay?" he calls out while hurrying over. The moment he sees his aunt, tears spring to his eyes. He quickly kneels beside her and draws her into his arms, only for her to stiffen as she shoves him away.

"She wants to hurt me. Get her away from me," she repeats, and Evan glances at me briefly before returning his focus to her.

"No, Aunt Mary, no one is going to hurt you. I promise." His voice is laden with emotion.

But Mary stiffens again, pushing him away with a strength that shocks both of them.

"No," she says. "She wants to hurt me."

Her voice is stronger this time, her breathing erratic.

Evan exchanges another glance with me. Who is she talking about? It can't be me, surely?

When Mary finally relaxes again and stops pushing us away, I help Evan get her back to her feet, and together we walk back to the house.

Mary keeps looking back in terror as though something is following us. Something only she can see.

NINETEEN

Evan is in the kitchen, making tea for Mary, and his hands are still shaking as he stirs the spoon. My heart goes out to him.

"You really scared me, Aunt Mary," he says. "You can't wander off like that. Do you realize what that does to me? I'm here to protect you."

Mary barely acknowledges him, clinging to her journal as if it were her lifeline. Although she still appears frightened, at least she has stopped repeating that someone wants to harm her. It's only been a quarter of an hour since we found her, and she's still agitated. I wish I could pull her into my arms and comfort her, but I stop myself, giving her space.

I sit down with them for a while, and Evan offers me a cup of tea as well.

I know he's overwhelmed right now, taking care of both of us. I wonder whether in moments like this he thinks about taking Mary back to the care home. As much as she wants to be around family, she would be safer there with round-the-clock supervision and care.

After taking a few sips of my coffee, I get up from the table and excuse myself.

There's a nervous energy in me, making my heart rate erratic. Maybe it's the remnants of the adrenaline from losing Aunt Mary.

As I walk down the hall, something catches my eye. Evan's office door is open. I guess with all the excitement of trying to find Mary, it slipped his mind to lock it. He keeps it locked most of the time, even when he's home. I guess as a psychologist, there are some important documents he needs to account for and protect.

Driven by a sudden, impulsive curiosity, I step inside, taking a quick glance down the hall first. As always, it's a tidy space, with an almost clinical sterility that contrasts with the rest of the house.

I breathe in the familiar scent of his cologne, leather, and polished wood. The bookshelves, perfectly arranged, the glass desk that gleams under the soft light, and the cue sticks lined up neatly in their rack on the billiard table.

Is the basement key hidden here?

Now I know Evan wants to surprise me with cleaning it up and turning it into a gym, but even so, it draws me. I wonder if I could find more answers about Margaret down there.

As I scan the room, my eyes land on a small, decorative box on the corner of his desk. I walk to the desk, carefully lift the lid of the box, and peer inside. It's filled with an array of small items, including a photo of him and Mary in what looks like a botanic garden. He's smiling into the camera, but Mary's gaze is focused on her lap.

I close the box and check the drawers, but except for neatly arranged papers and folders, there's nothing else.

The bookshelves are filled with psychology books and framed certificates. They all look so perfectly aligned and categorized by color and size that I'm afraid I might disrupt the order and not know how to put it back.

But then I look at the safe, and gasp. It's only very slight, but it's partially open.

From a distance I can still hear Evan talking to Mary in the kitchen.

I open the safe. Inside there is a stack of cash—a lot of it—and a folder with Mary's name on it.

I pull out the folder, flipping it open. Mary's medical records are inside, but there's also another page that catches my attention, a printout of a list of numbers and letters.

The list contains five rows, each consisting of two capital letters followed by a string of numbers, like RS1949. But two of the codes, KL1954 and MT1940, are crossed out with a bold red pen, and the remaining three are untouched.

Curiosity tugs at me, but there's no time to figure this out now. I fold the paper quickly and slip it into my pocket, telling myself I'll examine it more closely later, when I'm alone and can truly focus.

I take another look inside the safe. I can't see any key.

This is ridiculous. I shouldn't be here searching through my husband's things. I'm reaching into my pocket for the printout I took to put it back, when I hear Evan's voice sounding a little louder.

I hurry from his office and dash to the bathroom down the hall, shoving the printout back into my pocket and running the water at the sink.

Evan is in the corridor when I come out and his eyes dart toward the slightly open office door. "Are you okay?"

"Yes, I'm fine. Is Mary feeling better?"

"She is. I'm so relieved you found her. Thank you."

"You're welcome. But why was she so scared? Why did she think someone wants to hurt her?"

"It's because of the home. After she moved in with us, we later heard rumors of mistreatment there."

My stomach contracts. "Oh my God. They were hurting the residents?"

"Yes, and neglecting them, not feeding them properly, leaving them alone for hours without checking in on them. Some even had unattended medical needs. Of course, these are all rumors and allegations but..." His voice trails off and his hand curls into a fist. "I don't have solid proof, but that's what folks have been saying. And every time I visited Mary, she seemed... scared and upset. Investigations are underway, but I couldn't leave her there."

"Thank God she's safe now. I'll go and keep her company."

Mary is still at the kitchen table, eating cookies and washing them down with a glass of milk. She smiles when she sees me enter. "Did I tell you that my mother and I used to bake cupcakes for the neighbors at Christmas?"

"Yes, you did, but I love that story." I pull out a chair and lower myself into it. "Tell me more."

"Mama and I always baked them the night before and come Christmas morning we would pack them up and make them pretty with ribbons and bows. Then we'd go house to house, spreading holiday cheer."

"That's so lovely, Mary. You must have so many wonderful memories from your childhood." I hope when she remembers them they bring her some kind of comfort.

"Plenty of them." This time, instead of staring out into space, she's looking right at me, and I'm glad to see she's no longer afraid of me when I reach out to touch her hand.

A thoughtful silence stretches between us before she reaches for her journal, her frail fingers stroking the cover. "Would you read me my favorite poem from when I was a child?"

"Of course, Mary."

She flips through the pages carefully, then hands me the journal.

I begin to read, touched that she trusts me to read her words.

"The river moves, never stopping. Sometimes slow, sometimes rushing—"

My voice falters. Something tugs at the edges of my mind, and without thinking, I lower the journal and start again, my lips forming the next words from memory.

> *"The river moves, never stopping,*
> *Sometimes slow, and sometimes rushing.*
> *It hums a tune to the bending trees,*
> *A whispered song in the quiet breeze.*
>
> *"It carries with it dreams untold,*
> *The secrets of the young and old.*
> *The river moves, and as it goes,*
> *It leaves behind what no one knows."*

I don't remember learning this poem. I have no idea where it came from or why I know it, but the words feel like an echo from the past.

When I look up, Mary is smiling at me. "'The River Moves' by Isabel Winters, one of my favorites."

I clear my throat and force a smile back, handing the journal back to her. But inside, something remains, like a river carving its path through the cracks of my mind, carrying the memories with it.

They're coming. I know they are.

Before dinner, the atmosphere is tense with a lot of movement inside Evan's office, the sounds of drawers opening and being banged shut. And when he comes out, his usual warm demeanor is strained and his movements sharper.

As I help him cut the onions for the potato gratin, I sneak glances at him. "Everything all right, Evan?"

"Fine," he says, a little too quickly as he reaches for a dish towel, which he uses to wipe his brow. "Just… work stuff."

I pretend to accept his explanation but I'm nervous. He must know that I was in his office, that I took the printout. Why isn't he asking me about it directly?

He's quiet all through dinner and, later, after putting Mary to bed, he takes his phone and goes outside on the porch with it glued to his ear. Through the living room window, I hear him talking.

"Lina, when you came to the house yesterday, did you happen to go to my office?"

There's a pause, then he says, "Just checking. There's something missing."

He's quiet again as he listens. "Yeah, yeah. I'll check again, maybe it's misplaced… Thanks, Lina."

He ends the call and stays outside on the porch for a while longer, staring out into the darkness of the night. I watch him from behind the curtains. When he finally comes into the house, I pretend to be watching TV, but my heart is thudding. I don't even know why I took it. That was really stupid of me.

"Is everything okay, Evan?" I do my best to keep my voice steady, but the knot in my stomach remains tight.

He gives me a half-hearted smile. "Yeah, everything's fine. Except that I misplaced an important document for work." He glances around the room before his eyes land back on me. "Have you maybe—?"

"No," I say before he even finishes the sentence. "I haven't seen anything that looks important around the house. But if I do, I'll be sure to let you know."

He thanks me and says he's going to look again, while I say

good night and head upstairs. Locking the door to my room, I take out the paper, staring at it for a long time, trying to understand it.

At first glance, they look like codes. Maybe something professional, something tied to Evan's work. I try to picture him at his desk, typing these up.

Could they be initials and file numbers for his patients? Or maybe the numbers are their birth dates? MT... RS... KL... It seems plausible. But they could also be case numbers used for filing, with some kind of internal reference codes. Or maybe they mean something else—like labels for different mental conditions, or a coded system for diagnoses.

There are so many possibilities it makes my head spin.

Groaning, I pinch the bridge of my nose. It nags at me when I can't figure something out.

Two of the codes are crossed out in bold red ink. The others remain untouched. Why only those two? Were those patients he discharged?

The article I saw online about Evan resurfaces in my mind. Some critics found his research methods a little too unconventional, it said. Could these codes be connected to the book he's writing? Are these the names of his experimental therapy subjects?

I stare at the paper until the numbers begin to blur, frustration tightening around my neck. I have no idea how, but I'm determined to find out what this means.

TWENTY

Thursday, August 1, 2019

After lunch, I leave the house for the lake. The water shimmers and reflects the sky—beautiful, blue, pristine, and clear—while birds sing from the trees, their music like a promise that everything will be all right.

I settle onto a large, smooth rock near the shore and pull out my book, a cozy mystery I found on the small bookshelf in the living room. Something light but engaging to distract my mind and calm my nerves. Yet as I stare at it and flip through the pages, the words melt together into one big, chaotic blur.

My eyes skim over a sentence, but all I can think about is that paper I found in Evan's office yesterday with those mysterious codes. I give up on trying to read and reach for the thermos I brought with me and pour myself a cup of coffee.

Its warmth soothes me and I try to focus on the serene landscape and the gentle sway of the reeds, but my thoughts refuse to settle. They are like birds, flitting in every direction without pattern or pause.

What kind of unconventional methods does Evan really use

in his research? The article did not go into detail, so I did a quick search on that this morning, but found nothing further. That article made him sound like a scientist in a lab coat, not a psychologist.

I close my eyes and draw in deep breaths, trying to ground myself in the fresh, earthy smell of mud and water plants. I know I should be grateful for this slice of peace and try to enjoy it, yet the jittery energy within me won't allow it. My mind keeps circling back to those codes.

They have to be related to Evan's work. There's no point in me trying to figure them out. That paper must be important, and the right thing to do is return it to where I found it. I wouldn't want to risk interfering with something that could affect his patients' treatments.

I pack up my thermos, shove the book into my bag and walk back to the house over the rustling grass. The farmhouse looms ahead. Maybe I'll help Lina with one of her chores, or perhaps I could check on Evan. He might have wrapped up his meeting, even though he warned it could take a while. Afterward, he's going to work on his book and maybe I could keep him company.

What I really want to do is get into his office and find a way to return the page I stole. He has not forgotten to lock it again.

As I pass the barn, I catch a voice.

It's low, urgent. I slow my pace and feel my heart beginning to race. I wonder if Mary might have snuck out of the house again, but as I get closer, I know that isn't her voice.

The barn door is cracked open, enough for me to notice movement inside, even in the dim light. It's Lina, her phone pressed tightly to her ear.

One of her hands is tangled in her hair as she paces, clearly frustrated about something. Her back is turned to me, and her tone is tense. Suddenly, her hand drops from her hair, and she clenches it tight at her side.

"I told you I'd call you soon. Stop calling me at work," she snaps. "I can't mess this job up."

There's silence as the person on the other end responds, and Lina sighs sharply. Then her posture stiffens, and it seems like she might lose her temper. I have never seen her this way. She's always been so calm and collected, I always feel more relaxed around her. I guess that's the reason why I never told Evan that she was going through drawers in his office, why I don't want her to be fired.

"No, please, you need to be patient," she insists. Her pacing quickens and her voice grows louder.

"Fine, I'll meet you for lunch tomorrow. I'll call to tell you when and where."

I hesitate, torn between revealing myself, continuing to listen, or simply walking away. The latter seems like the best choice, but before I decide, Lina turns around and our eyes meet. She startles so hard that the phone slips from her hand and hits the ground.

For a heartbeat moment, we stand there staring at each other, her eyes wide. I was listening in to her call, and yet I swear there is a trace of guilt on her face.

"I'm sorry, I didn't mean to... I..." My voice trails off as I quickly go to pick up the phone for her since she appears frozen on the spot.

"Don't worry about it. It's fine. That was my boyfriend. He can be a bit overbearing sometimes." A soft, nervous laugh escapes her, but her smile doesn't reach her eyes. Then she wipes her phone with her hand and tucks it away.

A wave of relief washes over me; at least she doesn't hate me for being nosy. Which I am—like her.

As we go to leave the barn, I pause near where I found Margaret's locket chain.

"Hey, Cora, are you okay?" Lina asks, touching my shoulder and I jolt back to life.

"Yes. I'm just... I'm fine."

I trail after her into the house in silence, and we settle down at the kitchen table, each with a bowl of chocolate ice-cream, making small talk while Mary naps.

Then Lina nudges me lightly with her elbow. "Any new discoveries about Margaret? Or that photo of the bride?"

"No. With Mary disappearing, I guess I've been preoccupied." I swirl my spoon in my bowl absentmindedly. "But I'm still wondering where the chain that belonged to Margaret's locket has gone. I looked everywhere for it."

Lina's brows lift. "Yeah, I did a little searching for it too." Her tone is casual, but I have a feeling she is getting as invested in this Margaret mystery as I am.

She scoops up more ice-cream. "Okay, random question: Favorite movie?"

I blink at her, taken aback by the change in subject. "I—" Then my breath catches. A memory slams into me so fast it steals my words. "Oh my God."

Lina straightens. "What?"

"I remember." My heartbeat picks up. "I remembered my favorite movie without even thinking about it."

A slow smile spreads across Lina's face. "That's amazing, Cora. What is it?"

I press my fingers to my temple, doing my best to hold the memory in place before it slips away. "It's *Primer*, a science fiction film starring Shane Carruth and David Sullivan."

Lina's spoon clatters against her bowl. "No way. *Primer*?" She lets out a surprised laugh. "I tried watching that movie once. Couldn't understand a damn thing. You must be really smart."

Something inside me warms at the thought. I lost my past, lost my memories, but maybe I didn't lose everything. Perhaps, deep down, I'm still me.

"What about you?" I ask.

"Oh, nothing as brainy as *Primer*. I'm more of a *Miss Conge-niality* or *Legally Blonde* kind of girl. Life is serious enough already."

I chuckle and scoop up some more ice-cream. "I can respect that. What about your boyfriend? How long have you guys been together?"

Lina's smile dims a fraction. "A while," she says vaguely. "It hasn't always been easy."

I think of her tense phone call, the frustration in her voice. "Relationships rarely are," I say.

We finish our ice-cream, and Lina pulls out her phone, scrolling through movie options. "Maybe one of these days we could watch a movie together. Just no films that require a science degree, okay?"

"Deal. I'll think of something."

As I smile at her, something inside me settles. I might not remember my past, but for the first time since I woke up in this strange life, I feel like I'm starting to know who I am.

And that feels like a win.

When Mary wakes up, and Lina has to get back to work, I head to the living room to see if I can get lost in a TV program.

I have settled in to watch an episode of *Downton Abbey* when Lina peeks through the doorway. "Cora, I'm about to do laundry for Mary. Do you need me to add anything of yours?"

"No, I'm fine. You don't have to worry about that."

"I need to make up a full load; I'll just grab a few bits from your basket," she insists.

She looks like she's not going to take no for an answer, so I thank her.

Later in the evening, as Lina prepares to leave, she finds me sitting on the porch, soaking in the peaceful scene around me—

the distant chirping of crickets and a sky streaked with deep orange, fading into pink.

I almost feel compelled to take out my phone and capture the moment. Especially now that I know how fragile memories can be.

"Well, I'm off," she says. Then, taking a few steps forward, she suddenly turns back, revealing something in her hand. "Oh, I almost forgot, I found this in one of your pants pockets." She opens her hand to reveal a folded sheet of paper, the one with all the codes.

"Oh," I say, freezing. I reach out and shove it into the pocket of my jeans.

"It must be something important," Lina comments, raising an eyebrow.

I force a laugh. "Just an old note. Enjoy your evening."

"Right." Lina lingers for a brief moment, before casually shrugging and walking away. "Have a good evening, Cora."

As she reaches her car, she pulls out her phone and dials while sliding behind the wheel. As I listen to her muffled voice from inside the car, I wonder if she's talking to her boyfriend again. Before the door closes, our eyes meet through the windshield, and for some reason, my skin prickles.

TWENTY-ONE

Sunday, August 4, 2019

On Sunday afternoon, I'm standing by the office door, listening for any movement. Nothing. Just the occasional creak of Evan's chair. He's in there working on his manuscript while Mary is having her nap. I'm thinking of telling him I'm going out for a walk, but I don't need permission to go out.

As always, the bicycle is where I left it in the barn, leaning against the wall, waiting for me.

I throw my leg over and start pedaling toward Sabrina's farm, the warm afternoon air brushing against my skin. When I arrive, something feels off. The place is a little too quiet. No voices, no movement. Only the distant sounds of animals. I step off the bike and climb up the porch steps. When I knock, no one comes to the door. They must be out because the curtains are drawn.

A sleek black-and-white cat with piercing green eyes sits lazily on the wooden steps, its tail flicking in slow, deliberate motions. It watches me with an intensity that makes my breath hitch.

"Hey there." I kneel down. The cat studies me a moment longer before padding closer, rubbing against my legs like we've known each other forever.

I run my fingers through its soft fur, and a deep purr vibrates against my hand. Something about this moment makes my heart swell, like I'm on the edge of remembering something important—something buried deep in my mind.

Did I have a cat before?

The thought is fleeting, but the feeling lingers as I sit on the old porch swing. The wood creaks beneath me, its paint peeling at the edges, but the swaying is soothing. The cat curls up beside me, its purring a steady hum.

I close my eyes and take a deep breath, letting myself savor the moment.

But I can't stay long.

With reluctance, I stand, giving the cat one last stroke before heading back.

As I approach the house, the first thing I see is Evan emerging from the barn, and my stomach twists. His expression is unreadable for a second, but when I get closer and hop off the bike, leaning it against the barn, his eyes lock onto mine, and I see the fury, or shock maybe.

"Where the hell have you been?" His voice is low but sharp, each word laced with tension.

I step away from the bike and approach him. "I went to see Sabrina."

"Are you serious, Cora?" His jaw clenches. "I've been searching everywhere for you. I thought something happened to you."

"I told you—I went to see Sabrina."

His nostrils flare. "You can't leave without telling me. It's not safe out there for you. And you can't trust just anyone."

I cross my arms. "I'm not a child, Evan. I thought I made

that clear last time. And Sabrina and her family have been nothing but kind to me."

Something shifts in his expression, and I realize that he's putting two and two together.

"You've been going there a lot, haven't you?" His voice is quieter now, but it's edged with steel.

I don't look away. "Yes, several times."

A muscle ticks in his jaw, and charged silence stretches between us.

Then finally, he blows out a loud breath, rubbing a hand over his face. "I want you to be safe, Cora. You're safer here, at home."

I refuse to back down. "I will go where I want. It's my life."

His eyes darken. "And you're *my* wife."

I lift my chin. "Actually, no. I'm not your wife, Evan. Not really. Not until I remember who you are... who I am."

He simply stands there, his anger and hurt simmering beneath the surface.

Without another word, I storm past him, my heart pounding as I step into the house.

We barely speak for the rest of the day, and at dinner, I tell him I'm not hungry and he and Mary eat alone while I read a book in my room.

After everyone has gone to bed, I call Lina. Things were a bit awkward between us on Thursday when she handed me back the page I stole. And when she was here on Friday, I felt like she was watching me differently somehow. At one point I think she was eavesdropping on a conversation I was having with Evan. I can't prove it, but when I walked out of the room, I saw her disappear into one of the rooms upstairs. But even if she's nosy, Lina is my friend and I can't help but feel drawn to her.

I don't even wait for her to say hello before launching into a rant.

"Can you believe this? He acts like he owns me, like I need his permission to breathe."

"I totally get why you are upset, Cora. Really, I do." She clears her throat. "I'm sorry if I'm overstepping, but you're my friend and the way he talks to you sometimes—it's almost like he's analyzing you. Like he's trying to control how you feel."

Critics argue that his methods border on manipulation.

Could Evan be using his psychology background to control me?

After a pause she continues, "Hey, want to watch a movie like we said we would?"

I snort. "How? We're not even in the same house."

"Easy. We hit play at the same time and text about it. It'll be like we're watching together."

If she was trying to cheer me up, she succeeded. "All right. Let's do it."

After the call, I go downstairs to grab some microwave popcorn I saw in the cupboards. As I reach for a bowl, something falls from the counter with a small clink.

It's my bottle of sleeping pills, and it's not fully closed. I didn't leave it like that. In fact, I have not taken any sleeping pills at all since Doctor Rowe prescribed them. But the bottle is lighter. Did Evan take some for himself?

A pang of guilt tugs at me. Maybe I shouldn't have been so hard on him. He must be as terrified as I am, and that's why he overdoes it—constantly hovering over me, and insisting I get a lot of rest.

He cares too much—for me and for Mary. Maybe there really is a good reason why he did not want to tell me about Mary and Margaret. I'm sure he'll tell me everything when he's ready.

I put the bottle back in the cabinet, finish making my popcorn, and head back upstairs.

Lina and I decide to watch *Ocean's Eleven* and as we text

back and forth, commenting on the characters, guessing twists, and laughing at the witty dialogue, I forget everything and let myself relax.

After the movie ends, I go to close the curtains, peering outside into the darkness, empty and quiet. I can see the barn, its silhouette looming against the moonlit sky, and as I watch, it seems to grow darker somehow, its edges growing sharper, more threatening.

I wrap my arms around my body.

As I climb into bed, I can feel the shadows gathering in the corners of this very room, pressing in on me, and I can't shake away the image of that barn.

TWENTY-TWO

Monday, August 5, 2019

This morning, I felt an unusual heaviness in my limbs. Getting out of bed was a challenge, and now, as I recline on the living room couch, even sitting up feels daunting. A rhythmic pounding echoes inside my head, not debilitating but persistent, like a tiny drumbeat tapping at the edges of my consciousness.

The living room is softly illuminated by the late morning light that spills in through the sheer white curtains. Despite it being muted, the light still seems to pierce my eyes. I try to close them, hoping for a nap, but the noise from the basement makes it impossible. Evan is down there, doing whatever work needs to be done himself.

The dull ache pulses behind my temples as I curl up tighter on the couch, pulling a knitted blanket around me.

I wipe the sweat from my forehead, feeling like the house is stiflingly warm, even though the living room window is open.

Mary, settled at the other end of the couch, slowly turns the pages of her journal while a muted crime documentary flickers on the TV screen. She seems unfazed by the heat or the noise.

Earlier, she read a passage to me, telling me how she was homeschooled and her mother always made it so much fun, with science experiments in the kitchen and history lessons based on their family photos.

I close my eyes again, but as I'm about to doze off, a loud bang echoes through the walls, rattling the two oil paintings on the wall, of this very farmhouse in its glory days, when the paint was still intact and the fields around it were lush and vibrant. The initial bang is soon followed by a series of heavy hammer blows, each strike sending tremors through the floor beneath us. With a groan, I grab two throw pillows and press them to my ears.

Mary, on the other hand, shows barely any reaction. She glances up at the ceiling for a moment before returning to her journal. "He's been at it all morning," she says, then resumes scribbling furiously in her little book.

Finally, after another half an hour, the hammering stops, and Evan appears in the living room, coated in dust from head to toe. His white T-shirt clings to his toned chest, damp from all the hard work. I notice again how handsome he is even without his usual crisp suits and neat shirts and I feel an unexpected attraction surge inside me—especially when he leans down to gently kiss my forehead.

He goes to his aunt and presses a kiss to her forehead too.

"Are you feeling okay, sweetheart?" he asks, looking back at me. "You look pale."

I force a smile. "I'm fine."

From his narrowed eyes, I can tell that he knows I'm lying. He leaves the living room only to return shortly with some medicine and a glass of water.

"I think you forgot to take these. You really must take care of yourself, Cora."

He's aware I missed my dose because my pill organizer is neatly labeled with the days of the week.

"I forgot," I say truthfully, and reach for the pill he's holding, gulping it down with the water as he watches.

I'm feeling better when Lina arrives dressed in a casual summer dress that's in a soft shade of blue, her straight hair tied up in a high ponytail that sways at the crown of her head.

"I've already prepared lunch," Evan tells Lina. "But I'm afraid it will just be you and Mary for a couple of hours because I'm taking my wife out. It's the fifth of August, our anniversary."

"Oh, congratulations, you two." Lina beams at each of us in turn. Whatever doubts she had voiced about Evan on our call seem to be long gone.

Evan *did* mention our anniversary to me this morning, even showing me a calendar with the date circled in red. I wish I could feel a connection to this day, to him.

When we're ready to go, Lina practically nudges us out the door, insisting that we need this moment together.

She is right. We *do* need this, a chance to catch up on ourselves, revive our romance, and rebuild our connection. Today, I'll give Evan the benefit of the doubt. I'll try to open the door a little, and let him in.

But what if my memories of us never return?

TWENTY-THREE

We drive through the countryside, passing a few farms. Many have animals—sheep wandering freely and cattle grazing in the fields.

Eventually, we arrive at the town center of Cedar Hollow, and the atmosphere changes completely in the bustling yet charming streets. The town's heart is lively and quaint, with brick sidewalks, flower baskets hanging from lampposts, and historic buildings lining the roads. But what captivates me most is a tall clock on a church, its bronze hands ticking steadily.

I roll down the window, letting in the scents of fresh bread from the bakeries and the richness of roasted coffee from cafés. Small boutiques showcase handmade goods, and a bookstore with a weathered wooden sign catches my attention.

A customer exits, holding a steaming coffee cup and looking content. It's such a picturesque and comforting scene, and I'm grateful for the chance to experience it on such a beautiful day. The air drifting in is crisp and refreshing, a welcome change from the stifling indoor heat.

As Evan continues driving down the narrow streets, I take in the scenery outside.

"Are you okay?" he asks, a question I have grown so used to hearing.

"Better than before," I reply truthfully. Being here feels like exactly what I needed.

"I'm so glad to hear that." He reaches out to squeeze my hand without taking his eyes off the road. "Recognize anything?" I'm so glad he's still not bringing up our argument because I don't have the strength for it.

"Maybe." I stare back out the window, feeling a strange sense of recognition. Some places do seem familiar, but as usual, the memories hover out of reach. "I'm not so sure."

Evan points out spots he thinks I should know. "That's where we used to have brunch almost every Sunday." He gestures to a corner bistro with a cheerful bright-yellow wrought-iron patio. The name *Sunshine Café* is painted in a cheerful script on the window, and a few customers are sitting outside, sipping coffee and laughing at some shared joke.

"And over there," he continues, "is your favorite flower shop. You've always loved flowers, especially white lilies. Over the years, I've done my best to keep them coming."

I smirk as I notice the sign above the door: *Everpetals*. It brings to mind the white lilies from the wedding bouquet I saw in some of our wedding photos. "It doesn't look like there are many other flower shops around here. No wonder it's my favorite."

Evan chuckles. "That's true, but they still have the best blooms in town."

I laugh quietly and try to imagine myself as the woman he remembers—the one who strolled these streets, browsed these boutiques, and sat in these cafés. Did I feel truly free, or was I mostly confined, burdened by my illness?

After a while, we drive past a building displaying a sign that reads *Meadowbrook Assisted Living Facility*.

"Where Mary used to stay," I say to myself, studying the

place—its beautifully manicured gardens with elderly residents seated on sunlit benches.

The color of the building, a soft mossy green, blends with the lush grounds surrounding it, and brings out the vibrancy of the flower beds scattered throughout. I catch sight of an elderly couple, hand in hand, walking slowly along the stone path that winds through the garden.

"How long was Mary in there for?"

Evan's hands are clenched around the steering wheel, his knuckles white.

"She was there for about a year before we decided to bring her home. Actually, you were the one who pushed for that." He reaches out to squeeze my hand. "Even though you knew how challenging it would be to care for someone with dementia, you insisted that we should bring her home."

It comforts me to know I fought for Mary. I can hardly bear the thought of her in that facility, alone and vulnerable in a place that was meant to protect her. I feel a sudden surge of anger at the management of the home. What kind of monsters neglect those who are unable to care for themselves?

Evan glances at me. "I can't stop thinking about how scared she looked whenever we visited her. She was always so upset when it was time for us to leave. But I had no idea what was going on."

After a brief moment of quiet, we pass an ice-cream shop tucked between two brick buildings. Its sign reads *Sweet Sundae*, and through its large windows, I catch sight of black-and-white checkered floors, a gleaming wooden counter, and a chalkboard menu filled with vibrant flavors written in colored chalk.

A wave of nostalgia drifts out from the shop, prompting me to pause and take a deep breath. "What a sweet little place. It does seem familiar to me."

Evan gives my hand a gentle squeeze. "That's because it

used to be one of your favorite spots. You rarely came into town without stopping here for ice-cream."

"I can see why."

"You know what?" Evan suggests, wrapping an arm around me. "Let's grab lunch first, and then we'll come back for your favorite ice-cream, lavender honey."

I raise an eyebrow. "Well, that sounds delicious."

"You said it reminded you of your grandmother's house," he adds.

Knowing Evan remembers pieces of me I've lost—pieces he's desperate to recover—brings me comfort.

Eventually, we park the car in front of Willow Garden, a cozy restaurant bathed in soft golden light, where ivy winds around brick walls. Inside, every table is filled with quiet conversations and the soft clinking of silverware against china.

Evan finds us a secluded table in the back, near a wall adorned with watercolor paintings of the local scenery. The sounds of laughter float over from the bar, where a group of young people are gathered around, chatting and drinking.

"You always ordered the lemon butter salmon with rice here," he says as he orders for both of us. "Trust me—you're going to love it."

"Okay, that sounds amazing. Yes, please."

When our food is served, the enticing smell makes my mouth water instantly. And when I take a bite of the salmon, the flavors dance on my tongue. The buttery lemon sauce is decadently rich, and the salmon itself is tender and perfectly cooked. And the rice, which is lightly seasoned, provides a delicate balance to the richness of the salmon.

"You were right—this is delicious," I say, covering my mouth as I chew. "It doesn't bring back any memories, but I can see why I loved it."

As we eat, Evan entertains me with stories from our honeymoon in Bali.

"We got caught in a sudden downpour on our first day. It nearly ruined everything, but you insisted that we should make the best of it, acting as if we were in a romantic film. We sprinted through the rain back to the hotel, took a steaming shower, and then spent the entire day nestled in bed."

I smile and Evan appears pleased with himself, his attentiveness palpable as his fingers gently brush mine. I find myself transported back there with him, lost in dreams of us.

After our meal, as we prepare to leave the restaurant and head to Sweet Sundae, Evan excuses himself to use the bathroom, leaving his briefcase behind, sitting next to his chair. He takes that thing everywhere and I suspect his laptop is inside so he can type up notes for his book when inspiration strikes.

My eyes fix on it, and my heart begins to race as I fumble through my handbag. My fingers graze the piece of paper I took from him.

Since it's hard getting into his office, this could be my only chance at getting it back to him.

I quickly snap a photo of the paper before slipping it between some of the other documents inside his briefcase. Hopefully, when he discovers it, he'll simply assume he'd forgotten that he put it in there.

TWENTY-FOUR

Later, as soon as the farmhouse comes into view and Evan starts slowing down the car, I notice a commotion outside. Jill and Lina are on the porch and they look like they're arguing.

I squint at them as Evan slams on the brakes, the car screeching to a stop. He doesn't even bother turning off the engine before throwing open the door and charging toward the house.

"What the hell is she doing here?" he growls.

I fumble with my seatbelt and scramble out after him. Lina is speaking in hushed, urgent tones while Jill shakes her off, her silver hair wild in the wind. She's wearing a long floral dress that flutters around her ankles, and there's something almost ghostly about her.

Did she walk all the way from her farm?

Evan reaches them, his movements rigid.

"Get off my property. I thought I made it clear a long time ago that you should stop harassing us." His voice cuts through the stillness. To my surprise, he takes hold of Jill's arm and guides her off the porch.

"Evan!" I snap, shocked at his hostility.

Jill wrenches free, turning to face me. Her eyes, though unfocused, lock onto mine with startling intensity. "You know it's true, don't you?" she says, her voice raw and desperate. "Something happened to her. Something happened to Margaret." She clutches the locket at her throat, turning back to Evan. "You took her home away from her, and then something bad happened to her, and no one believes me. I need to speak to Mary. She will believe me. Mary!" she calls loudly toward the front door, and I know immediately that I'm the reason Jill is here.

I'm the one who dredged up memories of her friend, and the locket I gave her convinced her that something is very wrong. I'm the one who told her about Mary, who revealed her connection to Margaret.

Evan's expression hardens, his jaw tightening. "This is our home now. You have no right to be here, confusing my aunt. Get in the car. I'm taking you back to *your* home."

"Stop talking to her like that." I step between them. "She's upset, Evan. Listen to her. That's all she needs, for someone to hear her out."

But Evan doesn't hear me. His anger is a storm, sweeping everything in its path, and I find myself backing off. He moves toward Jill again, but before he can get close, Lina steps off the porch, placing herself between them. She's smaller than him by nearly a foot, but in this moment, she is a force, and her eyes blaze with an intensity I've never seen before.

"Enough, Mr. Harrison!" she commands, pushing a firm hand against his chest, the authority in her voice shocking. "I'll handle it. I'll drive her home. I know where she lives."

"No." Jill shakes her head stubbornly. "We need to call the police. We need to tell them that something happened to Margaret, something bad. Mary," she calls again, "you believe me, don't you?"

In that moment, I notice a shadow shift behind the living room window.

Mary is standing behind the glass. Her eyes are wide, her silver hair loose around her shoulders. One hand is clutching the curtain, and the other trembles against the windowpane as she leans in closer, her lips moving. Then she steps back again and is out of sight.

"Don't be ridiculous," Evan shouts back at Jill. "I need you to stay off my property or I will call the cops. I thought I told your daughter to keep you away." And with that, he strides up the steps, disappearing into the house.

Jill watches him go, her frail shoulders shaking. "I have to know what happened to Margaret," she whispers, her fingers ghosting over the locket.

Lina and I exchange a look before gently guiding her toward Lina's Toyota. She resists at first, but she eventually lets Lina help her into the passenger seat.

I turn to Lina as soon as she shuts the car door. "I don't understand what's going on here." I look through the windshield at Jill, who is now staring blankly at the house. "What if something really did happen to her friend?"

"Then we'll find out." Lina grips the door handle. "But first, I need to get her home, make sure she's safe. Then when I come over tomorrow, we can decide the next step." She slides into the car and slams the door shut.

I watch them drive off, then turn back toward the house.

Inside, I find Evan in the living room, sitting on the couch with his head in his hands.

"What the hell was that out there?" I demand sharply. "She's an old woman, Evan. She's missing her friend. What's wrong with you?"

For a long moment, he says nothing. Then, slowly, he lifts his head. His eyes are hollow, drained. "I thought it was over." He massages his temples. "When we first moved in, she used to come here every single day, disturbing us with her paranoia, refusing to accept that her friend moved on, which of course she did. You even called the police on her once."

I stiffen. "I did?" The words feel foreign on my tongue. "But I wouldn't... what kind of person was I?"

"A person who wanted peace in her own home. And you need peace and quiet, especially now that you're recovering. We can't have her barging in whenever she pleases. I won't stand for it. And you should stop going over there. She might see it as an invitation."

"Look, Evan," I swallow the lump forming in my throat, "I'm tired. I'm going to take a nap." This discussion is not over, but I have a lot to think about.

TWENTY-FIVE

The rain falls softly outside, and I try to concentrate on the gentle patter against the window, but my mind refuses to cooperate. I stare into the darkness of night.

It's as though the thoughts are all fighting for control, each one vying for my attention.

Jill's bewildered expression, Evan's fury, the paper I found in his office, all the things I found out about Margaret, Mary's frightened whispers of phantom cries.

I pinch the bridge of my nose, closing my eyes as the images flicker, like an old movie reel.

I jolt when I hear the rumble of thunder in the distance. A dull ache pulses in my chest as I think back to dinner, a few hours ago. Evan had been so different from the charming man who had laughed, cracked jokes, and opened up to me during our date, in a way that opened me up to him in return.

As we sat at the kitchen table, he was distant, his eyes locked onto anything but me, focusing instead on Mary. When he did speak to me, his responses were curt and almost mechanical. I wanted to talk about Jill again, to discuss how we can help find out where Margaret is and what really happened to her.

But I could almost feel the chill in the air that created an invisible barrier between us.

I need a break from my thoughts, so I pick up my phone to check my Facebook account. I'm surprised and happy to see that three of the people I sent a friend request to have finally accepted, but they have not responded to my message. But I also have a new friend request from someone called Donna Blaire. She has sent an accompanying message. I click on it and read:

Cora, what the hell is going on? I've been trying to reach you for weeks! Did you block me? And did you change your number? I don't get it. I know you were mad about what I said about your husband being controlling, but this? Cutting me off completely? We're sisters. We don't do this.

Mom and Dad are freaking out as well because they also can't reach you. You didn't even give us your new address yet. Please, Cora, I don't care if you're mad at me, please tell me you're okay. Let me fix this.

TWENTY-SIX

My mouth is very dry and I'm clutching my chest, struggling to breathe.

I read the message again and again, but the words remain the same.

We're sisters. Mom and Dad.

It feels like the ground beneath me has opened up and I'm on the verge of falling in. I have a sister and parents? Evan looked me in the eye and said I was an only child, that I was estranged from my parents. That they'd given up on me. He lied, like he lied about Mary and Margaret.

I cover my mouth with one hand, my mind spinning. Why would he do this? Why would he hide my family from me?

My throat is tight and my fingers are clammy as I grip the phone like it's a lifeline with the power to stop my world from shattering. Too late for that. This changes everything.

He's dangerous.

Whatever he claimed to feel for me has nothing to do with love.

My hands tremble as I look down at the phone again, ready to respond, to reach out for help, to tell my sister where I am and that I need them. That I need to come home, wherever that is.

I get as far as typing "I'm not sure what's happening—" when the quiet is broken by the soft creak of the house settling —every sound magnified in the stillness. Or is it footsteps?

I hold my breath as my heart thunders in my chest.

Now that I know what Evan is capable of, how manipulative he really is, I know I'm not safe.

I listen closely as the footsteps seem to approach and then gradually fade away as they pass by my door. I remain tense and frozen for a moment, then slide out of bed. It must be Evan going downstairs for a drink. It can't be Mary since her cane produces a distinct sound.

As I open the door, I catch sight of him heading toward the stairs, and the mere sight of him ignites a fire in my chest. I grip the doorframe, my nails digging into the wood, rage pulsing through every vein.

I could pack my bags right now and escape this place— maybe go to Sabrina to ask her and her family for help—but a part of me wants to know what other lies he's been telling, what more he's been hiding from me.

I'll stay long enough to uncover the rest. There's a lot going on that I need to get to the bottom of.

The fear buzzing inside me doesn't stop me from following him quietly, praying he does not turn around. Why isn't he turning on the lights? I see his figure, now a silhouette against the pale moonlight filtering through the windows, pause at the bottom of the stairs.

He doesn't go into the kitchen as I had thought he might. Instead, he moves toward the front door, grabs a raincoat from the rack, and steps outside.

I hurry downstairs and out the door after him, careful to keep a safe distance. Cold rain pelts my bare arms. The wind has picked up, hinting at an approaching storm. Any moment now, I'll be drenched. But I don't have a raincoat downstairs, and an umbrella would draw attention.

Unfazed by the downpour, Evan makes a beeline for the garage on one side of the house, but before entering, he pulls a flashlight from his pocket and turns it on.

The garage door opens with a loud creak, and he steps inside.

I move closer, keeping to the shadows as I peer inside to see that he is now rummaging through a wooden cabinet. His flashlight illuminates dust particles floating in the air. There's another Volvo XC90 parked inside that matches Evan's, and the whole place smells of stale gasoline and damp wood.

He pulls something from the cabinet, a toolbox, judging by its shape. Popping it open, he removes a set of keys.

As he makes his way back to the door, I quickly slip out of view and hide behind a stack of firewood piled against the side of the garage. I don't dare to move or breathe as I listen to the crunch of his shoes on gravel.

As it starts to rain harder, I follow him back to the house, where he marches in and heads straight to the basement door. He glances back over his shoulder before unlocking the door. So that's where he keeps the basement key, in the garage?

Why would he be going into the basement in the middle of the night?

Fearing being caught and what he might do to me, I hurry back upstairs to my room, to think of how to find out his secrets without putting myself in direct danger. I need to be very careful.

After drying myself off and putting on another set of warm pajamas, I lie on my bed, feigning sleep in case he comes in. I wait and listen for his footsteps. Now that I know where he keeps the key, I'll wait until he leaves the basement again—then I'll go down there myself.

It's an hour later that I finally hear him returning upstairs.

At the sound of his bedroom door closing, I'm tempted to jump out of bed and go back to the garage, but that might not be smart. So, I wait another hour. At 2 a.m., the storm is in full force, wind howling against the windows and rain pounding the roof. I open my door, step out, then lock it behind me.

The first thing I do is check under his door to see if the light is on. It's not. I hesitate, but something urges me to do this, to get the keys and go to the basement.

Using the flashlight on my phone, I tiptoe down the stairs, and wearing a coat this time, I step out of the house.

I'm relieved to find that he has returned the keys to the toolbox. Before I can talk myself out of doing this, I grab them and not long after, I'm standing in front of the basement door.

Taking a deep breath to steady my nerves, I try the first key on the set and nothing happens, but the second one turns in the lock with a soft click, and the door creaks open. I hold my breath, wait, and then step inside, closing the door behind me.

There's a light switch on the left side of the door and I'm about to flick it on but change my mind. I wouldn't want Evan to see light from under the door if he happens to come down again.

Thanks to my house slippers, my footsteps are muffled as I descend the stairs. I wonder if I should turn back in case he hears me, but my curiosity trumps my fear.

I use my phone's light to scan the basement, which—despite the storm—is quiet and smells faintly of paint. I'm surprised by what I see around me. Evan made it sound like a cluttered, unfinished space, forgotten and dusty. Instead, this place is neat, clean, and furnished. There's no real danger for Mary down here, except the risk of her falling down the stairs, of course.

Another bold-faced lie.

I take in the things in the room, which is made up of several cabinets, an old sofa leaning against one wall, an old-fashioned

TV set, and several other furniture pieces that are covered in white sheets and plastic. But everything is tidy and organized.

But then I shine the light in one corner to see a neat pile of broken wooden planks that look like they were part of some furniture pieces. There are quite a few, some of them with nails sticking out of them, which *could* actually be dangerous for Mary. Others are charred as if burnt.

I have a feeling that this is what Evan comes to do when he comes down here, and also that handyman—to break down the old furniture and, perhaps, destroy it. Or were they putting everything together to create new furniture? That would certainly explain the drilling sounds. But Evan wouldn't come here late at night to fix furniture.

Looking away to continue my inspection, I feel a chill that prickles my skin. It's as if the air in the basement is holding its breath.

I'm about to head back upstairs when I catch a sound. A faint and muffled sobbing.

Then I notice that one of the walls is freshly painted, unlike the others, and there's a door that almost blends in.

I move closer, my breaths shallow. Suddenly, the sobbing stops.

Then, slicing through the oppressive silence like a blade, a whisper breaks from the depths of the concrete, a woman's voice, drenched in desperation and terror.

"Help me. Please. That man... He's a monster."

TWENTY-SEVEN

GABRIELLE WALKER

Sunday, May 5, 2019

The mouthwatering smell of bacon fills the air as I stand at the stove, turning the strips over with practiced ease. I have a weakness for the crunchiness and saltiness, and for breakfast, I always crave something hearty to warm me up and get me ready to take on whatever the day brings.

My straightened hair falls from its ponytail as I move around, and I tuck it behind my ear. It's a mess, but I don't mind.

With a heavy sigh, I sit at the kitchen table and bite into a piece of toast smothered in margarine. For a moment, I let myself eat, not thinking about the problems in my life.

As I take my first bite, the door creaks open, and Linda, my roommate, steps in.

She's in her mid-forties, with tired but sharp features. Her dark hair is pulled into a neat bun, and she's still wearing her hospital scrubs, having returned from a night shift at Cedar Hollow Memorial Hospital. Linda is a nurse, and we have barely seen each other since I moved in six months ago.

I don't know how they do it, how these people spend nights and countless weekends caring for others, sacrificing their sleep and personal lives. The world runs because of people like her.

My heart aches for her when I see the dark bags under her eyes, and I'm frankly impressed that she's still standing and functioning. Healthcare workers really deserve more credit for what they do, and more pay.

"Morning," I say, glancing at the stove. "I made enough bacon if you'd like some."

"No, thank you." She crosses her arms over her chest, her face pulling into a deep frown. "Gabby. What the hell is going on? You quit your cleaning job last week?"

Of course she found out. After all, she's the one who helped me get that job. She spoke to some people she knew, pulled some strings, and now I've thrown it away without even telling her. I feel horrible for keeping it to myself, but I knew this is how she would react, and I needed time to prepare myself.

"I'm sorry," I say. "It really wasn't for me."

Linda shakes her head. "Do you really have a choice? Now that you've quit, we're going to be even more short on rent this month."

She's right, I haven't paid last month's rent either. I swear to myself that I'll make it up to her. I will get money. I have to.

While I search for something to say, guilt making my toast taste like sawdust, Linda steps closer and glares down at me. She doesn't speak again until I finally look up.

"I cannot believe you're putting me in this position, Gabby. You know I'm struggling too. My ex didn't exactly leave me much, and I've got a kid to take care of."

Linda has an eight-year-old daughter, but her mother helps care for her most of the time. I adore the little girl, even if I am normally clueless with kids, and sometimes I babysit her. This week, Isabella is with Linda's mother.

"I'm really so sorry, Linda," I say genuinely. "I promise I'll give you all the money I owe you. I'll be right back." Pushing back my chair, I get up and disappear into my room. When I return, I'm carrying my purse. I pull out fifty dollars and hand them to her. "Here... for now."

Linda looks even more upset. "It's not enough, and you know it." Then her voice softens. "If you can't pull it together... I'm sorry, but I'm going to have to find someone else. I can't keep doing this on my own."

My heart sinks. I don't want to lose this place. I don't want to be out on the street before I get another job. And I love staying with Linda. She's always been good to me, and I hate letting her down. She rented out the room I'm staying in because she was struggling herself. She needed extra income after her husband left her for a younger woman.

Feeling sorry for my friend and disgusted with myself, tears stab my eyes. "I know I messed up. But I'm going to fix this. You have my word."

I moved to this town six months ago after my boyfriend of three years, Mark, proposed. But I'd already been through a failed marriage—with my childhood sweetheart, no less. I was heartbroken to let Mark go, but I wasn't ready to be married again, so I ended things. And just like that, I found myself here. A fresh start, and a new purpose.

I'm grateful to Linda, not only for giving me a place to stay, but for helping me land my previous job, even though jobs here are scarce. Even though it barely paid the bills.

The thing is, I have to move to the next stage of my plan, and that cleaning job doesn't fit into it anymore.

Linda leans against the kitchen counter and rubs her temples. She looks exhausted, and I hate that I've added to her stress. I want to go over and give her a hug, but she's not exactly happy with me right now, so I stay where I am.

"You know what hurts the most?" She folds her arms again. "I helped you get that job. I don't know why I bothered."

"Yes, I know. And I'm sorry." I hate needing people to help me.

To break the tension, I head to the fridge and pull out a container of homemade sweets. I spent last night making them while thinking about my mother who taught me the recipe.

Linda raises an eyebrow. "You made these?"

"Yeah. They're for you. I thought you might like them."

I push the container toward her, and she picks one up, biting into it with a satisfied groan.

"Salted caramel toffees," she says between bites, her irritation fading. "You know... you should really sell these. You're good at this."

I laugh. "Maybe I should. But there aren't enough customers in this town to keep me in business."

And besides, I have other, bigger plans, that Linda doesn't know about.

She finally retreats to her room to get some sleep before her next shift.

It's time to get started. Time to put my real plan into motion.

After finishing my breakfast and cleaning up the kitchen, I head to my room to get dressed. I pull on a simple pair of beige pants and a loose white blouse. As I look in the mirror, my deep-set brown eyes stare back at me. They are tired, but determined.

Slipping out of the townhouse, I get into my beat-up Honda Civic and drive off. I don't pause as I drive straight through town, and eventually into the countryside. The wind rushes through my hair, and the fields stretch endlessly around me. For the first time in a while, I can't help but feel like everything is going to work out perfectly.

This next job is the key to getting my life back on track. I

don't know exactly what to expect, but I'm prepared for whatever it takes.

I hope my mother would approve of my choices.

TWENTY-EIGHT

As I step out of my car and make my way toward the Harrison farmhouse on Thistle Creek Ranch, a whirlwind of nerves and excitement takes over. My knees are unsteady, and my hands tremble.

The house looms before me, its age evident in the weathered wood and peeling paint, but it still has charm, with ivy climbing up its stone walls. My heart races wildly in my chest.

What if they don't need me because they already have someone to clean for them?

The door opens, revealing Evan Harrison. He doesn't know me, but I know him.

Despite being at home, he's wearing a suit, his hair impeccably styled, and his sharp amber eyes scrutinize me. He seems like someone who belongs in a sleek office building, not a rustic farmhouse.

"Can I help you with something?" His voice is smooth and polished, and the intensity of his eyes makes my skin crawl.

"I'm a housekeeper and I'm here about a job," I manage to say. "I saw an ad in the paper." It's a lie, but he can't know that. I've learned that if you sell a lie with enough confidence, the other person usually buys it. I try to push down the fear bubbling in my stomach.

"A housekeeper?" His eyebrows lift slightly. "But we didn't place an ad."

"Oh, perhaps I got the wrong address," I stammer, feeling the heat rush to my cheeks. It's what I expected to hear, but I'm here to convince them that they need me. "But considering the size of this place, I'm guessing you might need some help keeping it up? I'm hardworking, trustworthy, and efficient." My voice is more confident than I feel. I feel like a telemarketer, trying to persuade someone they need something they weren't aware they wanted.

The skepticism in his eyes doesn't wane as he crosses his arms over his chest. "Well, we haven't really thought about it," he starts, glancing over his shoulder at the sprawling house behind him. I take a deep breath and steady myself. His eyes flicker back over my body again in a way that sets my nerves on edge. I want to turn around and walk away, putting as much distance as possible between myself and this man.

But I can't deviate from my plan.

"Perhaps you might want to think about it now," I suggest as the door swings open wider and a woman steps out from behind the man. That must be his wife, Cora Harrison.

I know about her too.

She's striking, with sharp cheekbones, icy-blue eyes that cut through me like a blade, and black hair flowing loosely over her shoulders. But there's an air of authority about her, a coldness that makes her even more intimidating than her husband. She's breathtakingly beautiful, but distant. I wonder why her husband would even look at another woman, like he was clearly eyeing me just now. Then again, I am well aware that men can be pigs.

"Who is she?" she asks Evan instead of addressing me directly.

"My name is Gabrielle Walker. I'm a cleaning lady. I was wondering if you needed someone. I'm looking for a job."

"She said she saw an ad in the paper," her husband cuts in. "I told her we did not place one."

"I've come all this way, so I wonder if you might consider hiring me to help out," I counter, squaring my shoulders as I push my nerves aside.

Cora fixes me with an unwavering stare. The silence lingers for a moment before she shakes her head. "No, we don't need anyone," she says frostily. "I'm sorry you came all this way for nothing."

No way. This isn't how it will end. I will get what I came here for.

"If it's all right, I can leave my contact information and references."

Saying nothing, Cora goes back into the house, but Evan takes the references from my outstretched hand. "Please give me and my wife a moment."

He steps inside, leaving the door ajar. Through the gap, I catch snippets of a heated conversation. Cora's tone is sharp, while Evan's voice remains soft and persuasive.

"We can't just hire someone on a whim. We're capable of managing on our own," Cora insists.

"It's only cleaning, Cora. And you know this house needs it. We already have too much on our plate."

"But what if we can't trust her?"

"Why don't we hire her and put her to the test. We can always get rid of her. Besides, Cora, we do need some help, at least temporarily." Evan continues, his voice gentler now, "Honey, with your health, you really need to take it easy. I know you want to do everything yourself, but we can't risk you being overwhelmed. We both know what can happen if your condition takes over."

A silence follows. Just as Cora is about to respond, I notice an older woman leaning on a cane by the flight of stairs. She appears frail, tired, and almost ill as she watches me intently through the gap. Then she turns and walks away.

When Cora returns to the door to dismiss me, I speak before she can. "I saw you have an older woman living with you."

"My husband's aunt," she interrupts.

I nod. "Now I wonder, well, I can offer more than cleaning. I've cared for elderly people before."

Cora exhales loudly and shakes her head. "Sorry, no thank you. Goodbye."

Her tone leaves no room for debate. But as I drive away, I'm more determined than ever. I'm not someone who gives up easily. I will find a way to convince them to let me work for them.

They have no idea how far I'm willing to go for this job. How much I've already sacrificed to be here.

TWENTY-NINE

Thursday, May 9, 2019

It's 1 p.m. and I'm sitting at the kitchen table, a bowl of canned noodles steaming in front of me, when I get the call. It's Cora Harrison.

I made three more visits to the Harrison farm this week. The first time, the house was quiet and empty, with no one around. On my second visit, only Evan was there, and he promised to talk to his wife again about the housekeeping position as his eyes lingered on me uncomfortably long. When he offered me a cup of tea, I declined politely and left.

On my third visit—yesterday—the door creaked open to reveal a tired-looking Cora, who dismissed me with the same curt goodbye as last time and told me not to return. Her eyes avoided mine as the door closed with a definitive click.

"Hello, Mrs. Harrison," I greet her, attempting to keep the surprise from seeping into my voice.

"Please, call me Cora. Let's drop the formalities." Her voice, usually edged with sharpness, now carries a softer, kinder tone.

I push my bowl aside and lean forward with my elbows propped up on the table. "Hello, Cora. Did you call because—?"

"I'm calling about how I treated you. I know this is not an excuse, but I've been under a lot of stress lately. I shouldn't have brushed you off like that." She clears her throat. "I must admit, you're quite persuasive." I hear the sound of her shifting slightly on the other end of the line. "The thing is, I've had a challenging week, especially with my husband's aunt, Mary. She has dementia. She was in a home, but now she lives with us. I thought I could manage it all by myself, but... I think I was mistaken. You mentioned that you have cared for the elderly as well as cleaning. Can you tell me a little more about that?"

"My mother had cancer, and during her final months, I was her caregiver." I choose my words carefully and a knot of emotion forms in my throat. I swallow it down and reach for a dishcloth, wrapping my fingers tightly around it to help hold myself together. "Afterward, I lived with my grandfather and took care of him in his last days too. So I really know how to provide that kind of care."

"That's lovely," she replies. "What a wonderful human being you are to look after your family like that." I'm still surprised by her sudden change in attitude.

"Mrs. Harrison—I mean, Cora—I'd really love to help out. You need someone like me, and I need a job. I'm ready to start right away."

"Well, I've reviewed your references and made some calls. I do have one question." She pauses, and I hold my breath, waiting. "Since you came to Cedar Hollow six months ago, it appears you haven't held a job during that time."

That isn't entirely true. I simply chose not to mention the job I recently left.

"Yes, well, when I moved to this town, it was hard to find employment. I spent a long time searching but found nothing."

After a long silence, she finally speaks again. "You know

what? Maybe we do need each other." She laughs out loud—a high-pitched laugh. "How about you come by the house again this afternoon? We can talk more about the possibility of hiring you."

"Sure, that's not a problem at all. When should I come over?"

"As soon as you can. I'm home."

An hour later, I arrive at the farm to find the front door open. Cora stands on the porch, handing money to a dark-haired woman in jeans and a tucked-in black T-shirt, who gives her two bottles of milk in exchange before heading toward a blue pickup truck.

"That's Sabrina," Cora says, ushering me inside. "She and her family have a farm not too far from here. She sometimes brings fresh milk and eggs." She asks me to make myself comfortable in the living room while she takes the milk to the kitchen.

When she returns and sits with me, she asks more questions about my experience. It kind of feels as if she wants someone to talk to.

"Honestly, I should have given you a chance from the start. I'm really impressed with you. You seem like a strong person. The kind of woman I can get along with."

Before I can reply, there's a scream. We jolt upright.

"I think that's my husband's aunt, Mary! She might have fallen."

Cora scrambles to her feet and hurries to the stairs leading to the upper floor. "Please excuse me," she says abruptly, and in a flurry of skirts, she's gone.

"I can help if you'd like," I call after her.

She doesn't say a word, so I take that as a yes and follow right behind.

The older woman is sprawled out on the floor. Cora rushes over, trying to help her up, but Mary pushes her away.

"Leave me alone! Don't touch me!" she cries, clutching her elbow as if it hurts.

"She was napping. She must have fallen out of bed," Cora says to me, worry etched on her face.

I kneel down beside Mary, gently placing a hand near her shoulder but not touching her yet.

"Mary, are you hurt? Can you move your legs? Your arms?" My eyes scan her body for any obvious injuries. I gently guide her to sit up, while Cora stands a few feet off, watching us helplessly.

I sense this is my opportunity to demonstrate my skills.

"Let's check that elbow." I touch her this time and she doesn't push me away. "Can you bend it? Does this hurt?"

She shakes her head.

Once I'm sure there's no sign of a break or serious injury and Mary's breathing has started to calm, I smile at her. "Mary, do you like sweets?" I reach into my bag, and a spark of joy flashes in the older woman's eyes.

"I used to love mint toffees when I was a little girl."

"I don't have mint toffees, but I do have caramel ones. Would those work for now? I'll make some mint toffees for you another time." I glance at Cora, who mouths a silent thank you.

I then pull out a neatly packaged gift from my bag and unwrap it. Inside are some sweets—a gift I actually meant to give Cora, to thank her for considering me for the job. I take one of the salted caramel toffees and hand it to Mary before passing the box to Cora.

Mary bites into her sweet and closes her eyes as she chews. "My, my," she swoons, completely forgetting about her elbow. "Can I have another?"

Cora chuckles and hands her another piece and then takes one for herself. "You made these?" A delighted smile spreads across her face as she bites into the caramel. "They're simply delicious."

Thanks to the sweets, Mary calms enough to let me help her back onto the bed. "Everything's going to be all right," I assure her. "Why don't you get some rest?"

"Can I have more of those sweets later?" she asks, and I promise that she can. She lays her head back on the pillow and sighs with contentment.

Cora and I leave the room and return to the living room, where she thanks me and surprises me with a hug, not like I'm a stranger, but as someone she truly appreciates.

"I'm really sorry," she says, "Sometimes she can be unpredictable, and I don't always know how to handle it. It's embarrassing because she's family. I should be able to do this." As she pulls away, I notice tears in her eyes. She's clearly overwhelmed, and I really want to help her.

"You're doing the best you can," I say, crossing my legs. "So, about that job—"

"It's yours, if you still want it." She wipes her eyes, then plucks another sweet from the box, popping it into her mouth. "You know, if I hadn't already given you the job, this would've sealed the deal."

I clasp my hands together. "Thank you so much. I really appreciate this. When can I start?"

"How about tomorrow?" she says and not long after, we say our goodbyes.

Driving away from the Harrison house, I'm beaming. The first part of my plan has fallen perfectly into place.

THIRTY

CORA HARRISON

Monday, August 5, 2019

He's a monster.

The woman's words slam into me with the force of a freight train, and my breath is ripped from my chest. My stomach twists violently, and a wave of nausea crashes over me with such intensity that bile surges up my throat, threatening to choke me.

I stumble back, my head swirling with confusion. I could open the door, but fear holds me back. I'm terrified of what I might discover on the other side.

Before I can decide on a plan, I hear footsteps coming from upstairs. Panic grips my throat.

"He's back," I whisper as the footsteps draw closer, and then the basement door creaks open. I swiftly turn off my phone's light as a flashlight beam sweeps across the basement.

I duck behind a cabinet, covering myself with the sheet over it and pressing myself into the shadows. My breath catches as his footsteps come down the stairs.

When he reaches the bottom I hear him moving, pausing. I clasp my hands together so hard it hurts.

Fear like I've never known consumes me.

I wait for Evan to switch the light on, but even though I hear the switch being flicked, nothing happens. The lightning has probably knocked the power out.

"Damn storm," Evan mutters loud enough for me to hear, then he goes back upstairs, and the door closes again.

I take a deep shuddering breath, but then he's back, coming down the stairs. The faint glow from his flashlight bounces off the walls, stretching the shadows into grotesque figures.

My knees are bent slightly, my body coiled tight. Through the thin sheet, I see his tall silhouette. My jaw aches from being clenched and my blood is boiling, a deep, pulsing fury that begins in my chest and spreads through every inch of me.

This is the man I thought was kind and loving, the person I was beginning to trust despite all my doubts. I was beginning to believe the happy marriage lie he sold me. I swallowed the lies about my family. And all along he's keeping a woman captive down here.

There's no doubt in my mind now that the scratches in Mary's room were caused by someone's nails—desperate, clawing marks. I wonder if he kept the woman captive up there first, before dragging her down here.

"Cora?" His voice is soft. Again, closer now, "Cora?"

I shut my eyes and will myself to wake up from this nightmare, to be back in my room with the door locked.

This can't be true. I have to be dreaming.

Evan is my husband. The man who kisses my forehead before bed and every morning. The man who brings me breakfast in bed sometimes. Who covers me with a blanket when he finds me asleep on the couch. Who cooks for me and makes sure I take my medication. The man who...

The man who told me my family doesn't want me and I have no siblings.

The man who has a woman locked in the basement, a woman who is relying on me to save her.

He's a monster, she said.

My sister's words also echo in my mind: *I know you were mad about what I said about your husband being controlling, but this? Cutting me off completely?*

I clench my jaw tighter as my mind conjures an image of Evan the way he was only hours ago. Showing me our wedding photos, sharing a romantic lunch in town and telling me beautiful stories about our honeymoon.

I picture him upstairs, tucking Mary's blanket around her shoulders, hugging her when she's terrified, reading to her, loving her. Loving me.

My stomach twists even more, a deep, painful knot. The nausea rises fast, and it's bitter and burning at the back of my throat. I force it down.

Suddenly, Evan's flashlight beam cuts across the cabinet and I freeze. Every muscle in my body locks and my breath is trapped inside my lungs. I do my best to make myself small and turn myself into an immovable statue. But my heart is going wild, slamming against my ribs.

His fingers trail over a stack of crates. He nudges an old chair with his foot, sending it toppling over and hitting the ground with a loud clang. I think I hear a whimper, but I'm not sure if it's mine or if it belongs to the woman behind the wall—the woman with all the answers, the truth.

Evan mumbles something under his breath, too low for me to catch. His frustration is clear in the sharp, erratic way he's suddenly moving now, more urgent as his flashlight guides him to different parts of the room, where he knocks over more furniture and yanks down sheets to see what's hidden underneath them. It's only a matter of time before he exposes me, as he has been exposed.

But then he stops, and I hold my breath.

I hear something. A faint dripping sound. Is that a leaking pipe? A slow running tap? It's muffled. Maybe the sound is coming from the other room where that woman is hidden.

A woman I've unknowingly lived above, a woman who has been locked away while I went about my life as if everything was normal.

I don't move. I don't breathe as I wait for what comes next, what he decides to do.

After what feels like hours, Evan exhales loudly, then moves toward the stairs and starts to climb. I don't move, not yet. My body is still rigid.

But then he reaches the top, and his flashlight clicks off. The basement is plunged into darkness, a blanket of black swallowing everything whole. Then comes the creak of the door opening and the click as it closes, the lock sliding into place.

That's when I remember: I left the key in the door.

A shaky, frustrated breath escapes me as I mentally kick myself for being so careless.

Then, from behind the wall, a voice. "Is he gone?"

I don't answer. What if he's waiting outside the door, ears straining for any sound I make?

Silence stretches between us, two women on opposite sides of the wall.

Finally, I swallow the lump in my throat, and my legs wobble as I push away from the cabinet and lift the sheet. The air feels cooler now, as though a draft has swept through the space. My voice trembles as I force the words out. "Margaret... is that you?"

A long pause. More shuffling and then she responds in a weak but firm voice. "He's kept me locked up, and he's been drugging me with sleeping pills so that I sleep and don't make a sound. Before that I made a lot of noise and even whistled, hoping someone would notice. But then he reinforced the wall and told me no one would hear me anymore."

I think about the sound of birds singing, that sweet whistling sound I heard through the basement door. My bottle of pills that felt lighter somehow.

No wonder the crying and bird sounds stopped. And no wonder that wall looks freshly painted. It was probably that handyman who helped make it thicker that day he came over. And Evan drugged her to be quiet.

A sob breaks through, raw and trembling, and my heart shatters. This poor woman. What kind of a monster did I marry?

Margaret's breath is labored as she pleads. "Please get me out. I need to tell you... I know things about him. More than what he's done to me. There's so much more. I know everything."

"What things do you know about him?" I croak.

There's silence, so long that I wonder if she's passed out. But then she coughs, a dry, deep sound that makes my stomach twist. "I'll tell you if you let me out of here."

"I can't. He locked us both in. The key's outside."

Margaret makes a choked noise, frustration bleeding into her tone. "There has to be another way."

I go up the stairs and try the handle of the door to the basement, as though expecting it to magically open. But of course, it doesn't. I'm tempted to throw things at it, to break it down, like I've seen them do in movies, but how could I do that without making a noise that would alert Evan?

She is his prisoner, and now, so am I.

I look around the room and start stripping bedsheets from furniture, searching for something—anything—that could help. A tool? A spare key?

Margaret begins to sob. "I might not get this chance again. If you leave me here, if we don't escape, I know he'll kill me soon. And he'll probably kill you for finding me."

I keep searching and suddenly a box tumbles down, and an

album falls onto the floor, photos spilling out. I cringe, listening for him. Nothing.

I pick up a photo, shining my phone light onto it. It's a younger Margaret Tookes, smiling into the camera, leaning against Richard, who's dressed in a gray tweed suit, his black hair neatly cropped, his deep hazel eyes crinkling at the corners. Margaret is wearing a white dress with sunflowers embroidered across the bust, her hair in an elegant bun.

I look up and there, on the shelf where the box had been, is a white, dusty sewing machine.

And then I finally see it, under the shelf with the sewing machine. A bag filled with golf clubs. If Evan comes back, could I swing one of them at him, knock him down, and run past him?

My mind flashes to the woman trapped behind that door. She didn't have a chance against him.

But maybe I do.

THIRTY-ONE

GABRIELLE WALKER

Friday, May 17, 2019

The farmhouse stands tall and proud, the soft morning light making the land around it look golden and glorious.

I pull up my car under an old oak tree, where a red, weathered pickup truck is also parked. The tree's branches stretch wide for an embrace, its leaves trembling in the wind.

As I step out, my sneakers crunch on the gravel, and I inhale the earthy smell of damp earth.

It's another day filled with cleaning, cooking, and, most importantly, caring for Mary, who has always been my top priority here.

Using the key I was given when I started a week ago, so I can easily come and go every day, I unlock the front door and step inside.

The scent of polished wood mixed with a hint of lemon cleaner that I used yesterday to scrub the living room floors greets me. The house is quiet, aside from the steady ticking of the grandfather clock in a corner.

I don't call out for anyone because it's only seven and I would not want to wake Mary and Cora. As for Evan, he's probably been awake since six-thirty and is in his office already.

I drop my handbag onto the kitchen counter and tie an apron around my waist. I don't have an official uniform here but having worked in hotels and restaurants where uniforms were required, old habits die hard.

Today's schedule is simple—tidy up the shared spaces (excluding the living room, as I gave it a deep clean yesterday), vacuum both levels of the house, dust and polish the windows, and then make lunch. Mary is the only person I need to cook for; Cora and Evan typically handle their own meals.

Cora isn't much of a cook, so Evan is usually the one who prepares meals, especially on days when he's working from home. I haven't seen any clients visit their house, but I've overheard that he rents an office space in town for face-to-face meetings. He only holds virtual meetings at home.

As for Mary, despite her faltering memory and our limited time together, she has grown to like me.

She's the reason I'm here, but Evan and Cora must never know that.

I won't wake her, but I'm going to peek into her room, to see if she's okay.

Before I reach her bedroom door, I hear a sound.

I pause at the door, hand hovering above the knob, and listen closer. It sounds like she's talking to herself, a habit she tends to fall into when she's struggling with her memories. But no, there's another voice, Cora's. As I consider going back downstairs to give them time alone, I notice the crack in the door and peer into the room.

Cora is sitting in the chair next to Mary's bed, tucking the blanket around her frail shoulders. Mary's eyes flutter open, heavy with exhaustion, like she hasn't slept at all last night.

I watch as Cora helps Mary sit up, offering her a glass of water with a soft, soothing voice. "Just a sip, Mary. You'll feel better."

Mary takes the drink and then sinks further into her pillow.

Cora picks up Mary's white leather Bible from the nightstand and flips to a bookmarked passage. "Let's read something before you sleep again," she suggests.

I stand quietly, listening as she reads a psalm in a warm, steady tone, and when she's done, she leans in to press a gentle kiss on Mary's forehead. I notice for a moment that Mary flinches, a small reaction that happens sometimes when she forgets who her family is.

It will take time for her to adjust to living here, but I know it hurts Cora and Evan every time she forgets them.

"Sleep well, Mary," Cora whispers as she rises and moves toward the door. Noticing me standing there, she startles.

"Oh, morning, Gabrielle, I didn't see you there."

"I came to check if there's anything I can do to help with Mary before I get started with cleaning."

"Not necessary. It's all taken care of." She glances back at the door and closes it softly. "She didn't get much sleep last night. She had nightmares again. Expect her to sleep for most of the day. Maybe don't vacuum up here until lunchtime?"

"Sure."

"Would you like a cup of coffee before you start working?" Cora asks, wrapping her arms around herself as if she's cold.

"No, I'm fine. Thank you. I think I'll get started."

"I understand. I'm heading to the gym at the country club soon before coming home to work on my business plan."

"Business plan?" I cock an eyebrow, and she chuckles.

"I'm an interior designer, and it's always been my dream to set out on my own, to build something that's truly mine. But I wonder if I should put that on hold for a bit and tackle this place first. It's a little old-fashioned for my taste. And it doesn't feel like home yet."

I look around, taking in the faded wallpaper. "I think that sounds fun, to create a space that truly feels like yours. What better project to take on than your own home, right?"

"Right." Cora tucks a loose strand of hair behind her ear. "Anyway, I better get ready to leave. By the way, Evan's not home either, so it'll be just you and Mary for a couple of hours." Before walking away, she pauses halfway down the hall, her smile faltering. "Like I said, Mary had a rough night. Please let her rest, no disturbances. She suffers from nightmares, thanks to that care home in town where she lived before... we've heard whispers of neglect and even abuse. She's safe now, away from that dreadful place. But she needs time to heal. We simply have to handle her gently. Patiently." With that, she walks away in the direction of the master bedroom and, soon, she leaves the house.

Before returning to Mary's door, I wait until I no longer see Cora's Volvo in the distance.

My hand brushes against a small box in my pocket—a little silver-wrapped package filled with mint toffees, the kind Mary mentioned she used to love as a child.

To my surprise, when I enter the room, Mary is not asleep at all, but is sitting up in her bed, her Bible open on her lap.

"Good morning, dear," she greets me softly, her tired and pale face brightening. So much for sleeping most of the day.

"Morning, Mary." I lift the small box from my pocket and place it on the nightstand.

"For me?" she asks, her eyes brightening like a child.

"Yes, Mary. For you," I reply, watching as her thin fingers trace the contours of the silver package. She opens it gingerly, places one of the sweets into her mouth and closes her eyes.

I watch in silence as she finishes the first and takes a second one. She seems so happy and peaceful in this moment, and warmth spreads through me.

But then her expression shifts. Her eyes cloud over and drift shut, like she's disappearing into a memory.

Suddenly, they snap open again, locking onto mine. "I know why you're here," she whispers.

THIRTY-TWO

Friday, May 24, 2019

At 6 p.m., as I let myself into the house, I'm surprised to see the light on. Linda was supposed to have another late shift today. She's been having so many of those and we are rarely home at the same time these days. I find her at the kitchen table, slumped over with wrinkled scrubs.

She must have just gotten home and her daughter is with her mother again.

Not seeing Linda recently helped me avoid some tough conversations. It's been two weeks since I began working at the Harrison home, and I still haven't paid her the money I owe her for rent. But now it looks like I have no choice but to face her.

In front of her is a pile of unopened bills and when my eyes land on them, I swallow hard, but my throat is too tight.

"Hey, Linda." I set down my bag and remain standing, shifting from one foot to the other.

She looks up at me, her eyes rimmed with exhaustion, and tries to muster a smile. "Hey," she whispers, the word barely making it past her weary lips. "Gabby, we need to talk."

"Yeah, sure." I pull out a chair and lower myself into it. "I know what you're going to say, and I want to say... I'm sorry."

Linda sighs and starts to rub the back of her neck. "You know I've tried, Gabby. I've covered for you as much as I can. I've helped you out, but I can't do this anymore."

Her words hit me hard, and I grip the edge of the table to steady myself. This doesn't sound like it will end well for me.

"Look, I know things have been tight for you," she adds quickly.

"Linda, I promise you I'll get you the money. Evan and Cora still haven't paid me at all. They keep coming up with excuses."

"So, how can you make promises you can't keep?" Linda's voice is not angry, just tired. "How can you guarantee they will actually pay you?"

"They will. I promise I will talk to them again on Monday." I really pray they hand over my money this time. Every time I broach the subject of payment with Cora, since Evan keeps sending me to her, she changes the topic or promises she will sort it out but never does. If it was just about the job and I wasn't so desperate to be close to Mary, I would have quit.

Linda sighs and rubs her eyes. "It can't go on like this. I barely have enough for myself right now. Your rent is seriously overdue, and you need to figure something out soon."

"Yes, I will. I promise," I reply, even as uncertainty gnaws at my stomach lining.

"I hate doing this, but I can't support both of us." Linda gets to her feet. "I need you to understand that."

"I know, and I'm really grateful for everything you've done for me—"

"Just one more week, Gabby," she cuts in. "One more week, and I won't have any other choice but to find someone else."

With that, she leaves the kitchen, and I drop into a chair at the table, my eyes fixed on the bills as tears fill my face.

I know I should eat something, but I don't even have an appetite, so I head to my room and strip off my clothes. After a short hot shower, I climb into bed earlier than I normally do, a shoebox in my lap.

Opening it, my eyes land on several cutout newspaper articles from over the years. I dig through them until I find my mother's photo. Pushing the box aside, I press the photo to my chest as the dam of tears breaks.

"It's hard, Mom," I say under my breath. "But I'm doing it all for you. I'll never give up."

THIRTY-THREE

Monday, May 27, 2019

The thought of my upcoming conversation with Cora about payment tightens my chest as I get out of my car and walk toward the house.

Reaching the porch, I gather my resolve, and as I step inside, I'm met with the rich aroma of coffee and fresh bread, which Cora usually has delivered straight from the town bakery.

I find her in the kitchen, dressed in an oversized sweater and black leggings; her hair is still damp. When she sees me, she turns and offers a smile.

Cora is really kind, but I can't let her take advantage of my desperation. They knew how much I needed this job.

"Morning, Gabrielle. Are you okay? You look like you didn't sleep much last night."

"I'm fine." My eyes drift toward the kitchen table, where Mary is shifting her breakfast around her plate.

"You don't look fine." Cora pulls out a chair. "Come on, sit down for a bit."

I hesitate, fighting back tears, before accepting and sinking into the offered chair.

She pours me a cup of coffee, and I wrap my hands around the cup, the heat seeping into my fingers, which are always cold no matter the season.

Before I can take a sip, the words burst out before I have a chance to stop them. "I lost my place—the one I was renting. I couldn't pay the rent, and my roommate can't afford to keep me there anymore. I'm homeless." I freeze. Where did that come from? It isn't the complete truth, I still have a week to pay Linda before she considers kicking me out. But perhaps, by lying, I can push Cora to pay me sooner. "You haven't paid me since I started," I add, my voice firmer this time. "When do you think I'll be getting the money?"

I expect her to reach for her purse or at least promise a definite payment date, but instead she waves a hand. "Don't you worry. We will sort out the payment soon." Her face softens even more as she takes my hand. "But Gabrielle, I'm so sorry to hear you lost your place to stay." For a long moment, she studies me. Then her eyes light up. "I have an idea. Come and live here with us."

I blink several times, completely in shock. "Wh... What? You mean that?"

"It's the perfect solution." She squeezes my hand tighter. "Stay here until you figure things out, until you get back on your feet. We've got the space." Then she glances at Mary. "You've been so good to us. It's the least we can do."

The least they could do is pay me for my work. But to be honest, this is so much better. It means I get to spend so much more time with Mary.

Still, despite my strong desire to accept, a nagging feeling tells me something is off. This offer seems too easy, too good to be true. There have to be some strings attached, right?

"Are you sure?" I finally ask.

"Of course. You're welcome. You can take the guest room upstairs."

Before she changes her mind, I take the offer, and that afternoon, Cora shares the news with her husband. I expect him to object since she hadn't discussed it with him first, but he seems delighted.

"Well, that's great," he says, beaming, and his eyes linger on me a moment too long. "Gabrielle, we'd definitely love to have you."

My stomach twists. There's something unsettling about this man. He looks way too happy about me living here, like it's an opportunity for him as well as for me.

But Cora doesn't seem to notice as she gives my shoulder a reassuring squeeze. "It's settled then."

"Thank you so much." I force a smile, suddenly unsure if I've made the right decision.

That evening, I share the news with Linda, and to my surprise, she looks almost upset to see me go, even though I'd expected her to be relieved.

She wishes me well, and an hour later, I move into the Harrisons' upstairs guest room, a comfortable space with flowery wallpaper and a window overlooking the lake outside. I should be happy, feel safe here.

Lying on my bed, I'm exhausted to the point of not being able to sleep. And the room is too quiet. I guess I'm used to the constant hum of a busy town or city with traffic outside, the sounds of life.

Reaching under my pillow, I pull out a black-and-white wedding photo. I was twenty-eight—almost ten years ago—when I married Stephen, my high school sweetheart. Our marriage only lasted three years, destroyed by the demons I couldn't escape, demons that scared away any chance of long-lasting relationships after that. But I still cling to this photo, a reminder of one of the happiest days of my life.

I stare at it until I finally manage to drift off. But then I hear something, a voice, faint and muffled.

I sit up, holding my breath and listening closely. The sound intensifies, becoming more urgent. It's a jumble of words, indistinct at first, but it's coming from down the hall. Uncertain, I get out of bed and pad across the wooden floor to the door.

In the hallway, I discover that the sounds are coming from Mary's room. As I walk toward it, the voice grows clearer—agitated, full of desperation, and the words become distinct.

"No, no, please. Don't leave me here. I don't belong here. Don't touch me."

I open the door to find the older woman thrashing under her covers, drenched in sweat, her breath coming in ragged bursts. My heart jolts.

"Mary?" I sit on her bed and take her hand. "It's okay. You're all right."

Her eyes burst open—wild, unfocused, and still imprisoned by her nightmare. Her breathing steadies as she locks eyes with me. But just as fast, her expression grows tight and pinched.

"You," she gasps, her voice quivering. "I know you."

My pulse quickens, the thudding of my heartbeat loud in my ears.

"Yes, Mary. It's me, Gabrielle."

But Mary's gaze remains lost and unfocused. Then she slides her hand from mine and curls up in bed.

"You're not supposed to be here," she murmurs.

I let out a deep sigh. Poor Mary. She deserves peace, not fear and confusion, and I wish I could give it to her.

"It's okay, Mary. You're safe. You're home." I want to touch her again, but I don't know if she'll let me.

"What's going on?" The voice behind me startles me. I turn

to see Cora standing in the doorway, wearing a long nightgown. As soon as our eyes meet, she rushes to Mary's side, and I step away from the bed.

"Mary was having a nightmare. I didn't want her to wake everyone, so I came to check on her."

Cora brushes Mary's damp hair away from her forehead, speaking softly and reassuringly. "Shh, it's all right. It's me, sweetheart."

Mary clings to her arm, her breathing gradually calming. Finally, Cora turns to me.

"It's okay, Gabrielle. I've got this. Go back to bed." She pauses. "When she's like this, it's better for her to see a familiar face."

"Yes, you are right." With guilt and disappointment buried in my chest, I return to my room only to freeze in the doorway.

Someone is there, standing near my bed. Evan.

My heart races as I stare at my boss in his silk pajamas. "What are you doing in here?" I try to sound calm, but the words come out sharper than intended.

"Oh, Gabrielle. I didn't mean to scare you. I heard noises and thought it might be you."

"No, it was Mary." I narrow my eyes. "She had a nightmare."

I don't believe for one second that he thought it was me, and what gives him the right to come into my room?

Evan nods and moves toward the door. Stepping around him, I enter the room, keeping a safe distance, feeling uneasy about the whole situation.

Standing in the doorway, watching me, he says, "I've been meaning to thank you for everything you do for us."

"It's no trouble at all," I say quickly, desperate for him to get out of my room before Cora leaves Mary's. I wouldn't want her to come to the wrong conclusions.

Evan continues to stare at me, long enough to make every hair on the back of my neck stand up. Then to my relief, he smiles and closes the door.

As soon as he's gone, I lock it. Creep.

THIRTY-FOUR

Monday, June 10, 2019

I'm in the kitchen, cradling a warm cup of black tea between my hands before my workday starts. The air is laced with the smell of aged wood and faint traces of last night's dinner.

My eyes follow the morning light as it filters through the lace curtains and creates soft patterns over the speckled granite countertops with their edges worn smooth by years of use.

It's been two weeks since I moved in with the Harrisons, and I've more or less settled into my routine on the farm.

Occasionally, I assure Cora that I'm on the lookout for a place to stay and have already checked out several options. All lies.

The good thing is, they have finally paid me the money they owed me, and I could easily go back to Linda to beg her to take me back in.

But I'm trying to delay moving out of this house as much as I can. I need to stay close to Mary, and I don't intend on going anywhere soon. Evan still makes me uncomfortable with his stares, but at least I haven't found him inside my room again in the middle of the night.

The work itself is demanding but manageable. I've been a cleaner for most of my life, after all. But the best thing is that Mary seems to appreciate my presence, especially since she's not been feeling too well lately. In fact, it's 10 a.m. and she's still in bed.

Her condition seems to be worsening. She's become more forgetful and is often lost in her thoughts, shutting the world out. She also flinches at unseen things and mutters under her breath—things we do not understand, sometimes even in her sleep. And sometimes, she seems afraid of us, only to immediately catch herself and apologize, looking confused.

Doctor Rowe, the family doctor, comes now and then to check on Mary's condition, but he always says the same thing—that it's normal for her to be this way, that unfortunately, it will get worse and all we can do is try to keep her comfortable.

Cora does everything she can, staying up late most nights to tend to her. But I do notice that she's not coping well herself.

She had an episode a week ago where she was so low that she didn't get out of bed, totally depressed. Two days later, she was up and almost hyper, filled with energy and doing way more than was expected of her, even visiting Sabrina's farm to get the eggs and milk.

I've seen Sabrina quite a bit—whenever she brings milk and eggs, often accompanied by her son, Owen. Sometimes Evan or Cora call her because her mother, Jill, has wandered off and we find her outside the house, saying things that don't make sense, something about wanting to find her lost friend. I keep asking Cora what she means, but she just says Jill is old and gets confused sometimes.

Last Friday, when it happened again, Evan was so pissed off that he told Cora to stop buying their products, to stay away from them. But Cora refused, insisting that Sabrina had become a friend to her. She told him if he didn't want her coming over, she'd start visiting them instead, and he couldn't stop her.

I really wish Evan could be more loving toward his wife. She's clearly lonely. He works most of the day or is at the country club, and disappears a lot in the evenings, leaving her alone.

A week into living with them, I started to wonder if he's having an affair, and not long after, I heard them arguing behind the bedroom door, Cora accusing him of that very thing, and him denying it, saying he's sticking to their arrangement.

Whatever arrangement that is.

But I wouldn't put it past him to flirt—he does it with me almost every day. And I guess if I gave in, he'd probably take the next step.

When Cora comes into the kitchen, she smiles at me.

"Hi, Gabrielle. Could you do some dusting today?" She pauses and reaches for a glass, filling it with water. "I noticed Mary has been sneezing quite a lot lately and it gets so dusty around here."

"That's one of my top tasks today." I drain my cup and stand up from the table to rinse it.

"That would be great, thanks." Cora opens a cabinet and reaches inside for her medication. She takes it without water, swallowing hard and wincing slightly.

Before leaving the kitchen, I hover in the doorway. "How's Mary doing?"

"I don't know, Gabrielle." Cora turns to look out at the barren field while one arm is wrapped around her middle. She looks tired, sad, and lonely. "It's so hard watching her slip away a little more every day."

"That's true," I say. "It's so sad."

Cora has been around Mary so much that I don't get as much time with her as I'd like. The few times I did spend with her when she was lucid, she told me about her childhood and how she climbed the ladder of success as a businesswoman with an impressive career in the insurance industry, even showing me newspaper clippings featuring her. A part of me felt a twinge of pain, jealousy perhaps, but I brushed it away.

I told her about my childhood as well, and we bonded some more over our love for poetry, the smell of fresh rain on a sunny day, and how the first bite of a peach in the summer can be so sweet it almost feels like a sin. We even discovered that we both had a soft spot for the scent of old books. But those moments together were fleeting. We need more time together.

"By the way, I'm going to play tennis today." Cora interrupts my thoughts. "Can you watch out for her?"

"Yes, of course," I say a little too quickly. "You've been taking care of Mary so much. You need a little time for yourself."

Cora shrugs. "I really don't mind. It's just that a few friends have been calling a little too much, and I've been canceling. But Evan urged me to get out today, so I promised him I would. But I won't stay long. He's meeting a client in town but should be here in maybe an hour or two."

As Cora goes to get ready, I hope she will be back home before Evan returns; I hate the idea of being alone with him in the house.

That said, even though I like Cora, I'm glad to have her out of the house because when she's here, she's hindering my plan, standing in the way between me and Mary. And every chance I get with her gone, I make the most of it.

As soon as she drives off, I head to Mary's room. She's not sleeping anymore, just staring at the window.

"How are you feeling, Mary?"

She doesn't even look at me.

"I made some of those sweets you like." To please her, I was busy last night after everyone was in bed.

At hearing that, she looks up and smiles. "My favorites?"

"Yes. Do you want to come to the kitchen so we can enjoy them together?"

When she agrees, I help her out of bed and guide her out onto the porch instead of the kitchen, then I make her a glass of lemonade and set the sweets in front of her.

The thing about Mary is, if you force her to talk, she shuts down. So, I tread lightly. She makes all the right sounds as she eats her sweets.

I begin to ask her about her life in her younger years, but she doesn't want to talk about that. Then, even though she often avoids the topic of her health, this time, she opens up about her condition and expresses her fear of dying.

"You still have many years ahead of you, Mary. So don't talk like that."

"You're not a very good liar, are you?" She pats my knee in an affectionate way. "Will you come to my funeral when I die?"

"Of course, Mary." I swallow the lump that has formed in my throat. "But let's not dwell on such things right now."

We continue to sit in companionable silence before I take her to the kitchen table, where she starts piecing together a new puzzle, while I get on with my dusting.

Since moving in, I've noticed the dining room is rarely used —the curtains in there are almost always drawn. But I suppose there's little need for it; the kitchen is spacious, bright, and the large table more than accommodates everyone.

I start in the empty room downstairs, then make my way to the living room. Eventually, I find myself at the basement door.

Cora said it wasn't necessary to clean down there, but today I decide to anyway. As I step inside, a strange chill prickles my skin. The air is cool and stale. My eyes go over all the covered furniture and then to my surprise, I see a white door opening into a room I didn't know about.

I've been down here maybe twice before but never saw that door. Actually, there used to be a large shelf on that wall, which blocked the door from view. I approach, my curiosity piqued. The first thing I notice as I enter the room is that the wall is very thin, only a few inches thick. And the space itself is small, almost claustrophobic, like it might have been used as a pantry or storage space.

There's no window and the walls in here are empty—no shelves, no furniture. But there's a thin, bare mattress on the floor against the far wall, and at the foot of it is a crumpled blanket. There are no pillows, no signs of comfort at all. The mattress also has a dark ring on it, as though someone has urinated there.

I notice a silver bucket in one corner. Confused as to why it's in here, I approach it and it's empty, but stained. But why would it be here?

This doesn't look like a normal room at all. It doesn't look like a storage space either. It feels like someone was living here. The mattress would explain that. I rub my arms to chase away the chill across my skin.

Another thing that catches my attention is the wall opposite the one with the mattress. There are scratches on it, small horizontal lines, like someone had been marking the days, the way prisoners sometimes do.

Suddenly, the light flickers, and I jump. My body tenses.

When I step out of the room, I'm surprised to see Evan coming down the stairs. I totally lost track of time. But now, he's standing there, watching me with a deep frown etching lines in his forehead. His eyes, usually light and jovial, are dark and inscrutable.

"What are you doing down here?" he asks casually, though his eyes are intense.

"I was cleaning. I... never noticed this room before."

Evan steps closer with a slight smile, glancing at the door I exited.

"We only moved in a couple of months ago." He leans

against the staircase and crosses his arms. "Haven't had a chance to clear out the entire place yet."

"Yes, I thought I might help tidy up a bit." Remembering the mattress on the floor, my mouth turns dry.

Evan remains silent, studying my face intently. I desperately want to leave this basement and never return.

"You don't need to clean down here," he finally says. Then, without another word, he walks past me and locks the door to the hidden room with a key I didn't know he had.

He gestures for us to go back upstairs. I walk ahead of him, feeling him watching me with every step.

There's a primal instinct in me, screaming right now.

Run.

THIRTY-FIVE

Thursday, June 13, 2019

It's three days later when Mary has another nightmare, and I wonder whether I should go to her or if Cora will hear her as well.

Ever since I stepped into that basement, I haven't been able to stop thinking about it. That creepy room, and the stained mattress. The scratches on the wall. I shiver every time the image flashes through my mind. Was someone living down there at some point?

Whatever the truth is, for now, I've stifled my fear and buried my earlier instinct to run for one reason only. Mary. I need to be here for her, to watch out for her.

I can't let the poor woman suffer on her own for one second longer. So, I swing my legs out of bed and pull on a sweater.

I want to grab this moment with her without Cora knowing, so I tiptoe down the hall, careful not to make a sound, even though the old floorboards betray me at times.

I find Mary talking in her sleep, her voice trembling, and I don't catch the fragmented words. She's inside her world again, trapped in a nightmare.

"No, please... I don't want... don't—"

Even with the light on, her eyes are shut tight. I move to her bedside and gently touch her arm. She jolts awake, grabbing my arm. Her pupils are dilated, and she's shivering as she sits up in bed.

"Mary, it's okay. It's me."

Her breathing slows as she calms down. Then her expression softens into relief. "Oh dear... it's you." She settles back against the pillows, closing her eyes again for a brief moment before opening them again.

I reach for her hand and hold it. "What were you dreaming about, Mary?"

"A terrible, terrible dream," she says.

"About the care home?"

Her eyes widen. "Terrible people."

I stand up and go to the dresser, pick up her brush and head back to the bed. Then, I sit down next to her, unraveling her two braids that hang down her shoulders. I start to brush her hair the way Cora does it for her.

"I used to have the most beautiful hair," she sighs, and her shoulders sag.

Finally, she closes her eyes, and I take my time plaiting her hair up again into the two braids she likes. When I'm done, she traces them with her fingertips, her eyes sparkling with joy. "You're a sweet girl." She studies me as if seeing me in a new light. "Tell me about yourself, dear. Your childhood. What was it like?"

My hand stills on her shoulder. A thousand memories press against the back of my mind, most of them sharp and heavy.

I go on and tell her the happier ones—climbing trees, scraped knees, chasing butterflies in summer—and she listens intently.

"Such precious memories." She watches me for a moment longer, as if she senses there's more I'm not saying. But some stories are best left untold.

"Why don't we create another precious memory?" I pull out my phone. "Let's take a picture together."

Mary looks surprised but she allows me to lean in beside her, snapping a quick selfie.

Then, I pull up the photo and quietly add it to an album on my phone labeled *Mary*.

The next morning, I wake up to find myself still in Mary's room, having drifted off in the chair while she sleeps soundly in her bed.

I'm about to stroke her cheek when I feel a presence in the room. I look up to see Cora standing at the open door, watching me.

"Gabrielle?" She takes a step into the room. "What are you doing in here?"

"Oh, I... She was having a bad dream. I didn't want you to lose any sleep, so I checked on her. You were so tired yesterday."

Cora's eyes flit between me and Mary, who's stirring in bed now. "You should have woken me."

"I know. You're right. But I didn't want to disturb you."

In that moment, Mary opens her eyes and Cora forgets our conversation, hurrying to her bed to tend to her.

"I'm so sorry you had a bad dream, Mary. I'm here now." With a single look, she signals me to leave them alone.

Over breakfast, Cora lingers by the counter, and she keeps watching me as she sips her coffee in silence. Mary is sitting at the kitchen table, but she's not touching her scrambled eggs and toast; she just sips tea and refuses anything else.

Cora calls me to follow her out of the kitchen and closes the door behind us.

She crosses her arms in front of her chest. "Gabrielle, I appreciate everything you do."

"Of course. I don't mind helping out at all. You have quite a lot on your plate."

Cora shakes her head a little and dips her head to the side. "I do think it's best if I take over Mary's care completely. You already have enough to do. This house requires a lot of maintenance. I don't want you to be overwhelmed."

Ice spreads through my stomach. "I really, really don't mind, Cora. Mary is easy to take care of. She doesn't take up too much of my time at all. I want to help. You've done so much for me, and I'd love to do more."

"I know you do want to help and that's very kind of you. But since I'm not working at the moment, I don't have much to do around here. My priority is Mary. Please focus on what we hired you for." Her lips spread into a smile, but it does not look genuine.

"Of course," I say, faking a smile back. "No problem at all."

"Good. It's not that I don't appreciate what you do," she continues. "It's just that we have so little time left with Mary, and I'd like to make the most of it."

What Cora doesn't know is that Mary may be her priority, but she's mine too.

And she's not going to stop me from getting close to her.

THIRTY-SIX

Saturday, June 15, 2019

I'm seated at a table outside a little café located in the town square, right beside Sweet Sundae, which Cora once mentioned serves the best ice-cream.

The café has a rustic charm, with its mismatched wooden tables and colorful chairs placed under a faded awning. A few plant pots nearby are filled with flowers, adding splashes of color to the sidewalk.

As I sip my tea and eat a sandwich, I watch people as they stroll past, their faces not yet familiar to me.

An older couple stops at the ice-cream shop, laughing as they good-naturedly argue over what flavor to share. A little boy with a mop of curly hair races past while his mother hurries after.

Ever since I began working for Cora and Evan, I have rarely left the house, even on my weekend days off. But two days ago, Cora made it abundantly clear that I should leave Mary's care to her, and since then, things have shifted in the house. Cora has changed.

The warm-hearted woman I used to know has disappeared, replaced by a colder, harsher version, like the first impression she gave when I came to the house asking for work. Her voice has taken on an icy tone, and it feels like she's constantly watching me.

She also makes a point of ensuring that Mary and I aren't left alone together for long periods. I cannot let her come between me and Mary. But I also have to be careful not to get on her wrong side and possibly end up losing my job and being banned from Mary's life completely.

I needed to step out, to clear my head and reflect on what my next steps are. Besides, since I'm not paying rent, I can afford to spoil myself a little. I might even do a little shopping.

Taking another bite of my sandwich, I bring my attention back to the people around me. They're all carrying on with their lives, their priorities so different from mine.

A young couple strolls by, hands intertwined and laughter enveloping them like a warm blanket, and I feel a small twinge even though romance is not my priority right now. Maybe one day when I've healed from the pain in my past.

Looking away, this time I notice a little girl, her hair in two braids as she excitedly tugs her mother toward the ice-cream shop. Memories of my mother instantly flood my mind and an ache burns its way up my chest. I want her back so badly it takes my breath away.

I take a deep breath, attempting to push down the wave of sadness, but the memory of her face, the crinkling of her eyes when she smiled and the soothing sound of her voice when she sang me to sleep, only intensifies my longing.

I blink back the tears that threaten to spill. The pain of losing my mother never really leaves. It simply dulls over time, occasionally flaring up at unexpected moments. And right now, in the middle of this busy town with children's laughter in the background, it burns through me.

I finish my food, pay, and walk to the ice-cream shop, where I grab two lemon scoops. I enjoy the treat while wandering aimlessly among the crowded streets, the tangy sweetness a small comfort.

Just as I'm finishing my ice-cream, I pass by a thrift shop with various items spread out on a table outside. Among the items, a well-worn leather wallet catches my eye. It's old and slightly battered, but there's something about it that draws me in. The rich, mahogany color reminds me of the one my mother used to carry, and I end up buying it.

On the way to my car, I come across the Turning Pages bookstore, and even though I don't want to spend any more money today, I come to a stop in front of it. I've always been a booklover but it's been a while now since I've been absorbed in a good novel.

I give in to the temptation and step over the threshold into the store, enjoying the familiar smell of musty pages and leather bindings. My eyes skim over the shelves stocked with books, some old and worn, some pristine.

Moving from aisle to aisle, I pick up a few, flipping through the pages.

I'm in the fourth aisle when I hear a familiar voice. I glance around a corner and my heart stutters in my chest.

It's Evan but he's not alone. He's with a woman with brown hair and glasses and they are bent over a book, their heads too close together for me to think there's nothing going on between them.

Cora said he's at the country club this afternoon playing golf.

I watch as he closes the book and puts it back on the shelf. I recognize it immediately: *The Dynamics of the Mind*. He's the author of that book.

Then he reaches out to tuck a loose strand of hair behind

the woman's ear and leans in to kiss her neck. She giggles loudly.

So, Evan is unfaithful to Cora. Does she know? If so, no wonder her moods swing so wildly from day to day. I suddenly feel a deep sympathy for her.

How could he do this to her, while she spends most of her days at home caring for his aunt?

The disrespect turns my stomach and indecision grips me. Should I tell Cora? Or does she already know?

I take out my phone and snap a quick photo in the exact moment their lips meet. I might need it.

Despite Cora's illness—and everything on her plate right now—I feel compelled to tell her. She never told me she has bipolar disorder, but I overheard her talking to Evan about it once, and I looked up some of the medications she takes.

Even though our relationship has been strained lately, she has been kind to me, giving me a job and a place to stay.

Still feeling weak and sick to my stomach, I go back to my car.

During the drive, a deep dread settles over me as I anticipate the conversation, and when I finally pull up in front of the house, I remain in the car for a bit, gazing at it through the windshield. I picture Cora inside, and I imagine explaining what I saw, a vision that ends with her breaking down in front of me.

I despise the way Evan is treating her, and I loathe how he flirts with me at every opportunity. I bet that woman is not his first affair.

I find Cora in the living room, leafing through a house-keeping magazine while Mary watches TV next to her.

"Cora, do you have a minute to talk? It's kind of..." I glance at Mary. "...a bit personal."

We go to the kitchen and take a seat at the table.

Cora folds her arms on the table. "What is it, Gabrielle? What's so important it can't wait?"

I clear my throat. "It might not be my place, but I believe you need to know."

Cora waits for me to continue, her finger tapping impatiently on the table.

"It's about Mr. Harrison," I begin.

"What about Evan?"

"You said he would be playing golf at the club today. But I saw him at the Turning Pages bookstore. He was with another woman. I'm so sorry, Cora."

To my surprise, she lets out a loud laugh. "Oh, Gabrielle. Are you saying my husband is cheating on me?"

"Yes, I... I thought you should know," I stammer, taken aback.

Cora stands up. "Well, Gabrielle, it's really none of your business, but my husband and I have an agreement."

I'm stunned into silence. So, their "agreement" is an open marriage?

However, later when I pass by the bathroom, I hear her quietly crying inside. And after everyone is in bed, I hear yelling coming from their bedroom, along with the sound of objects hitting the wall.

Whatever agreement they might have had, it's clearly shattered.

THIRTY-SEVEN

Tuesday, June 18, 2019

The afternoon is peaceful with no tension in the house since Cora and Evan are out, leaving Mary and me alone at home. They were invited to a charity event organized by one of Evan's clients.

Cora seems to enjoy such gatherings, always dressing up elegantly, eager to socialize with people of their social standing.

It's rare to have them both gone, and I feel buoyed and free. It's good to have this alone time with Mary, giving us a chance to chat away. Mary is having a nap, but she has been sleeping for a while, and I feel it's okay for me to wake her.

But before I bring her up a tray with some tea and ginger snap cookies, I decide to vacuum the downstairs hallway, something Cora asked me to do before she left.

I push the vacuum cleaner out of its closet and plug it in. As I begin to move it back and forth over the carpet, I notice that Evan's office door is closed and probably locked—as it always is —but the key is inside the lock. In their hurry to leave and not be late, he clearly forgot to remove it.

So far, I've been allowed to clean everywhere in the house except the basement and that office. In fact, I have never stepped foot inside it. But now the key is dangling tantalizingly in the lock. A part of me feels guilty but another part, a more curious one, gets the better of me.

My heart pounds as I grip the doorknob and turn the key. With a soft click, the lock releases, and I carefully push the door open. The room is filled with bright light and a fresh, airy feel, carrying different scents: a blend of leather, a trace of Evan's cologne, and a hint of old paper.

Everything here appears new, a marked contrast to the rest of the home, which hasn't been renovated since they moved in. For now, Cora wants to focus on Mary.

An entire wall is occupied by bookshelves with all sorts of books, neatly organized. From where I stand, I notice hardcover psychology textbooks—likely ones Evan studied during university—alongside various research materials. And of course, his own book displayed prominently in the center with its cover facing outward.

The space is really tidy and in the center of the room is a large glass desk.

I know I shouldn't be here. If I get caught, this will be difficult to explain. What would I say? That I was cleaning, even though I'm not supposed to?

Ever since I arrived at this house, I've been even more fascinated by Evan and Cora. I'm sure there are more secrets than I know about here, things lurking underneath their supposedly happy marriage, their "arrangement."

I take several deep breaths before moving toward the desk. I run a finger along its surface, and in the process, my hand shifts a stack of papers, revealing a small metal key underneath.

My breath catches as I glance at the drawers on one side of the desk—they're all locked.

I try to open each one, and the key turns smoothly in the third.

But I pull out the drawer, only to find it empty.

Why would someone lock a drawer that has nothing of value inside it?

Running my fingers along the inside of the drawer, I feel a slight unevenness along one side. I press down and hear a soft click, followed by a tiny section of the drawer's base lifting slightly. A bead of sweat slides down my spine as I lift the false bottom to reveal a matt black USB stick, labeled *Research*.

I pick it up, staring at it in my palm. Is this something I could use to my advantage at some point?

I'm about to slip the USB stick into my pocket and head to my room to check its contents on my laptop when I spot something else on the desk—a small open box in the corner filled with nearly identical, unused USB sticks.

Thinking quickly, I peel the label off the original USB and stick it onto one of the blank ones. I place the decoy back in the drawer, ensuring everything is as it was before.

Clutching the real USB in my hand, I quietly leave the office, closing the door softly behind me, locking it and leaving the key where it was.

I quickly dash upstairs to my room, plop down on my bed, and reach for my laptop. Soon enough the screen lights up with its background showing a photo of me and my mother from our last vacation together in Canada.

It was the last time we were together, years ago. I shake off the wave of sadness and hold my breath as I insert the USB into the slot on my laptop.

A folder suddenly appears on my screen, containing one PDF file named *List* and a folder labeled *Archive*.

I open the folder first, to find three subfolders inside. I'm shocked when, inside the first, I see nearly thirty thumbnails of photos featuring Evan.

They might have seemed harmless, except that in every picture, he's with a different woman, the most recent one being the woman I saw him with at the bookstore.

In all of them, it's clear that he is far more than a casual acquaintance to these women. His arm is draped over their shoulders, and he's even kissing some of them.

I click through the images, my stomach turning.

The next folder contains more than pictures. There are also photos and screenshots of emails, text messages, even hotel receipts.

I'm about to click on the third folder marked *Videos*, but the thought makes me nauseous.

Feeling sick to my stomach, I exit the parent folder and click on the lone PDF document, but it's a list with nonsensical codes, and they offer no context—no names, just a sequence of seemingly random strings of numbers and letters. They could be passwords, financial details, or any number of things.

I switch off the laptop and pull out the USB.

I need to return it to Evan's office right away.

Grabbing my laptop bag, I stuff the computer inside, but when I look up again, my stomach drops.

Mary is standing in the doorway. How long has she been there?

THIRTY-EIGHT

Wednesday, June 19, 2019

As I step out of the shower and dry myself off, I try not to think about yesterday.

I can't shake the feeling that Mary was standing in the doorway for a while.

For the rest of the day, she had this knowing look on her face whenever our eyes met, like she was holding onto some secret. And when I went up to bed, I caught her lingering near the door to my room, almost as if she wanted to go inside. Or like she had already been inside. I couldn't tell, but something in the way she hovered there made me uncomfortable.

But there's no doubt she's curious about what I saw on that laptop screen. She must have seen the shock and horror on my face when I was going through the files.

I tried to make light conversation with her, postponing returning the USB to Evan's office. But then before I had the chance to do so, he and Cora returned home early as Cora wasn't feeling well.

Now I've decided I'll act normal. I'll pretend nothing happened, like everything's fine.

After getting dressed in black jeans and a plain white T-shirt, I head downstairs, expecting to find Mary at the table. But no one is in here and the table is empty.

"Poor Mary took a turn for the worse last night," Cora says when she comes in a few minutes later, finding me emptying the dishwasher.

"I'm sorry to hear that." I straighten up, holding a small black-and-white plate in my hand. "And you? I hope you feel better today."

"A bit better, thank you." She moves to the cupboard and takes out a packet of tea bags. "I'll make Mary some tea."

"No, let me make it, then you can take it up to her." I set the plate down onto the counter with a soft clink.

She hesitates first, but then, with a sigh, she leans against the counter, watching as I set the kettle on to boil. Her arms are wrapped around herself as if she's cold even though it's warm in here.

I pull Mary's favorite mug, a pastel-pink one with a faded picture of a cat, from the cupboard and place it on the counter.

The silence in the kitchen is filled only with the soft hum of the kettle heating up. We don't say anything to each other at all until I hand her the tray, and she leaves the kitchen.

I turn back to the dishwasher to continue my task, then turn to find Evan standing outside the door, wearing a blue striped suit, staring at me. His eyes narrow before he turns and walks away.

I slump back against the counter, feeling the cool surface of the cabinets seep through my shirt. I think somehow, he knows I was in his office.

Stupid. Stupid. What the hell was I thinking?

· · ·

Late in the morning, Mary comes downstairs, and Cora settles her in an armchair by an open window. My stomach knots as I take in how fragile she looks. She appears to have aged even more overnight.

While I'm cleaning another window, I hear her talking softly to herself. Every few minutes, she jerks, startled by something unseen. Sometimes she also wraps an arm around her stomach like she's in some kind of pain.

"I'm sorry, Gabrielle," Cora says. "Why don't you go and tidy up upstairs for now? I think you have some vacuuming to do. Mary needs some peace and quiet."

"Sure, of course." I watch as she hovers around Mary, tucking the blanket around her frail body, adjusting the throw pillows.

Just as I'm about to leave, Evan comes in, barely acknowledging my presence as he pulls up a chair beside his aunt and clasps her hand. I've never seen him so unsettled and distressed; he always seemed so composed.

Shortly after lunch, the doorbell rings, and I walk over to open it, finding Doctor Rowe standing on the doorstep.

"I'm here to check on Mary," he informs me just as Cora appears behind me.

"Thank you so much for coming so quickly, Daniel," Cora says as she guides him into the living room, where Mary is now curled up on the couch.

Cora quickly shuts the door behind him, leaving me outside. To keep my anxiety at bay, I start rummaging through the pantry, even though it's already tidy.

Eventually, I find myself back at the living room door, pressing my ear against the wood, straining to catch words through the muffled voices.

"She's not well," Doctor Rowe states calmly but firmly. "It might be best to take her to the hospital for observation."

After a long pause, Evan replies, "No. My aunt is staying right here. She hates hospitals."

Doctor Rowe sighs. "Evan, you need to consider what's best for her. This could be serious. Those abdominal pains she's experiencing—"

"I am thinking about her best interest," Evan retorts, his tone tight and controlled. "She's comfortable at home. We'll monitor her for a few days, and if she doesn't improve, then we'll take her in."

Following another lengthy, heavy silence, it seems the doctor has no choice but to respect their decision, and he finally leaves. As soon as he's gone, Cora and Evan vanish into the office, and I hear raised voices making their way down the hallway.

I dare not get too close, but from where I am in the hall, I catch fragments of their argument. Mary's name keeps coming up.

I'm not entirely sure, but it sounds like Cora is opposing Evan's decision to keep Mary at home instead of taking her to the hospital.

"If you don't do it, I will," she eventually declares, and I can tell she's near the door, ready to leave. "This has been going on for too long."

Just a few seconds later, the door swings open, and she storms out. I quickly jump into the guest bathroom before she has a chance to see me.

After a few minutes I make my way to the kitchen.

Cora is standing at the counter, her shoulders rigid and fists clenched at her sides. She stares at the tiled backsplash like it's personally offended her.

Before I can speak, she grabs a plate from the drying rack and hurls it against the wall.

THIRTY-NINE

Thursday, June 20, 2019

A heavy, oppressive silence hangs over us at dinner, the only sound coming from Mary, who keeps quietly murmuring over her food. She looks better but is still a bit pale for my liking. But at least she's strong enough to sit at the dinner table.

As we eat our steak and salad, I keep a close eye on Cora. She appears completely exhausted; the dark bags under her eyes are impossible to conceal with the thick layer of makeup she's wearing.

I overheard them arguing again late last night, and today she barely managed to get out of bed.

I still remember the sound of that plate shattering against the kitchen wall yesterday. I'd never seen Cora like that before, like something inside her had finally snapped.

But despite how low she feels, she still manages to get up and care for Mary. The few times she left the bed today were to tend to Mary's needs.

I really wish she would follow through on what she said to Evan and actually take Mary to the hospital. This morning, when Evan was not nearby, I casually told her that I thought Mary really needed medical attention, and even offered to take her myself if she didn't have the time.

Clearly irritated, she reminded me again that Mary's care was her responsibility. I let it go then, but if they don't do something soon, I will.

Cora exhales heavily as she raises her glass of orange juice to her lips and when she sets her glass down, it nearly topples over, but Evan catches it in time. He places an arm around her shoulders, but I notice her flinch.

She clearly doesn't want anything to do with him right now, but she's also determined not to create a scene.

I can't take the silence anymore. This dinner is unbearable —Cora barely lifting her head and Evan sitting stiffly across from me. The tension is suffocating.

When dinner is finally over, and they leave the table—Cora gently guiding Mary out of the room—I sigh with relief.

Wasting no time, I quickly clear the dishes and put them in the dishwasher, scrub the sink, and retreat to my room. The moment I shut the door behind me, I lean against it, eyes closed, forcing myself to calm down.

I've been on edge all day, especially around Evan, wondering if he's noticed that the USB is missing. If he knows it was me.

Since I have access to the master bedroom for cleaning, I'll slip the USB into one of the drawers tomorrow. Or better yet, I'll tuck it into Cora's closet, hidden among her belongings for her to find.

Even though I hate the thought of hurting her even more, she deserves the truth, and proof along with it. But it won't come directly from me.

Once she sees what Evan has been hiding, she'll surely leave him—and Mary—behind. And Evan? He won't be capable of caring for Mary himself since Cora mostly did that on his behalf. He'll probably put her back in a home, one safer than the last. Then I'll find out where she is and visit her as often as I want, continuing to look after her the way I always intended.

Hope and adrenaline surging through me, I drop to my knees beside the bed, reaching for my laptop bag underneath. I quickly unzip it, and my hands dig inside, searching.

But they come up empty, and my throat clenches.

The USB is gone.

Heart hammering, I rip through the bag, yanking out papers and pens.

Finally, I sink onto the floor, my bag's contents strewn around me. Running a hand through my hair, panic rises in my throat.

Could Mary have taken it? Maybe she really *did* go into my room when I saw her standing outside the door.

I need to talk to her.

When I'm sure Evan and Cora have been in bed for a while, I swing my legs out of bed, slip into a robe, and tiptoe to the door.

The house is silent, except for the rhythmic ticking of the grandfather clock downstairs. I hold my breath as I step into the semi-dark hallway. Then I see him.

Evan.

He's closing Mary's door. As soon as he sees me, he stands there motionless, his figure illuminated by the moonlight from the window at the end of the hall.

A chill snakes down my spine, and for a moment, neither of us moves.

I open my mouth to speak, but before a sound comes out, he turns to walk away, and I'm left standing there, confused and unnerved.

I head down the hall toward Mary's room. As soon as I reach it, I notice a sliver of light beneath the door, and hear Cora talking on the other side.

I go back to my bedroom, and my mind circles back to Evan, the way he had looked at me from across the hall.

He definitely knows I've uncovered some of his dirty little secrets. He may not have said a word, but that look said plenty. I could be mistaken, but it looked like a warning.

FORTY

By the next morning, there's no chance for me to speak to Mary because she's not feeling well. Her stomach issues have worsened significantly since last night, and she can barely keep any food down.

As I clean the microwave, I watch her struggle to eat her cereal at the kitchen table. Her frail hands shake violently as she attempts to lift a spoon to her lips. It clatters against the bowl, sending tiny droplets of milk splattering onto the tablecloth.

With Cora urging, she tries again to eat, but after only a few bites, she grips her cane and hurries to the bathroom like she did once before.

Cora is on her feet in an instant, pushing her chair back sharply, to go and help Mary, even though I'm dying to do it.

They're gone for a long time, and when they return, both are dressed, as if they're about to go out. Cora has on a pair of white-washed jeans and a pink blouse, the same shade as Mary's favorite mug. Mary is wearing a simple blue dress that hugs her frail frame and her face is pale. One of her braids has almost come undone, making me want to reach out and fix it.

"I'm taking Mary to the hospital," Cora announces, determination written all over her face as she betrays her husband. I wonder if she told Evan, who has been in his office all morning in meetings, and I haven't even seen him yet today. I doubt it. And they will probably have another huge argument when he finds out.

Cora looks so worried, barely holding herself together, and her lips are pressed into a thin line, her eyes shimmering like she's about to cry.

"That's good." I use a dry dish towel to wipe my hands. "Is there anything you want me to do while you're gone?"

Cora taps her lips with a finger, thinking. "Oh, yes. I'd love it if you could clean the rest of the windows downstairs. I think they need it."

That's not true. I cleaned them a few days ago, and they still look spotless. Still, I nod, and they leave.

As much as I appreciate that Cora took Mary to the hospital, it also means I'm now alone in the house with Evan.

He's still in his office, speaking in that low, measured voice of his.

Trying not to think too much, I gather the cleaning supplies and start with one of the hallway windows.

Dunking the cloth into the bucket of soapy water, I squeeze out the excess liquid, then I press the rag against the glass, scrubbing at invisible dirt, my movements tense and aggressive as I remember last night, seeing Evan in the hallway watching me.

No matter how much I scrub, I can't shake the anxious energy crawling under my skin. Any moment now, he will be out of that office, and we will come face to face.

I keep wiping, long and forceful strokes, the moisture streaking the glass before I buff it dry. My breathing is shallow and as I exhale, the glass fogs slightly from my breath. My reflection stares back at me, wide-eyed.

After a while, my arms start to grow sore from the repeated motions, and I try to focus on them rather than my thoughts.

I wonder what the doctors will say at the hospital. What if it's worse than an upset stomach? What if Mary doesn't get better? What if we don't have more time together?

No. I can't think like that. She will recover and get her strength back. I need more time with her.

From my position at the window, I hear Evan inside his office. His deep voice is slightly raised and it carries through the closed door.

I move closer and strain my ears to hear.

"Like I said, I will let you know when it's done."

His tone is clipped and firm.

A pause.

I move away quickly and back to the window where I continue wiping the glass.

I can still remember the dread I felt last night when he watched me. It was as if he saw through my facade... knows my own secrets.

Are his secrets worse than mine?

The sound of his office door opening makes me freeze, my fingers tightening around the cloth.

"You're working very hard." His voice is so smooth.

I force myself to turn and look at him. He's standing behind me—a little too close—with his hands tucked into his pockets. And he's smiling. But there's also a sharpness in his eyes, a knowing glint that makes my skin feel prickly under my clothes.

"Hi," I say, keeping my tone neutral. "Is there anything I can help you with?"

"Yes, in fact, there is. There's a box downstairs in the basement, inside the storage room. The one I found you in recently."

He pauses, watching me. "I need you to bring it upstairs for me."

Blood rushes to my head, the sound of it roaring in my ears.

Why is he sending me down there now when, before, he locked the door to keep me from going back? Why doesn't he get the box himself?

"Umm... Cora asked me to clean the windows. Maybe I—"

"I really need that box," he interrupts, his voice as smooth as ever, and that grin still pasted to his face.

"Sure. Okay." I step away from the window and drop my scrubbing cloth into the bucket. Every nerve in my body screams at me to refuse. But I don't feel like I can.

"Glad to hear it." His smile widens, and he steps aside, gesturing to the short hallway.

With unsteady legs, I make my way to the entrance of the basement, rest my hand on the cool knob of the door, hesitating for a moment.

"Thank you, Gabrielle." His voice echoes from behind me, but there's a cool undertone.

I don't turn around, don't acknowledge him. Instead, I push down the knot in my stomach and turn the doorknob. The door is unlocked.

Next, I place one hesitant foot on the top step, gripping the handrail tight, and without looking back, I descend.

As I step downward, the air grows cooler, heavier. It feels like the walls themselves are pressing in on me. Each step echoes, very loud in my ears.

The room looks exactly the same, except that the dirty mattress is no longer on the floor but propped up against the wall, the stain on it on full display. And it's sunken in places. My eye moves to the bucket in the corner. This place creeps me out.

There's no box in here. What is he playing at?

I turn only to come face-to-face with Evan. He's come down here with me, and he's closing the door.

"Gabrielle, I think we need to talk."

FORTY-ONE

CORA HARRISON

Monday, August 5, 2019

I'm positioned at the bottom of the stairs, hidden by a cabinet. I hear the key slide into the lock, the click as it turns. The door groans open. A second later, the light flicks on, flooding the basement with a harsh glare. The power must have come back on by itself, or he fixed it.

My pulse races. If this plan fails, it's over.

My hands grip the handle of the golf club, a film of sweat making my palms slippery. I clutch it, fully aware that this moment is a matter of life or death.

His footsteps echo as he steps onto the stairs and I can feel the vibrations through the floor beneath me.

When he reaches the bottom, he halts, the silence deafening.

"Cora," he calls out.

Every muscle in my body is taut.

"Cora, are you here?" His voice wavers.

He's not sure, but he definitely suspects I'm down here. He

found the key in the door, after all. Would he really think he forgot to lock it?

A shiver trickles through me when he begins to move again.

And then, as I had hoped, he heads to the locked door, the one hiding the other woman.

If he turns slightly to the left, he'll see me.

I grip the club tighter and when he pushes the key into the lock, I raise it.

Before I have a chance to think, I swing.

The club connects with the back of his head with a sickening thud.

One pain-filled grunt, then he crumples to the floor.

Breathing hard, I stare at his motionless body. He's sprawled out, the set of keys still clutched in his hand.

Oh God. What have I done?

My legs start trembling and my knees threaten to give way. I reach for the wall to steady myself and the club slips from my hand and falls to the floor. My hand flies to my mouth, smothering the gasp that has clawed its way up my throat.

I didn't know I was capable of this, of hurting someone. The sound of the metal head hitting his skull replays in my mind and I feel like throwing up.

I might have just killed a man, or at least seriously injured him.

My stomach churning, I take a step back, then another, distancing myself from my act of violence. Then I gingerly move toward him again and bend down to peel the keys from his fingers.

As shocked as I am right now at what I'm capable of, I need to open that room, to save Margaret. I have to know that I didn't do this for nothing.

I turn the key in the lock and the heavy door creaks open, revealing a damp, foul-smelling space. The stench hits me first, a mixture of mold, sweat, and something sharp and metallic.

The woman is sitting on a filthy mattress against one wall, her hair tangled and matted, hanging in greasy strands around her gaunt face. It's so dirty I can't tell if it's light or dark in color.

But as I continue to watch her, my throat closes up and my body goes cold like someone has poured a bucket of freezing water down my back.

This can't be right. The woman in front of me is not Margaret.

She's much younger, in her forties maybe. I blink several times, willing her face to transform into the one I expected. But it doesn't. It's not her.

My head feels like it's spinning and my heart is pounding too loudly in my ears, like a warning drum. What is going on? Who is this woman?

Whoever she is, she's afraid. And she needs me.

Ignoring the stained mattress she's sitting on, the scattered paper plates with dried food, and an empty bottle of orange juice near the door, I meet her eyes.

"Tell me what you know about Evan, please." I need to know the whole truth now about the man who is now bleeding out on the floor, thanks to me.

She blinks once, then twice. "Evan is a con artist," she finally manages through cracked lips. "Mary... she's not his aunt. He finds vulnerable elderly people like her, people with no family. He targets them for their money.... gets them from a health care facility, a place run by his sister, Lilian Holloway. There's one right here in town."

My entire reality is cracking apart piece by piece.

But she's not done talking. Even though her voice is weak, she continues, and every word hits me like a knife to the gut.

"I'm not the only one he's locked up," the woman continues. "He did it to someone else before me."

"Who?" I croak.

"Margaret Tookes, the woman who owned this farm." She squeezes her eyes shut. "And then he killed her."

FORTY-TWO

A sharp, searing pain grips my chest, like something inside me is tearing apart. My knees buckle, and I grab onto the nearest surface to keep from collapsing.

Evan *killed* Margaret Tookes?

The woman I had been so obsessed with. The woman I was made to believe had simply left, seeking an easier, quieter place to spend the rest of her days.

Oh my God.

A strangled sob pushes its way up my throat, but I push it back down, my body trembling as the force of the truth seeps into my every pore.

Jill was right all along. That gut-wrenching desperation in her eyes and the fear in her voice when she said something had happened to Margaret. All that wasn't paranoia.

She knew. She felt it. And that's why she kept coming here.

The air feels even thicker and more suffocating. I press a shaking hand to my mouth, trying to hold myself together, but my mind is spinning, unraveling.

"You're lying," I whisper as a cold sweat breaks over my skin, and the room feels like it's moving.

I don't want to be the fool who believed Evan, hung on his every word, trusted him. I hate that losing my memory meant I had to depend on others to tell me what was fact or fiction. Was everything Evan fed me really all made up?

Suddenly, I have a blinding flash in my mind of Mary inside her room, frail and confused, unaware of what's going on. All this time, I thought Evan loved her. The way he took such great care of her. Is he really such a great liar?

He did make you believe the lies about your family, didn't he? a little voice tells me when I remember the Facebook message I received.

But something else is eating at my stomach lining, something more toxic and corrosive than fear. It burns like hot acid and spreads through my insides like wildfire.

How much did I know?

Before I lost my memory, how much did I know of what was going on, what Evan was doing? What if I had seen the signs and ignored them, or worse—what if I had been a part of it, complicit in his crimes?

The thought sinks in like a stone that threatens to pull me under. I pray I'm innocent in all of this because the idea that I could have been blind to it all, or was involved in any way... I don't think I could live with myself.

"I'm telling you the truth," the other woman pleads. "You have to believe me. Evan killed that poor woman for her money. As soon as he tricked her to put him in her will, he didn't want to wait until she died naturally. Look, we need to get out of here now, to take Mary somewhere safe, away from this place. If Evan wakes up, she will be in danger."

I glance at where Evan is lying next to the stairs, and a wave of dread turns my blood cold. What if he's dead? What if I killed someone? I feel lightheaded, and I try to steady myself, but there's nothing to hold on to but the lies, the betrayal, the reality that I could be a killer.

No. No, I couldn't have. I didn't.

But if he's still alive and I didn't kill him with that blow, he could come to any second. If he has murdered before, if he killed an innocent old woman, what would stop him from doing the same to us?

"Okay. We have to hurry." Still shaken but having made my decision, I reach for the woman's hand, and her fingers grasp mine.

As I lead her out of the room and we step over Evan's body, her pace is much slower than mine and the climb up the stairs seems to take an eternity.

Upstairs, I do the first thing that comes to mind—I lock the basement door so Evan won't be able to follow.

What if I'm now a murderer like him? The thought sneaks in again, but I shrug it off. I have to stay blinkered. I can't think about that right now.

"I'll be right back," I tell the woman and rush to Mary's room.

To my surprise, she's awake, sitting up in bed, clutching her blanket with both hands. Fear lingers in her eyes, but when she sees me, she relaxes—just a little—though she doesn't release her grip, holding the blanket like a shield.

I close the door softly behind me. I have to hurry, but I don't want to scare her more than she already is.

Breathing hard, I sit beside her, forcing myself to stay calm. If I panic, she'll panic.

I gently take her hand in mine, covering it with both of mine.

"Mary... is Evan really your nephew?" I bite down on my bottom lip as I wait for her answer.

Her reaction is instant. Her eyes widen further, and she shrinks back.

I squeeze her hand. "Please, Mary. This is very important."

I hope she remembers, that this particular memory isn't lost in the haze of her mind.

After a tense pause, she says something, and I lean in closer. "What did you say?"

"I was an only child," she whispers.

I promise Mary I'll be right back, then I run upstairs to my room, grab my cell phone, and dial 911. Whatever other secrets Evan has buried, they will be revealed.

Feeling slightly calmer knowing help is on the way, I head back downstairs to check on the woman I rescued, to comfort her.

I find her in the hallway, in the direction of the guest bathroom.

"Hey," I call gently because she doesn't see me at first and I don't want to frighten her. Being locked up for God knows how long would leave someone in a perpetual state of fear.

As expected, she jumps and spins around, her eyes wide as they meet mine.

I raise my hands in a calming gesture, approaching her slowly. "It's all right," I reassure her, quickly moving to her side and wrapping an arm around her shoulders. "I've called the police. They're on their way. They'll handle him. You're safe now."

"No, I'm not," she whispers, her eyes filled with panic. Suddenly she pulls away and dashes toward the front door. I chase after her, in time to see her snatch Evan's car keys from the hook by the door.

While my mind is still reeling, she jumps into the vehicle and drives off. That's when it dawns on me—I never asked her name.

But now, with her face clear in my mind, I recognize her.

She's the woman from the torn wedding photo I found in the trash bag.

FORTY-THREE

Sitting on the porch with Mary huddled next to me—her journal hugged to her body—I barely register the flashing lights of the police cars and the ambulance, the officers rushing inside, their heavy boots stomping across the floor.

Everything seems muffled, like I'm watching it all from far away.

A detective approaches us and asks to speak to me. While someone else stays with Mary, I lead him into the house, the living room, where we both take a seat on the couch.

He asks my name, his expression stern but not unfriendly. He's a man in his thirties, blond with sharp eyes.

"All right, Mrs. Harrison. I'm Detective Black. Can you tell us exactly what happened tonight?"

To ground myself, I try to focus on his face, the small mole on the side of his chin, but my thoughts are scattered, and my hands are trembling. I clasp them together. "I—" My voice cracks and I clear my throat, forcing myself to think, to speak. "I snuck into the basement after Evan... my husband... after he was in there." Wringing my hands in my lap, I glance toward the doorway. "Is he... is he okay? Oh my God, I—" My breath catches. "Is he dead?"

"Don't worry, ma'am," Detective Black says in a calm but firm voice. "The paramedics are attending to him right now. Please continue."

I close my eyes for a moment and open them again. "There was a locked room in the basement. And there was someone in there."

The detective raises an eyebrow, his pen raised over his notebook. "Someone? In a room?"

A lanky officer with a buzz cut steps into the doorway, listening in. I glance at him briefly, then turn back to Detective Black.

"Yes. She—she didn't tell me her name, but she told me Evan had been keeping her there for a long time, holding her prisoner." Immediately, memories of that room flood back to haunt me and I know they will for a long time to come, if not forever. "I let her out and she told me... everything." I bite into my lower lip, afraid to say more. What if I really am involved somehow and end up implicating myself? But if I lie, things could get even worse, right?

"What did she say, Mrs. Harrison?" the detective presses as he scribbles into his notebook.

"She said Evan killed Margaret." My voice falters. "He... he wanted her money."

Detective Black's pen scratches furiously on the pad. "Margaret?" He looks at me for confirmation.

"Yes. Margaret Tookes," I repeat and massage my temples. "She lived here before we—The woman said Evan is a con artist. He steals money from vulnerable people like Mary."

"Who's Mary?" the detective asks, leaning in closer, eyes squinted.

"The elderly woman outside. She's his aunt." I shake my head. "No, he told me she was his aunt. But..." I take a deep breath and try to form the next sentence. "He lied. He's a liar." The last word shoots out of my mouth like a bullet.

From below in the basement, I hear the sound of footsteps climbing the stairs. Then, the officer in the doorway steps aside, and through the door, I see the paramedics pushing a stretcher with Evan on it. His face is turned to the side and his eyes are unfocused but open. I go still, my breath hitching in my throat, and I feel the blood draining from my face.

"Ma'am, your husband will be fine," the officer in the doorway tells me, as if that should be good news.

"Mary was not your husband's aunt then?" Detective Black attempts to bring back my attention to him.

"No, Mary was his target. He removed her from a care home, where she stayed because she has dementia. He pretended to be her nephew."

A sob breaks through me, causing me to shudder. I'm trembling so hard now that I have to clutch my arms around myself to try and stop it.

But what if I'm like him? What if they think I know more? What if I knew about Mary?

And what if Evan manipulates the situation and pins all the blame on me? What if he tells them everything, bad things about me I don't even remember?

Even if he doesn't, the bottom line is I'm his wife. The police might find it hard to believe I was unaware of my husband's actions, especially since he was holding someone captive in our basement.

"And you don't know who the woman in the basement was?" Detective Black asks, his voice softer, but I can detect an urgency in his tone.

"I... I don't know her," I gasp out between sobs. "I feel like I do, but I can't remember." Then it hits me that the detective knows nothing about my memory loss, so I fill him in.

"I'm very sorry to hear about that. Do you have anything, anything at all that could help us find her?"

I immediately remember the torn photo that I had patched back together the best I could. I'm one hundred percent sure it was her. I can't believe I didn't think of it sooner. I quickly head upstairs to get it, and when I return, I hold it up to Detective Black, my sweaty fingers barely able to grip it.

"This is her, I think." My voice is shaking as much as my hands.

He takes the photo carefully, his brows furrowing as he studies it, probably wondering why it's torn. Then he passes it to the other officer, who squints at it, then back at me.

Detective Black clears his throat. "That's the woman?"

"I can't be sure because she was dirty and thin, but I think so. When I called nine-one-one, she ran off with my husband's car."

Detective Black asks me to describe the car and I do.

"Okay," he says finally, closing his notebook. "We'll need to talk to you again when you feel better." He hands me his card. "For now, try to rest and if you remember anything else that could be important, give me a call." He opens his book again and writes down my phone number.

Instead of leaving immediately, they go outside and try to ask Mary some questions, but she's so much in shock that she struggles to string together coherent sentences.

When Detective Black shows her the photo, and asks if she knows the woman, Mary blinks, then shakes her head. "I don't remember."

"That's all right. We can talk another time. We'll get you checked out at the hospital, okay?"

As soon as the detective is done talking to Mary, I remember to tell him about the scratches in Mary's room, and that I suspect they were caused by someone's nails.

Then I glance toward the ambulance waiting to take Mary

to the hospital, and I think of Evan's eyes. A sense of dread pools in the pit of my stomach.

He's not dead. I didn't kill him.

In some ways, that realization terrifies me more than the thought of him being gone. What will he do when he recovers? What will he do to me?

FORTY-FOUR

The hospital corridors are quiet, the soft hum of fluorescent lights the only sound breaking the stillness. In this small town, emergencies must be rare. The waiting room is nearly empty, and the lone nurse at the reception desk flips through a magazine.

I insisted on coming with Mary because at the house, she wouldn't let the paramedics take her away, clinging to me as if terrified, though the people who would take her were the very ones who could protect her.

In the ambulance, she barely spoke, staring out the window in silence. But now something about her has changed.

She grins as I go to sit in a chair next to her hospital bed, after a nurse leaves, having checked her to make sure she's all right.

Mary, inside her bed, looks small, but she seems completely different from the fragile woman I know. She's thoroughly enjoying all the attention with the nurses treating her like she's royalty.

You would think she's in a luxury hotel, not a hospital. She's more lucid than ever, cheerfully chatting away and thanking me over and over again.

"God will bless you for what you did, my dear." She squeezes my hand.

"You don't need to thank me." I hesitate, then decide to go ahead and ask. "Mary, did you know all along that Evan wasn't your nephew?"

I expect her to get all confused again or to evade my question.

"My memory isn't always so bad," she says after staring at the wall for a long time. "Sometimes my mind is very clear. But I thought I'd be better off in a fancy home, so I checked myself in." A pause. Then she sighs, her smile dimming. "I was wrong. It was awful. The nurses were abusive and barely paid attention to us. Then Evan showed up, claiming to be my long-lost nephew, offering me a home... and I couldn't remember clearly enough to see that he was lying. I guess maybe I also let myself believe it even though often I knew, in moments of clarity, that it wasn't really true. The thing is, I wanted a family. I should have married." The regret is thick in her voice. "But I put my career first. And now look where it got me."

Just as quickly as she seemed sharp, her mind slips again, and her words become disjointed.

I wonder what she's thinking, where she is right now in her mind.

"When I had flashes of clear memories about my past," she suddenly continues, catching me off guard, "I knew I didn't have a family, I didn't have a nephew. And Evan was constantly pestering me about writing my will. I knew I'd made a terrible mistake, and that he had tricked me, that he was not a good man. I didn't always know what was happening, but when I did I wanted to call the police, to make them come for me, but I was too confused, too scared. He threatened me. Said he'd kill me if I breathed a word to anyone." She shakes her head, then beckons me closer, lowering her voice to a whisper. "There are so many secrets in that house. In that barn. Too many to count."

Her words leave me frozen, but before I can ask her to tell me more, she's gone again.

When another nurse comes in carrying a bowl of pudding and starts fussing over her, she forgets all about me. But before turning to accept the food, she brushes a gentle hand over my cheek.

I stay at the hospital a little longer, making sure she's all right. Finally, when she falls asleep, I leave, telling the nurses I'll return in the morning.

As I step out of the hospital, I'm overwhelmed, confused, and exhausted. It's still dark outside, and the night's events swirl in my head. The basement. The woman who escaped.

I suck in a deep breath, trying to steady myself before returning to that place of horrors. Then I call a taxi and slide into the back seat, my eyes drooping with sleep, but I need to stay awake and alert.

Before we left in the ambulance, Detective Black told me the farm is now a crime scene—that I should find another place to spend the night until it's cleared. And even though I did book a room at a local motel in the center of town, I need to know now what Mary was talking about... what the other secrets are.

And where did that woman go? Is she safe?

Like Mary, she's already been through so much. Both of them were prisoners of Evan, the monster I married.

When we reach the farm, it's still crawling with police. They won't be pleased to see me back at the crime scene, so I decide to return in the morning.

"Please take me to the Radio Motel," I tell the taxi driver.

I have a little money in my purse—around one hundred and fifty dollars in cash. I found it in the kitchen drawer, where Evan keeps an envelope of money for when we order in. It should be enough for a night or two in a place that isn't too fancy.

Finally, we arrive at the motel. It's small and unassuming, its neon sign flickering like an old TV set, but it will do fine for the night.

I thank the taxi driver, pay him, and step inside. The receptionist barely looks up as she hands me a key. She's young— probably nineteen or twenty— and is reading a novel when I walk in.

Dragging my feet down the hall, exhaustion weighing me down, I know the first thing I'll do when I reach my room: drop onto the bed and sleep. My mind needs clarity, and I need silence. But tomorrow, I'll go to the station to find out if they've learned more about Evan.

They might be surprised that I'm not going to check on my husband, that I'm not asking to see him in hospital. But he's a stranger, now more than ever, and he's the last person I want to see. I might have been his wife once, but I'm not now, no matter what any piece of paper says.

I push the key into the lock and step inside. The room is simple and sparsely furnished, and when my eyes land on a bed with stiff sheets, I'm instantly reminded of that mattress in the basement that woman had sat on, was forced to sleep on. This one feels like a king's bed in comparison. There's a small TV, a coffee table, a desk, one chair by the window, and not much else.

I lock the door behind me and double-check it. Then I get ready for bed, washing my face, and my underwear so it can dry overnight.

When I'm back in the room, I remember the message I received from my sister. Deleting what I had started to write earlier, I type out a new one:

I never meant to ignore you. I fell down the stairs and lost my memory. Evan told me I didn't have siblings, and my parents want nothing to do with me. He told me so many lies. So much has happened, awful, unthinkable things. I can't explain it all here. Please... can we talk on the phone?

I hit send, and a second later, I type out my new phone number and send that too.

Later, as I lie down, staring at the ceiling, Mary's words echo in my mind.

So many secrets in that barn.

FORTY-FIVE

Tuesday, August 6, 2019

When I wake up in my motel room, sunlight is streaming through the windows. I didn't close the curtains last night because I fell asleep so fast. Even though I managed to get some rest, I still feel exhausted.

Blinking the fog from my eyes, I take in the room: the plain beige walls, the desk and chair, a wooden dresser I don't remember noticing yesterday. There's also a mini fridge in the corner, humming softly.

I inhale the faint scent of bleach mixed with what seems to be old cigarette smoke lingering in the worn carpet. Then, I sit up and reach for my phone on the bedside table.

It's 9 a.m., and I have eight missed calls. Five are from an unknown number, which I suspect is the police, or my sister. The remaining missed calls are from Lina. She probably knows about Evan's arrest already, or perhaps she went to the house to work and discovered it empty. But this morning I just don't have the energy to talk to anyone. There's one thing on my mind, somewhere I know I need to go.

Forcing myself out of bed, I take a quick shower, dress in yesterday's clothes, and call a taxi.

Twenty minutes later, the taxi pulls up in front of the farmhouse, which is cordoned off with yellow crime scene tape.

My heart pounds as I step out into the blinding sunshine. As the taxi pulls away, anxiety and fear twist within me, even if Evan is in custody and can't do anything to me. Still, I feel afraid to be here alone. But I need to do this.

I come to a halt where the tape creates a border that keeps anyone out, my pulse hammering in my ears. I know it's illegal to enter a crime scene and I should respect the law.

But I can't. I need to know what Mary was talking about, so with a deep breath, I grip the tape, pushing it up just enough to slip under.

My foot catches on the bottom strand, and for a second, I panic. But I steady myself and step free, hurrying to the front door. I avoid the basement at all costs, not ready to relive those memories.

The house has been ransacked, with furniture scattered all over the place, but I ignore that and head straight to the kitchen, where I find all the cabinets thrown open and my pill bottles in the sink, one of them open and the medication spilling out.

As I reach for one of the closed bottles and stare at it, doubt creeps in. I feel so different, so clear, even though I didn't take them yesterday or this morning. What if I take them now and the clarity disappears and the fog returns? Evan said I hated taking them because they made me feel like a different person. And he was right.

Without thinking, and hoping I won't regret it, I put them back in the cabinet and walk out of the house.

With no time for hesitation, I make my way toward the barn.

The barn doors are slightly open and inside the air is thick with dust and the scent of hay. But something is different. Bales of hay have been overturned, and wooden crates shoved aside. I wonder what the police were looking for in here.

I walk to the farthest corner, my shoes crunching against the dirt floor. My gaze sweeps over everything, even the wooden beams above, and the feed troughs.

I scan the walls and the floorboards. And then, when I'm about to give up, something catches my eye and I approach it.

A small, faded marking on the bricks of the supporting wall near the back of the barn. A clover. Painted in green ink. I instantly remember two things. Mary's birthday dress that her mother sewed for her—that I read about in her journal—had clovers on it. The day I found her hiding at the back of the barn, her fingers had green paint on them. Did she paint this?

I run my fingertips over the rough brick, then press against it. It shifts slightly under my touch, and I hold my breath as I wedge my nails into the edge before pulling. It comes loose, revealing a small, narrow gap.

For a moment, when my fingers reach inside, I feel nothing but dust and grit, and then something small, smooth, and solid. Inside, nestled in the hollow space, is a small black USB stick.

A cold shiver rushes through me as I clutch it in my palm.

I hurry back into the house and head straight to my bedroom to find my laptop. But it's missing. I close my eyes for a second and take a few deep breaths.

The police must have taken my laptop as evidence, which could mean they suspect I may have committed the crimes with Evan.

Evan's office is in complete chaos. The police really tore through the space, leaving it in disarray. Every desk drawer has been pulled out, their contents carelessly strewn across the floor in messy heaps. His once neatly arranged files are now scattered around the room, with some pages partially torn and others trampled on.

The bookshelves, which used to be orderly, are now in

shambles and some books have cracked spines and lie open, while others have been pulled out and tossed on the desk or the floor. Even the filing cabinet is wide open, its folders bent and rifled through.

I step forward carefully, my shoes crunching over scattered paperclips and shards of glass from a photo frame lying broken at my feet. When I pick it up, I swallow a lump in my throat. It's a photo of Evan and me from our wedding day.

The glass is shattered, with a jagged crack slicing right through Evan's face. I place the frame back down, and turn my attention to the desk. Evan always kept his laptop here, conveniently placed in the center.

Instinctively, I start lifting scattered papers, opening drawers, and searching beneath piles of folders and notebooks. But it's gone, which doesn't really surprise me since mine is missing too.

My stomach clenches as I crouch to check under the desk, running my hands along the cold metal frame beneath the glass, searching for anything hidden. Nothing.

As I turn to leave the office, I notice the safe, and it's open and emptied out. The money I saw inside it last time is gone, and so is everything else. The police must have taken it all as evidence as well.

I call another taxi, and when it arrives, I ask to be taken back to the motel.

At the front desk, I approach an older woman who has replaced the night clerk. Her name tag reads "Edna," and her eyes are kind and understanding.

"How can I help you?" she asks, putting away the red lipstick she had been applying.

"Good morning," I say. "I know this is a weird request, but do you happen to have a computer I could use? It's really important."

"No problem. You can use this." She reaches under the counter and pulls out a pink laptop.

"I only need a minute." I reach for it gratefully and take it with me to a small lounge area with a worn-out couch and a low, coffee-stained table. After several deep breaths, I plug in the USB.

The device boots up quickly, and the first thing that catches my eye is a folder titled *Archive*, alongside a PDF document named *List*. As soon as I open the PDF, I instantly recognize its contents.

It's identical to the page I found in Evan's office, the one with the list of numbers, except this one has none of them crossed out.

I click the folder next to it, which contains three subfolders. The first two are numbered 1 and 2, and the third is labeled *Videos*.

In the first folder, I expect to see photos related to Evan's book research—photos, notes, maybe articles. Instead, what I find is something that turns my stomach. Lots of photos of him with random women. Some look like they were taken without their knowledge.

Did I really not know about any of this?

To make matters worse, the second folder contains photos of hotel receipts and screenshots of messages exchanged between him and the women he was unfaithful with.

As I'm closing the folder, repulsed by what I've seen, my eyes land on the *Videos* folder.

As much as I would rather not click on it, something compels me to do so. So, I pull in a deep breath and brace myself for what I might find. My entire body is numb with dread as I open it.

Only one video file is inside, and I hold my breath and click it.

In the grainy footage an elderly woman is lying in bed in a dimly lit room, her eyes wide with terror, reminding me of Mary's when I went to her room after escaping the basement.

Shortly after, another woman appears on the screen, her back facing the camera. But from her movements and mannerisms, she seems younger.

Initially, I assume she's there to help the woman in the bed, but to my shock, she picks up a pillow and covers her face with it.

The frail woman struggles weakly, but the younger woman continues to apply pressure until the older woman becomes motionless.

She continues to hold the pillow in place for a few more moments until the door suddenly flies open and Evan charges in.

"Cora, what the hell are you doing?" he demands, shoving the woman aside.

Cora?

The world tilts as the woman turns around. It's not me at all.

It's her. The woman Evan had kept locked in the basement.

But if she's Cora...

No. This has to be a mistake.

But I don't have time to process it because I'm still staring at the horror scene unfolding in front of me. Evan is frantically trying to revive the old woman, but it's too late. When he turns back to the woman he called Cora, his expression is pure rage.

"We may be many things, Cora, but we are not murderers," he shouts.

"Stop pretending to be a saint." She brushes him off. "It was time, and you know it. We got what we want. Why wait longer?"

As soon as she speaks those words, the video ends, leaving

me breathless. I can't think, and I'm shaking all over, my back coated with sweat.

Seeing that woman's face triggered something inside me, opened a door that has been locked for a long time.

Suddenly, like a light switching on in a dark room, I remember everything.

I know the truth—about them, and about me.

FORTY-SIX

GABRIELLE WALKER

Friday, June 21, 2019

As soon as Evan locks the door, I hear something, a voice. Cora.

My heart leaps to my throat, but I'm still trapped in here, with him.

But Evan seems thrown off as well. His face is tense, his jaw working as if he's grinding his teeth. I guess his wife has derailed whatever plans he had for me.

Either way, this is my chance to get out of here. Before he can recover and come up with plan B, I ball my hands into fists and call out Cora's name as loud as I can.

"We're down here!" I shout, my eyes locked on Evan's, challenging him.

His fists clench. Whatever he had in store for me in this room isn't going to happen because I'm going to make damn sure Cora hears me.

Standing there, frozen, he says nothing, but I can feel the frustration radiating off him. After a tense moment, he steps aside, allowing me to open the door and bolt out of the room. I don't waste a second as I race up the basement stairs.

I pause outside the kitchen, forcing my breathing to still. I need to calm down and plan my next move wisely. I've come this far, I'm not going to ruin everything now. I don't even know what Evan was trying to do, although my guess is he wanted to coerce me into joining his long list of women he's slept with.

"There you are!" Cora says when I come into the kitchen, where she's giving Mary a glass of water. "I was looking for you."

"I was just cleaning. You're back early." After that unsettling moment with Evan in the basement, every part of me wants to spill it—to tell her what I found on the USB, so she can leave him and Mary can return to a home, where I can have unrestricted access to her.

But I hold back for now. I need to be careful, to figure out exactly how to say it. There's also a chance that Cora might take Evan's side. If she does, I could get kicked out and lose everything. My place in this house. My access to Mary.

"Mary had a meltdown," Cora whispers. "She refused to go to the hospital. It was a disaster." Then she looks at me closely, her eyes narrowing. "What's got you so flustered?"

"Nothing. I... I just..." I stammer. "I'm fine. Do you want me to do anything for you?"

Cora gives me a small smile. "Yes, could you please go lay Mary down while I get her medicine? I shouldn't have dragged her out of the house like that. I know how much she hates hospitals."

Glad for a chance to be alone with Mary, I get to work, tucking the older woman in and even reading her a psalm. She stares into space, looking deeply troubled. She's here, but at the same time, she isn't.

When Mary is settled in her bed, I go into the kitchen, and from the doorway, I see Cora preparing tea in Mary's favorite pink mug.

I'm about to say something when she glances quickly over her shoulder. Not seeing me, she retrieves a small bottle of liquid from her pocket and adds a few drops into the mug. She places the mug on a tray next to Mary's medication, then slips the bottle back into her pocket like she's hiding it.

Why the pocket? If it's part of Mary's treatment, shouldn't it be stored with the rest of her medications in the cabinet?

Something isn't right. But is it possible I'm overreacting? Maybe it's some new supplement or something I don't know about.

It doesn't make sense. None of it does.

Unless that bottle isn't supposed to be part of Mary's treatment at all.

My heart pounds as I shrink back from the doorway and hurry upstairs, where I pace the hallway, listening for Cora's footsteps as she climbs the stairs. When she finally reaches the landing, I step directly into her path, blocking her way.

I need to know what she put in that mug, and I pray to God that there's a harmless explanation.

At first, I decide to try a subtle approach. "Hey, Cora. You must be exhausted. How about I take this to Mary?"

I hope Cora will let me, since she allowed me to care for Mary earlier.

But she hesitates this time, narrowing her eyes and tightening her lips into a thin smile. "Not necessary. I think I need to spend a little more time with her today. I promised we'd start a new puzzle together."

"Okay." I look down at the tray, then back up at her, trying to sound casual. "By the way, I saw you put some drops into her tea. What was that? Just curious."

For a split second, her face goes pale, and then she forces a soft, unconvincing laugh. "Oh, that? It's ginkgo and lemon balm, a custom herbal tincture from a local wellness shop." She shrugs, as if it's no big deal. "Ginkgo biloba helps with memory and blood flow to the brain. And the lemon balm is calming. It can really help with anxiety, especially when Mary gets agitated... like today. I want to help her feel better any way I can."

But something in her eyes tells me she's lying. I can feel it, deep in my gut. Her fingers are also too tight around the tray's edge.

"I'm sorry but I don't believe you." The words leave my mouth before I can think and they hang heavy in the air between us. "Drink it. Drink the tea yourself."

She gives me a forced smile, one that doesn't reach her eyes. "What are you talking about, Gabrielle? Why would I drink Mary's tea? It's hers, not for me."

But I see it. The slight tremble in her fingers, the way her throat bobs with a hard swallow.

She tries to move past me, but I don't let her, trapping her on the landing.

"You're drugging her, aren't you?" I accuse, folding my arms across my chest. All those times Mary has been sick, the stomach issues.

It disgusts me to even think it, but could it be that Cora has been drugging her for a while? Is that why she's so insistent on being the one to care for Mary, bringing her tea, giving her meds? Was it to make sure no one else has control over what she's taking?

The mask drops and Cora's expression twists into fury. "You have no idea what you're talking about."

"Then drink the tea. If you didn't put anything in there, drink it yourself first. Taste it."

Before I can react, she swings the tray violently to the floor, and the mug shatters, liquid seeping into the floorboards as Mary's medication bottles roll away.

"What is *wrong* with you?" I ask through gritted teeth. "You want to poison Mary. She's become too much for you to handle, and you want to get rid of her."

All this time, she acted like she cared for the woman, but maybe Mary became more of a burden than she wanted.

Still, something doesn't add up. If Cora was poisoning her, why take her to the hospital?

Unless... she didn't.

"You didn't take Mary to the hospital, did you, Cora?" I whisper. "You know what I think? I think you just took her for a drive, then came back and fed me that story about her having a meltdown."

I was frantic with worry for Mary, and Cora knew it. When I told her Mary needed medical attention, she must've realized that if she didn't act fast, I would've taken Mary to the hospital myself without her knowing. And I would have.

Cora stiffens, then juts out her chin. "You're insane, Gabrielle," she hisses, planting her hands on her hips and getting in my space. "Who do you think you are?" But her eyes tell me I'm right. She lied about the hospital.

I take a step back, trying to get past her, my goal clear. I need my phone, which I left in the living room. "I'm calling the police."

Cora's body tenses. I can feel it even more than I see it. And before I can move, she shoves me, her hands slamming into my shoulders with a force that takes my breath away.

The next thing I know, my feet slip on the slick floor and my arms are flailing as I try to grab the handrail but fail.

I twist and tumble backward, the world flipping upside down, while Cora stands at the top of the stairs, not making a move to help me.

Soon, my spine collides with the sharp edges of the wooden steps. At the bottom, my head snaps back, hitting the ground hard.

Darkness swallows me whole.

FORTY-SEVEN

GABRIELLE WALKER

Tuesday, August 6, 2019

I remember it all, so clearly. My name is Gabrielle, not Cora. My fall was no accident. The woman in that video pushed me down the stairs. She is Evan's wife, not me. And that woman I wrote to on Facebook is not my sister because I *am* an only child.

I can't breathe. No matter how much air I inhale, my lungs refuse to expand, and an invisible hand seems to have clenched around my chest, squeezing the life out of me.

It's all flooding back.

I see myself arriving at the farm three months ago, looking for that housekeeping job. I see Cora turning me away only to call me a few days later for an interview. I see everything now, with none of those bipolar medications to cloud my thoughts either.

I do not have bipolar, but Cora does. Evan was doing everything he could to get me to adopt Cora's identity. And having me taking medication for an illness I do not have definitely skewed my sense of reality.

Feeling shaky and barely able to move, I stand up and give the laptop back to the receptionist, barely registering the woman's words.

"Are you okay?" she asks, but it sounds like she's talking from miles and miles away.

Without saying a word because my mouth refuses to work, I walk away to my room. And with each step, the weight of everything drowns me. The other woman in the video must be Margaret Tookes. It was Cora who killed her, not Evan.

And I rescued her from that room. I let her go. I thought she was the victim.

Oh my God, what have I done?

A few minutes later, my mind races as I pace my small room, my hands clutching my hair as flashbacks continue to flood my mind—Cora's false innocence, the photos of Evan with other women, Cora putting poison in Mary's tea.

They're as bad as each other.

She and Evan were in on this scheme together, conning old people for their money, and Cora wanted to send Mary to the grave sooner than planned, just as she did with Margaret Tookes.

And Evan—he locked her up and made me believe I was his wife in her place. What kind of sick people are they? What did I get myself into?

It was my huge mistake to let Cora go. Now I need to do something about it, to make things right.

Fixing wrongs is what I do. I remember that now. They had no idea who they were dealing with, when they thought they could destroy me.

I rush out of the motel and walk to the police station, which is only about ten minutes away.

The bright lights inside the building make me dizzy. I approach an officer at a desk and ask to talk to the detective who gave me his card last night.

When Detective Black shows up behind the desk, I give him the USB stick and tell him everything I know about Cora and Evan, including the fact that I'm not his wife—how he brainwashed me into believing I was.

He doesn't look the least bit surprised, which tells me they've likely already figured out who the real Cora is, possibly from the photo I gave them. What does catch him off guard is when I tell him I believe she's the one who killed Margaret. At least, I think the woman in the video was her.

"I appreciate you coming in and bringing this." He holds up the USB, then wraps his fist around it. "I'll have a look right away." He hesitates for a moment, then adds, "What Evan Harrison did to you was a crime too. Rest assured, we'll make sure justice is served."

"Thank you, detective, I appreciate that." Just then, a uniformed officer escorts someone into the station, their handcuffs clinking as they shuffle past. My attention briefly shifts to the new arrival. I glance over, but quickly force my focus back to Detective Black. "Did you find her... Cora?"

"Not yet, but we are actively tracking her down, both her and anyone else involved in this."

My head jerks up. "There are others? Like who?"

He folds his hands on the desk and offers a controlled response. "Unfortunately, I'm not at liberty to share details about an active investigation."

Of course he can't. But that only sharpens my curiosity. My mind sifts through every detail, every name that's come up in the past few weeks.

I already know about Lilian Holloway since Cora revealed that she supplied Evan with victims, and I shared that with the detective.

But another name hits me like a jolt and I lean forward. "What about a man named Daniel Rowe? Was he involved? He's supposed to be one of the doctors in town."

Evan must have told him to support the lie that I had bipolar disorder. So he's either a corrupt doctor... or a fake one.

Without flinching, Detective Black simply repeats that he can't share any details at the moment.

But something flickers in his eyes. It's barely there, but it's enough to confirm my suspicion.

"Is there anything else you want to share that you think might help us find Cora Harrison?" he asks. "Anything at all?"

I'm about to say I don't, but then I remember the Facebook message I got last night. "It's possible she ran to be with her family. Someone named Donna Blaire messaged me last night. I thought she was my sister at first, but now I'm sure she's Cora's."

He writes the name in his notebook. "Thank you. That's helpful."

I leave the police station feeling lighter, relieved to have finally remembered myself, my own identity, no matter how awful this situation is. But I won't fully relax until I know that Cora is behind bars and can never hurt anyone again.

I head to the hospital next to check on Mary, who I find resting in her bed, flipping through a gardening magazine. She seems so at peace in this place.

As I stand outside the room, watching through the glass as a nurse adjusts the pillow behind her back, I feel comforted in knowing that Mary is safe and well cared for, at least for now.

When the nurse comes out, I ask how she's really doing.

"Really well mostly." The nurse glances at Mary through the glass partition. "She's such a trooper. She'll be transferred elsewhere later today."

"Thanks for taking care of her."

"Of course." The woman smiles and walks away.

Left alone, I enter the room and sit down with Mary. We talk about the magazine she's reading and the weather outside. And then, out of nowhere, she gets confused again, drifting in and out of focus, forgetting what she said, and repeating things.

Occasionally, she stares at the door as if expecting someone to enter.

I stay with her for a bit longer, trying to engage her in conversation, but it's stilted.

After a while, I say goodbye with the promise that I will come and see her at her new home.

Just as I reach the door to leave, she calls for me.

"Gabrielle." Her voice is almost a whisper, but I hear it very clearly.

I whip around in shock and rush back to her bedside, taking her frail hands into mine. "You knew? You knew all along that I wasn't Cora?"

"I did." Her eyes flicker toward the door again. "Sometimes I remembered everything, but he told me he'd kill me if I told you the truth. I'm sorry."

When she was lucid, she must have been so terrified.

Mary reaches for her journal beneath her pillow, the one she's always been jotting things into, the one she kept forgetting around the house.

"This is for you." She places it in my hand.

Not understanding, I start flipping through the pages, reading about Margaret, and also about Mary's childhood. Then I stop.

A passage about making cupcakes with her mother, giving them away to the neighbors on Christmas.

The childhood stories she told are not her memories at all.

I flip through more pages and discover that they are mine. This is *my life* she's been jotting down; the things I told her in our conversations before I fell.

During our time together, I told her about the birthday dress my mother sewed for me, and the fireflies I used to catch with my grandfather, the same grandfather who taught me to swim. Now that I remember my childhood, I realize that everything is right here.

That's why she kept leaving the journal lying around. It wasn't because she was forgetting it, but because she wanted me to read it. She wanted me to know about Margaret and discreetly uncover the secrets hidden in that house.

But more than that, she wanted to help me remember who I am. No wonder I always felt that pull, that quiet connection to the things she wrote. And *The River Moves*, the poem she asked me to read to her? That was my mother's favorite, and I told Mary that once.

Mary may have forgotten most of her own life, but she remembered mine.

Before I leave, she tells me the real reason she tore up Cora's wedding photo. The night Cora pushed me down the stairs, Mary overheard me confronting her. She heard me accuse Cora of wanting to poison her. She knew everything.

"She deserves to pay for what she did," Mary says.

I couldn't agree more.

FORTY-EIGHT

After leaving the hospital, I head straight for the farm, which is still a crime scene, but there are no police there. As soon as I let myself into the house, I go straight up to the guest room, the same room I used to stay in when I was the housekeeper, the same room Evan stayed in when he pretended I was his wife and claimed he was giving me space to recover.

Thanks to the police search, the room is as messy as the rest of the house. Closet doors stand wide open, hangers are empty, the dresser drawers are half-pulled out with clothes spilling onto the floor. The bed is no longer neatly made, the sheets are crumpled, and the mattress is slightly skew.

I search the room and miraculously find what I'm looking for under the bed—one single, half-closed suitcase with clothes spilling out as if someone had rifled through it in a hurry. It's stuffed with everything that belongs to me. Evan must have packed my life away, probably planning to destroy it so I never remembered who I am.

My belongings are in complete chaos with everything crumpled and tangled.

I pull out my clothes and my purse, relieved to find some

money in my wallet: three-hundred dollars, the only money I have left to my name.

I pack everything back in the suitcase, except for my purse, and put it by the door. Then I go to the master bedroom to get some toiletries out of the mess left behind by the police. Inside the bathroom, things are tossed everywhere—even the shower curtain has been pulled down and now lies crumpled on the floor. But I manage to dig up two bottles of shower gel, toothpaste, and my toothbrush, which is not on the floor but sitting on the open shelf above the sink.

As I reach for a small jar of hand cream on the floor, something shimmers in the corner of my vision. Tucked into the narrow space where the wall meets the baseboard, barely visible unless you're looking from the right angle, is a delicate glint of something.

I crouch down and gently ease it out.

The rusty, broken chain. It must have fallen through a crack at the back of the drawer and landed down there.

I wrap it in a piece of tissue and shove it deep into my purse, not even sure what I plan on doing with it now.

I'm on my way back to the guest room for my suitcase when I realize that I'm not done here yet. I know the police are actively searching for Cora, but I can't sit around waiting for news.

Thinking back to the safe in Evan's office—and the cash that used to be inside—an idea strikes me, and I suddenly know what I have to do.

Last night, after we escaped the basement and I found Cora in the hallway downstairs, I suspect that she was headed for Evan's office at the end of the hallway. Maybe she knew he kept money in the safe and wanted to take it before anyone else could.

Evan is in custody, and she has nothing. She didn't get a chance to grab money, IDs, or anything else she might need to make a run for it. If she's truly desperate, she might risk coming back, thinking the money might still be in there. And I will be right here waiting for her.

The house is quiet as the sun sets eventually and I make myself some canned soup from the kitchen. My stomach is too troubled to be hungry, but I know I need to get some nourishment inside me. I'll need my strength for what's coming next.

Returning to the living room after my quick meal, I know I'd rather be anywhere else but here. This whole house, not just the basement, creeps me out, but it helps to know that it's the last time I will be surrounded by these walls.

Still, at the back of my mind, I feel ridiculous. How long could it be before she returns? What if she never does?

The longer I wait, and as the darkness outside thickens, my anger grows, fueling my determination. I can never give up. They need to pay for everything they did.

I wake up to the sound of a car engine outside, and I sit up from the couch, heart in my throat.

Peeking through the blinds, I see two policemen stepping out of their car, walking toward the front of the house.

It looks like they're taking down the crime scene tape. I'm surprised they're only doing it now, but I guess with everything that went on in this house, it took time to collect all the evidence they needed.

I have to hide—fast. If they catch me here, I could be arrested. When I entered this place it was still an active crime scene, so I shouldn't be here.

I grab my purse and rush out of the living room, my bare feet silent against the wooden floor. I don't have many options.

The guest room? No, they might check the rooms first. The basement? No way.

Then I remember the pantry in the kitchen—a small space, but big enough for me to squeeze into. I dash inside just as the front door creaks open.

Footsteps echo through the house as the officers enter and move through the house. I hold my breath, pressing myself against the back wall of the pantry, praying they don't stay long.

They don't, but I don't move until I'm sure they're gone.

It's close to midnight when my patience is finally rewarded.

I'm sleeping on the couch in the dark, but the moment I hear the key in the lock, I'm wide awake.

My adrenaline is pumping as I rush to Evan's office and sit on the couch. Without switching on the light, I call the police and whisper on the phone that they should get here fast. Then I press another button and push the phone inside my pocket.

The lights are off, and Cora is about to get a nice little surprise.

As brave as I try to be, my hands betray me, trembling as I press them against my knees. My breath hitches at every creak of the floorboards. I have to admit that I am a little terrified of her, after learning about everything she's capable of.

She enters the office, flicks on the light, and heads straight for the safe, like I thought she would. She's so focused on what she came here for that she doesn't even notice me immediately.

A sharp intake of breath when she finds it empty, then, as though she finally senses my presence, she whirls around.

"Hi, Cora. Looking for something?" My eyes on her, I push myself up from the couch and take a step forward.

She's still wearing the same clothes she left in, looking disheveled. I wonder where she spent the night. Outside on the streets, perhaps?

"What are you doing here?" she asks through clenched teeth.

"I thought you might come back." I push my hands into the pockets of my jeans. "I figured we could have a little chat, now that I remember everything."

Her expression hardens as I continue. "You're a murderer. You pushed me down the stairs. You killed that woman, Margaret Tookes. Not Evan."

Her eyes flicker, and then she shrugs.

"Okay, you're right. I killed Margaret Tookes and wanted to get rid of Mary." Cora claps her hands. "Well done for figuring it all out. But I'm not stupid. I don't believe you have any proof."

"Oh, the police do have proof, and now they're going to have even more." I pull my phone from my pocket and press play.

Cora's face falls as her own voice plays back at her, bouncing off the walls in the room.

"The evidence the police already have is a video of you murdering Margaret Tookes. Your lovely husband was kind enough to record everything. I guess he didn't trust you."

Cora's eyes flash. In a blink, before I can react, she pulls something from her jacket pocket.

A gun.

She points the barrel directly at me.

Then, a click.

FORTY-NINE

I'm frozen, my whole body gone cold as I stand there, trying to process what happened, staring as Cora crumples to the floor in slow motion, the gun slipping from her grasp and clattering away.

Then I see the blood. But as soon as I do, my mind catches up.

Spinning around so fast I feel dizzy, I find the person standing behind me, her weapon still raised, her stance steady and professional.

It's Lina. She is no longer dressed in the simple dresses she wore whenever she came to look after Mary. Instead, she's wearing practical clothing—dark jeans, a fitted leather jacket, and lace-up ankle boots. A badge is clipped to her belt, and a gun holster rests at her side.

I part my lips to speak, but nothing comes out.

"I'm sorry," she says, lowering her weapon. "I'm sorry I wasn't honest with you."

"You're a cop?" Swallowing through my dry throat, I wrap my arms around myself.

"Yes. I'll explain everything, I promise."

Without wasting a second, she strides to where Cora lies groaning on the floor and kicks the weapon safely out of reach. She had only shot the hand that was holding the gun.

She scoops up the gun, tucks it into her belt, and pulls out her phone to call for backup and the ambulance.

As she kneels beside Cora and begins administering first aid, I stand there, hollowed out by disappointment. Lina, someone I thought I could trust and had confided in, had been lying to me all along. I really thought she was a friend.

I stay buried in that feeling until more police officers arrive, and paramedics flood the house. Everything is chaotic, loud, and overwhelming.

In the middle of all the chaos, Lina places a hand on my shoulder and leads me to the living room just as Cora is taken away in an ambulance.

She sits beside me, turning to take my hand in hers. "Again, I should have told you, but I didn't want to ruin the investigation."

"What investigation?" I slide my hand away from hers. We haven't been friends for long, but I feel betrayed. I've been fooled by so many people.

"We've been investigating Evan and Cora Harrison for a while now, gathering evidence of their crimes."

"Did you know who I was? Were you investigating me too?"

"You're Gabrielle Walker." She glances down at her hands, then looks up again. "I knew who you were from the start, but I wasn't allowed to jeopardize the investigation by revealing your true identity. I had to play along. And of course I wasn't investigating you. You did nothing wrong."

"Did you know about Cora? That Evan had locked her in the basement?"

"No, I didn't. We were looking for her, but we had no idea

where she was. And now, because of you, we found her. We didn't know Evan and his wife were killing people. We thought they were only running elaborate cons."

"Is your name really Lina?"

"No," she says, offering a small smile. "My name is Detective Nina Park."

"I can't believe this." Shaking my head, I stand up and walk to the window. Outside, two police cars are still there, one officer behind the wheel.

"Did they find Margaret's... body?"

She shakes her head. "Not yet. We looked everywhere on this property and found nothing. But we won't stop." She rises to her feet. "I need to get back to work. But, Gabrielle, I like you, and I hope we can still be friends, go to the movies maybe?"

Friends?

I don't respond.

A friend would be nice. The world is a scary place without anyone by your side.

But the thing is, I have remembered something else about myself and my past.

And it will make it very hard to be friends with a police detective.

I'm standing on the porch with my suitcase next to me, waiting for my taxi.

I'm so ready to leave this nightmare behind. But when my ride arrives, it's followed by a pickup truck, which I soon recognize as Sabrina's. As the cars come to a halt next to each other in front of the farmhouse, I ask the taxi driver to give me a minute and walk over to Sabrina as she's getting out of the truck.

Soon she's standing in front of me, but she looks so different. The confident, strong, and cheerful woman is nowhere to be seen. Instead, she's a bit of a mess, her shoulders hunched and her eyes sparkling with tears that are illuminated by the porch light. She's wringing her hands in front of her like it's the only thing holding her together.

"Sabrina? What are you—?"

Her eyes meet mine and a sob escapes her. "I heard what happened. That Margaret is—I thought my mother was worried for nothing. I really thought Margaret had just moved on. Evan... he really killed her? She's really dead?" She almost chokes on the words, and I feel my stomach drop.

"Yes, she is. But it wasn't Evan who did it. It was his wife, Cora. But Evan was part of it. They both conned Margaret. And they will pay for it. I'm sure they will go away for a long time."

Sabrina's face goes pale, like the life is draining right out of her. She presses a hand to her mouth and shakes her head slowly, as if she's refusing to believe what I said. "Oh God, I didn't know. I thought—"

"Sabrina," I say before she can continue, "why didn't you tell me that I'm not Evan's wife? You knew I wasn't Cora." Biting into my lower lip until it aches, I take a step back. "You knew, and you didn't tell me?" Things were so hectic in the last couple of hours that I didn't even think of Sabrina until now.

"I'm really sorry," she cries. "Evan—he paid me. He gave me money to stay silent, to act like you are Cora. He told me things about you."

"Like my favorite kind of music?" Evan knew I loved listening to Michael Learns to Rock, as I often played their songs while cleaning.

"Yes." She blinks away tears. "He also gave me that chocolate and the John Grisham book."

"You lied to me... for money?"

"No." She purses her lips to stop herself from crying. "At

first, I refused the money. Even if we really needed it... to help us save up for my mother's eye surgery. But then he threatened to kill my son if I said a word to anyone, even my brother, or went to the police."

The air shoots out of my lungs like I've been punched and my knees wobble. "He threatened to kill Owen?" A child. An innocent little boy. I now know that Evan is a monster, but this... this knocks the breath from me.

"Before I agreed, he came to our farm in the middle of the night to scare me. It was terrible. He had a gun. Raymond wasn't home and I was so scared. That's when I said yes to the offer. I never told my brother."

"Oh my God. I'm so sorry." I almost reach out to touch her arm, but then I end up dropping my hand again.

"Thank you. I hope you understand that I had to do whatever it took to protect my child."

I nod. I may not be a mother, but I can imagine the sheer terror of being forced to choose between doing something unthinkable and losing your child.

"But didn't you ever wonder where Cora was?"

"Not really. Evan told me she left him. And I believed him because the last time she came over, she was upset. She thought Evan was having an affair. I didn't have her phone number. I had no way to check on her. I can't... I can't believe she's a murderer. Poor Margaret." Tears are streaming down her face and her shoulders are shaking uncontrollably now. "I was so stupid. Please forgive me for the part I played in all of this. What I did was awful and I'm so sorry. I never wanted to hurt you. I didn't want to be part of this. I was confused and desperate and scared for my son."

The longer I look at her, the more something inside me shifts. "I forgive you, Sabrina," I say finally, my voice weak. "I have to go now. Goodbye."

Soon, I'm sitting in the back of the car, staring out the

window as the farmhouse gets smaller with Sabrina standing in front of it in the darkness.

I blow out a breath, trying to steady myself. Like me, she was another one of Evan's victims, and there's been enough suffering, enough innocent people caught in the crossfire. The ones who deserve to pay will soon answer for it.

FIFTY

Wednesday, August 7, 2019

The next afternoon, I'm sitting on the edge of the motel bed, chewing on a sandwich from the gas station across the road. The white bread is a bit stale, but I barely notice.

My eyes are fixed on the small TV bolted to the wall.

"Cedar Hollow is reeling from the shocking discovery that Evan and Cora Harrison have been arrested for the murder of seventy-nine-year-old Margaret Tookes. The con artists allegedly manipulated the elderly woman into changing her will, leaving all of her assets to them."

A photo of Margaret flashes on the screen. Her hair is loose, her eyes bright, and her teeth white as she smiles at the camera.

I immediately feel a pain in my chest. After being so obsessed with her and her life, I almost feel like I knew her.

"Authorities believe Tookes was murdered shortly after the change to her will. Her body has yet to be recovered."

Lowering the sandwich to the napkin on my lap, I pick up the remote and increase the volume to better hear the brunette newscaster.

"In a chilling twist, investigators say the Harrisons attempted to repeat their scheme with another elderly woman, seventy-year-old Mary Saunders, who suffers from dementia. The couple convinced her and the staff at Meadowbrook Assisted Living Facility that Saunders was Evan Harrison's aunt, and they brought her to live with them at the Tookes farmhouse."

Another image appears on screen, this time of Mary outside what looks like a museum.

"Thankfully, authorities were able to rescue Saunders before harm could come to her, and she is currently doing well. Both Evan and Cora Harrison are now in police custody. We will keep you updated as the story unfolds."

The news segment comes to an end and is replaced by a story about a Cedar Hollow church that's being restored. As I switch off the TV, something flicks in my mind.

Margaret Tookes. Mary Saunders.

My mind wants to tell me something that I don't quite understand yet.

I stare blankly at the wall for a moment, then get up and dig through my handbag. My fingers come out holding a crumpled old receipt, and I pull it out. I grab the pen lying on the night-stand and scrawl both names down on the back of the receipt.

There's something there, tugging at the edge of my memory. I close my eyes and breathe deep. Then I write the initials next to the names:

MT and MS.

Wait.

A rush of adrenaline shoots through me and I grab my phone and scroll through the gallery until I find it—the photo I took of the paper I stole from Evan's office, the list of codes that had not made sense to me.

MT fits. That's Margaret Tookes. And 1940? That would make her seventy-nine, like the newscaster said.

But there's no MS on the list, just RS. So it can't be Mary.

Still staring at the small screen I suddenly remember. She goes by Mary, but officially, she's Rosemary. Her full name, the name on her documents and her pill bottles. Rosemary Saunders. RS.

The hairs on my arms rise as I finally figure it out.

RS1949. That would make her seventy, a match to the age mentioned on the news.

It's clear now, and sickening. The codes weren't client IDs or patient files.

They were a list of Evan and Cora's victims. And the ones crossed out in red have to be the ones that are dead, Margaret being one of them.

I throw on my clothes and rush out the door, heading straight to the police station.

The next morning, Mary greets me at the door of her temporary hotel suite wearing a white cardigan over her nightdress. A private nurse lingers in the background, flipping through paperwork near the window.

"There you are, sweetheart," Mary says, her face lighting up. "Come in, come in. I was about to have some tea. Let's have some together."

She's moving slowly, but with surprising determination, shuffling toward the small kitchenette, more alive and independent than she was with Evan and Cora around.

The nurse offers me a polite smile, then steps out to give us privacy.

"I found the USB," I tell Mary as I take a seat at the small round table by the window.

She looks over her shoulder, distracted as she pulls down two mugs. "Hmm?"

"Yes, the one you hid in the barn. I found it."

"Oh, good." She fumbles with the kettle, while I stay on alert should she need help. But she manages fine, and continues,

"There's got to be more in there... in that barn." She trails off and sets the mugs down, joining me at the table. "I—I heard them talking about it, you know?" Her brow creases. "Cora and Evan. Arguing." She pauses. "It's fuzzy... but I remember something about them saying the barn wasn't the right place. If they should move it. It sounded strange."

Move *it*.

My stomach flips over as the pieces begin to fall into place. I'm one hundred percent sure that Cora and Evan weren't debating storing a piece of furniture or another farm-related item. They were deciding where to hide a body.

Margaret Tookes.

FIFTY-ONE

Thursday, December 19, 2019

Even though it's freezing outside, the jail is colder than I expect, and the air is thick with the stale scent of disinfectant and something metallic that lingers at the back of my throat. The bright lights above shower the place with an artificial glow, making the empty block walls feel even more lifeless.

A thick pane of glass stands between me and Evan Harrison as I sit down opposite him, the phone receiver feeling icy against my ear.

He looks different. His hair has grown out and looks messy, and the usual cocky glint in his eyes is dulled by the orange jumpsuit and the weight of his situation.

But when he smirks at me, it's clear he still believes he's in control. "I have to admit," he says, his voice smooth even with the static crackling through the line, "I didn't expect to see you here."

I clutch the receiver tighter. "I needed answers."

He tilts his head slightly, considering me. "Ah. Curiosity.

The very thing that got you tangled up in this mess from the start."

I don't take the bait. I just stare, waiting. "Why did you pretend I was your wife?"

Evan sighs, then chuckles. "I won't lie to you, Gabrielle. When you came to work for us, I was intrigued. You were sharp, observant. Beautiful." His eyes trail over me, and my stomach tightens with disgust. "Then when the opportunity presented itself, I wanted to see how far I could push you into believing something that wasn't true. It was all in the name of research, for my book, *The Chameleon Effect*, which was going to make me a lot of money. I did everything to make sure I convinced you of your new identity. You have to admit I did a darn good job." He scratches his bushy beard. "Technology is an incredible thing. It was so easy to doctor our wedding and vacation photos—thanks to Photoshop—and to create a fake Facebook account. The truth is, Cora was never interested in social media and was only going to build an online presence because of the business she wanted to start."

"Research," I repeat flatly. "Were all those women you cheated on your wife with also research?" I spit out. "I saw the photos." I'd rather focus on the others rather than being made to remember that he made such a fool of me.

"Yes, for other projects I was working on. You see, my marriage with Cora was built on an understanding. She knew I needed firsthand experience for my writing. I could date other women if it was for research. We used to play games like that all the time."

My mind flashes to Cora's face the day I told her I saw Evan with another woman. She hadn't looked pleased, and she had cried in the bathroom after that. Had she really agreed to this twisted arrangement? Maybe at one point, but I have a feeling Evan took things too far. The photos of him and those other women weren't only for *research*. Maybe Cora finally realized that too.

I will myself to stay focused. "So that's what I was to you? A game?"

Evan exhales sharply. "It wasn't that simple. And let's not pretend you didn't enjoy parts of it. The attention, the mystery—"

I slam the receiver down for a second, composing myself before picking it up again. "Let me guess. You're going to tell me that, deep down, you really did care for me."

He smirks, but it falters at the edges. "I suppose you wouldn't believe me if I said yes."

"No." My voice is icy cold as it cuts through the line. "You weren't just using me for 'research.' You were keeping me close because you knew I might remember what happened. You knew Cora had been poisoning Mary and that she pushed me, as you'd caught it all on camera, and if I remembered and went to the police, you'd go down with her."

I never got to see the video of Cora pushing me down the stairs, but the police did. They found it buried deep in Evan's hard drive.

He doesn't deny it and I laugh, an empty, humorless sound. "Your plan didn't work, Evan. I did remember. And tomorrow, you will be found guilty and will pay for every single one of your crimes."

I stand, my pulse steady and my resolve stronger than ever. I press my palm flat against the glass, leaning in just enough so that he has to hear my final words.

"You always thought you were the one pulling the strings," I whisper into the receiver. "But in the end, you were another piece on the board. And I won the game."

For the first time since I've known him, Evan Harrison looks small, defeated.

I turn and leave, stepping out of the cold, sterile prison and into the fresh air.

The moment I leave the courtroom, I close my eyes and tilt my head up to the sky, taking a deep breath. I don't even mind the cold as it slaps my face. The tense months of waiting are behind me, and it feels like the first time I can truly breathe.

The trial is over, and justice has been served, at least in the eyes of the law. Cora was revealed to be the mastermind behind the operation, manipulating and murdering vulnerable elderly people for financial gain. As it turns out, it was her idea from the start, and she convinced Evan to participate.

Before all this, Evan and Cora were drowning in debt, living way beyond their means. Their fancy lifestyle in Charlotte had drained their finances. Even with the huge advance Evan got for his published book, they still craved more.

When questioned by the police, Lilian Holloway—Evan's sister—revealed that the idea first came to Cora one day when they were talking, and Lilian mentioned to her how an elderly woman had passed away at Meadowbrook and left her entire fortune to one of the carers. It was then that Cora came up with the idea to find sick, elderly people with no families and trick them into leaving them their money. She convinced Evan and Lilian that it was easy money, and they could all live the lives they'd always dreamed of.

Their first victim was Keith Landon from Charlotte, where Meadowbrook operates another facility. He suffered from dementia and had no family. Posing as his daughter, Cora moved him out of the care home. Six months later, Keith died from a mysterious fall down the stairs in the middle of the night. KL1954, the other name that was crossed out on the list.

After being proven to be an accomplice, Lilian is now

awaiting trial as well. So is Doctor Daniel Rowe, a real but corrupt doctor and a close friend of Evan's.

Evan was complicit, but never wanted the murders to happen. He had planned to let the old people die naturally and profit from their deaths, but Cora was not patient like him. She was a sadist.

Evan revealed that whenever he traveled, and Cora was left alone with Margaret Tookes, she locked the old woman inside that basement room, that was once a pantry, and was terribly cruel to her, starving her for days.

I passed on the information about the barn to the police, and sure enough, Margaret's body was found there. I was there when it happened—along with a crowd of reporters—and watching the woman I feel like I knew being carried out in a body bag hit me so hard I could barely stand. I still remember that night vividly: the sirens, the flashing lights, the stretcher being rolled toward a white van with no windows.

It all happened because of me. If I hadn't gone to work for Cora and Evan, Margaret's mystery might never have been solved. She wouldn't have been in a body bag that night. She would still be in the ground, hidden and forgotten.

And that rusty chain I discovered? What looked like rust was actually dried blood. At some point—likely during a struggle earlier in the day—Margaret must have been dragged by the chain, and the cut bled just enough to stain it.

After helping her cover up Margaret's murder, Cora's second kill, Evan made her promise she would never do it again. So when he saw the video of me accusing her of poisoning Mary, he finally decided to do something about it and he locked her away in the room in the basement.

When asked how long he intended to keep her down there, Evan couldn't give a straight answer, just that he felt it was his duty to protect others from her.

It was quite a sight, watching husband and wife turn against each other in the courtroom, each trying to secure a lighter sentence.

A major piece of evidence was a jar of liquid cyanide that was found among Cora's belongings. That sealed her fate.

Feeling liberated and ready to move on, I walk away from the courthouse toward my car that Evan had abandoned in a deserted lot far from the farm.

After all this time, I still grapple with everything that happened, but as I slide behind the wheel, exhaling slowly, excitement buzzes through me.

I'm not done yet.

"I'm coming for you, Cora."

EPILOGUE

One Year Later

When I visit Cora in prison, I find her with a busted lip so swollen it makes it hard for her to speak. She's paying for her crimes in more ways than one.

As I sit across from her in the visitation room, the once-confident woman before me is reduced to silence and stillness. She doesn't look like herself at all. Her hair is a nest, there are dark bags under her empty eyes, and her hands won't stop shaking.

"I'm sure you're surprised to see me here," I say, smiling at her. "I'm not staying long. I came to let you know that Mary Saunders has passed away. Peacefully. At the new care home where she was well taken care of."

I lean back in my chair, ready to deal her the next blow, an ironic twist. "She left me her entire fortune." I pause, letting the words sink in before adding, "It was a thank you for saving her and for being by her side until the very end. In fact, I was holding her hand when she closed her eyes for the last time."

We grew really close during that time, and she confided in

me that she had indeed followed me to Evan's office when I took the USB. She'd watched as I'd connected it to my computer, and when she'd seen the shock on my face, she'd realized that it must hold terrible facts about Evan. So, in a moment of confusion but desperate to do something, she had taken the USB and hidden it in the barn, hoping it would be found there along with the barn's other secrets.

What nobody knows is that I knew Mary well before I started working at Thistle Creek Ranch. I was employed at the care home as a cleaner under a different name, before they took her out. Once Mary left, I resigned from that job and followed her to the Harrisons' farm, or more accurately, to Margaret Tookes's home.

Cora tries to say something, but the pain must be too great. She puts a hand over her mouth, her muffled words turning into gibberish.

"It's okay, Cora. You don't have to say anything. I'll do the talking."

From my pocket, I pull out a passport photo of an elderly woman and place it on the table between us. "She's dying of kidney disease, and I've been her housekeeper for the past two months, and also her carer. To be honest, I'm the closest thing she has to family right now."

I don't tell Cora the woman's name, or that I've been using a fake one myself. A brand-new identity, complete with forged documents, a fabricated backstory, and just enough history to pass a background check.

Cora's eyes widen slightly, but she remains silent, waiting for me to continue.

"The poor woman is in the hospital right now. She won't be living much longer." I slip the photo back into my pocket and smile. "I need to keep playing my cards right. And when the time comes, I'll make sure the money she leaves me as her sole beneficiary doesn't go to waste."

"What are you talking about?" Cora finally manages, though her words are distorted. She winces, touching her swollen lip again.

"I mean exactly what you think I mean, Cora." I lean in slightly. "I learned from the best. You and I—we're not so different. But we're motivated by different things." I rise to my feet, smoothing my shirt. "Goodbye, Cora. I don't think we'll see each other again."

Without another glance, I walk away, leaving her to stew in her own confusion and rage.

After leaving, I drive to Westledge—a small town also in North Carolina, just two hours from the prison—and find myself standing at my mother's grave.

The weight of my past presses down on me as I remember her—our endless hours in the kitchen, baking, creating memories that have kept me going for so long.

I run my fingertips over her name. Angela Walter. A cold breeze ruffles my hair and chills my scalp as I pull my hand away.

My mother's death wasn't just a tragedy. It was an injustice, caused by a corrupt insurance company that refused to pay for life-saving treatment after she had paid into it for years. That company was called Providence and Guardian Insurance. The same company Mary Saunders co-founded.

"It's all going to be fine, Mama," I say softly. "I'll make sure I get it all back."

I clear away the dead flowers and leaves from her grave, reflecting on my calling. My mission to reclaim the wealth stolen by those who built their fortune on the suffering of others, and to funnel it into cancer research and other worthy causes.

I don't want anyone to go through what my mother and I have endured.

No one should suffer the same fate. No one should be robbed by the system.

Once I'm done, I sit down in front of her grave and pull out my own list from my pocket, along with a red marker.

I cross out Mary Saunders's name.

A LETTER FROM LIZ

Dear Reader,

Thank you so much for picking up *Not His Wife* and taking the journey with me to Cedar Hollow. I'm so grateful you chose to spend time with Cora, Evan, Mary, and the rest of the cast. Writing their tangled, tension-filled story kept me on the edge of my seat, and I hope it did the same for you.

It was a refreshing experience to explore a new setting with this book, and I especially loved bringing Thistle Creek Ranch to life. Roaming its grounds through Cora's eyes was a thrill—an eerie, unsettling one at times—and I hope it added a fresh layer of suspense and atmosphere that you enjoyed.

If you had a good time unraveling the secrets of *Not His Wife*, I'd be so grateful if you left a review. Reviews not only help other readers discover the book, but they also mean the world to authors like me.

If you'd like to be the first to know when I release a new book, please sign up for my mailing list using the link below. Your email will always stay private, and you can unsubscribe at any time.

www.bookouture.com/l-g-davis

Connecting with readers is one of my favorite parts of this journey. Whether you want to share your thoughts about the book or just say hi, you can find me on Facebook, Instagram, X, or through my website. I'd truly love to hear from you.

Thank you again for reading.

Much love,

Liz xxx

www.lgdavis.com

facebook.com/LGDavisBooks

x.com/lgdavisauthor

instagram.com/lgdavisauthor

ACKNOWLEDGMENTS

Writing a book is not always easy, but writing one without support can feel impossible. I consider myself incredibly lucky to have had the right people in my corner as I brought *Not His Wife* to life.

A heartfelt thank you to the amazing team at Bookouture for believing in me and this story. I'm especially grateful to my editor, Rhianna, whose insight, patience, and sharp eye helped shape this book into what it is. Your encouragement means more than words can say.

To my husband, Toye—thank you for your endless love and for holding down the fort when I disappeared into my writing cave. And to my sweet kids, Simon and Dara, thank you for being my sunshine and inspiration. You remind me every day why I do what I do.

And finally, to my readers, thank you for picking up this book and welcoming my stories into your world. Your messages, reviews, and support mean everything to me. It's a joy writing for you.

With love and gratitude,

Liz

PUBLISHING TEAM

Turning a manuscript into a book requires the efforts of many people. The publishing team at Bookouture would like to acknowledge everyone who contributed to this publication.

Commercial
Lauren Morrissette
Hannah Richmond
Imogen Allport

Cover design
The Brewster Project

Data and analysis
Mark Alder
Mohamed Bussuri

Editorial
Rhianna Louise
Ria Clare

Copyeditor
Donna Hillyer

Proofreader
Emily Boyce

RAISING READERS

Books Build Bright Futures

Dear Reader,

We'd love your attention for one more page to tell you about the crisis in children's reading, and what we can all do.

Studies have shown that reading for fun is the **single biggest predictor of a child's future success** – more than family circumstance, parents' educational background or income. It improves academic results, mental health, wealth, communication skills, and ambition.

The number of children reading for fun is in rapid decline. Young people have a lot of competition for their time, and a worryingly high number do not have a single book at home.

Our business works extensively with schools, libraries and literacy charities, but here are some ways we can all raise more readers:

- Reading to children for just 10 minutes a day makes a difference
- Don't give up if children aren't regular readers – there will be books for them!

- Visit bookshops and libraries to get recommendations
- Encourage them to listen to audiobooks
- Support school libraries
- Give books as gifts

Thank you for reading: there's a lot more information about how to encourage children to read on our website.

www.JoinRaisingReaders.com

Printed in Dunstable, United Kingdom